More Than I Love My Life

David Grossman

Translated by Jessica Cohen

JONATHAN CAPE
LONDON

1 3 5 7 9 10 8 6 4 2

Jonathan Cape is part of the Penguin Random House group of companies
whose addresses can be found at global.penguinrandomhouse.com.

Penguin
Random House
UK

Originally published in Israel as *Iti ha'chayim mesachek harbeh*
by Ha'kibbutz Ha'meuchad, Tel Aviv, in 2019. Copyright © 2019
by David Grossman and Ha'kibbutz Ha'meuchad.

Translation copyright © Jessica Cohen 2021

David Grossman has asserted his right to be identified as the author of this
Work in accordance with the Copyright, Designs and Patents Act 1988

First published by Jonathan Cape in 2021

penguin.co.uk/vintage

A CIP catalogue record for this book is available from the British Library

ISBN 9781787332935 (Hardback)
ISBN 9781787332942 (Trade paperback)

Printed and bound in Great Britain by Clays Ltd, Elcograf S.p.A.

The authorised representative in the EEA is Penguin Random House Ireland,
Morrison Chambers, 32 Nassau Street, Dublin D02 YH68

Penguin Random House is committed to a sustainable future for
our business, our readers and our planet. This book is made from
Forest Stewardship Council® certified paper.

Also by David Grossman

FICTION

A Horse Walks into a Bar

Falling Out of Time

To the End of the Land

Her Body Knows

Someone to Run With

Be My Knife

The Zigzag Kid

The Book of Intimate Grammar

See Under: Love

The Smile of the Lamb

NONFICTION

Writing in the Dark: Essays on Literature and Politics

Death as a Way of Life: Israel Ten Years After Oslo

Sleeping on a Wire: Conversations with Palestinians in Israel

The Yellow Wind

More Than I Love My Life

More Than I Love My Life

❧

RAFAEL WAS FIFTEEN YEARS OLD when his mother died and put him out of her misery. Rain poured down on the mourners huddled under umbrellas in the small kibbutz cemetery. Tuvia, Rafael's father, sobbed bitterly. He had cared for his wife devotedly for years and now looked lost and bereft. Rafael, wearing shorts, stood apart from the others and pulled the hood of his sweatshirt over his eyes so that no one would know he wasn't crying. He thought: Now that she's dead, she can see all the things I thought of her.

That was in the winter of 1962. A year later his father met Vera Novak, who had come to Israel from Yugoslavia, and they became a couple. Vera had arrived with her only daughter, Nina, a tall, fairhaired girl of seventeen whose long face, which was pale and very beautiful, showed almost no expression.

The boys in Rafael's class called Nina "Sphinx." They would sneak behind her and mimic her gait, the way she hugged her body and stared ahead vacantly. When she once caught two kids imitating her, she simply pummeled them bloody. They'd never seen such fighting on the kibbutz. It was hard to believe how much ferocious strength she had in her thin arms and legs. Rumors started flying. They said that while her mother was a political prisoner in the Gulag, little Nina had lived on the streets. *The streets,* they said, with a meaningful look. They said that in Belgrade she'd joined a gang of feral kids who kidnapped children for ransom. That's what they said. People say things.

The fight, as well as other incidents and rumors, failed to pierce the fog in which Rafael lived after his mother's death. For months he was in a self-induced coma. Twice a day, morning and evening, he took a powerful sleeping pill from his mother's medicine cabinet. He didn't even notice Nina when he occasionally ran into her around the kibbutz.

But one evening, about six months after his mother died, he was taking a shortcut through the avocado orchard to the gymnasium when Nina came toward him. She walked with her head bowed, hugging herself as if everything around her was cold. Rafael stopped, tensing up for reasons he did not understand. Nina was in her own world and did not notice him. He saw the way she moved. That was his first impression: her quiet, sparing motion. The limpid, high forehead, and a thin blue dress that fluttered halfway down her shins.

The expression on his face when he recounted—

Only when they got closer did Rafael see that she was crying— quiet, muffled sobs—and then she noticed him and stopped, and curved inward. Their gazes entangled fleetingly and, one might sorrowfully add, inextricably. "The sky, the earth, the trees," Rafael told me, "I don't know . . . I felt like nature had passed out."

Nina was the first to recover. She gave an angry puff and hurried away. He had time to glimpse her face, which had instantly shed all expression, and something inside him coursed toward her. He held out his hand after her—

I can actually see him standing there with his hand out.

And that is how he's remained, with the outstretched hand, for forty-five years.

But that day, in the orchard, without thinking, before he could hesitate and trip himself up, he sprinted after her to tell her what he'd understood the moment he'd seen her. Everything had come to life inside him, he told me. I asked him to explain. He mumbled something about all the things that had fallen asleep in him during the years of his mother's illness, and even more so after her death. Now it was all suddenly urgent and fateful, and he had no doubt that Nina would yield to him right then and there.

Nina heard his footsteps chasing her. She stopped, turned around, and slowly surveyed him. "What is it?" she barked into his face. He flinched, shocked by her beauty and perhaps also by her coarseness—and mostly, I'm afraid, by the combination of the two. That's something he still has: a weakness for women with a bit—just a drop—of aggression and even crudeness. That spiciness. Rafael, Rafi—

Nina put her hands on her waist, and a tough street girl jutted out. Her nostrils widened, she sniffed him, and Rafael saw a delicate blue vein throbbing on her neck, and his lips suddenly hurt; that's what he told me: they were literally stinging and thirsting.

Okay, I get it, I thought. I don't need the details.

Tears were still glistening on Nina's cheeks, but her eyes were cold and serpentine. "Go home, boy," she said, and he shook his head no. She slowly moved her forehead toward his head, tracking it back and forth as if searching for precisely the right point, and he shut his eyes and then she butted, and he flew back and landed in the hollow of an avocado tree.

"Ettinger cultivar," he specified the name of the tree when he told me the story, so that I wouldn't forget, God forbid, that every detail in the scene was important, because that is how you construct a mythology.

Stunned, he lay in the hollow, touched the bump already growing on his forehead, then stood up dizzily. Since his mother's death, Rafael had not touched anyone, nor had he been touched, except by the kids who fought with him. But this, he sensed, was something different. She'd come along to finally open up his mind and rescue him from the torture. Through the blinding pain, he shouted out what he had realized the moment he'd seen her, though he was amazed when the words left his mouth, insipid and crude. "Words the guys used," he told me, "like 'I wanna fuck you,' that kind of thing." So different from his pure, scrupulous thought. "But for a second or two I saw on her face that, despite the dirty language, she got me."

And maybe that is what happened—how should I know? Why not give her the benefit of the doubt and believe that a girl born in Yugoslavia, who for a few years really was, as it later turned out, an abandoned child with no mother or father, could—despite those opening stats, or perhaps because of them—at a moment of kindness glance into the eyes of an Israeli kibbutz kid, an inward-looking boy, or so I imagine him at sixteen, a lonely boy full of secrets and intricate calculations and grand gestures that no one in the world knew about. A sad, gloomy boy, but so handsome you could cry.

Rafael, my father.

There's a well-known film, I can't remember what it's called right now (and I'm not wasting a second on Google), where the hero goes back to the past to repair something, to prevent a world war or something like that. What I wouldn't give to return to the past just to prevent those two from ever meeting.

—

Over the days and, mostly, the nights that came afterward, Rafael tormented himself about the marvelous moment he'd squandered. He stopped taking his mother's sleeping pills so that he could experience the love unclouded. He searched all over the kibbutz, but he could not find her. In those days he hardly spoke to anyone, so he did not know that Nina had left the singles' neighborhood, where she'd lived with her mother, and expropriated a little room in a moldering old shack from back in the founders' days. The shack was like a train of tiny rooms, located behind the orchards, in an area that the kibbutzniks, with their typical sensitivity, called the leper colony. It was a small community of men and women, mostly volunteers from overseas, misfits who hung around without contributing anything, and the kibbutz didn't know what to do with them.

But the notion that had germinated in Rafael when he met Nina in the orchard was no less impassioned, and it wrapped itself tighter and tighter around his soul by the day: If Nina agrees to sleep with me, even once, he thought in all earnestness, her expressions will come back.

He told me about that thought during a conversation we filmed an eternity ago, when he was thirty-seven. It was my debut film, and this morning, twenty-four years after shooting it, we decided, Rafael and I, in a burst of reckless nostalgia, to sit down and watch it. At that point in the film he can be seen coughing, almost choking, scouring his scruffy beard, unfastening and refastening his leather watch strap, and, above all, not looking up at the young interviewer: me.

"I have to say, you were very self-confident at sixteen," I can be heard chirping ingratiatingly. "Me?" the Rafael in the film responds in surprise. "Self-confident? I was shaking like a leaf." "Well, in my opinion," says the interviewer, sounding horribly off-key, "it's the most original pickup line I've ever heard."

I was fifteen when I interviewed him, and for the sake of full disclosure I should say that until that moment I had never had the good fortune to hear any pickup line, original or trite, from anyone other than me-in-the-mirror with a black beret and a mysterious scarf covering half my face.

A videotape, a small tripod, a microphone covered with disintegrated gray foam. This week, in October of 2008, my grandmother Vera found them in a cardboard box in her storage attic, along with the ancient Sony through which I viewed the world in those days.

Okay, to call that thing a film is somewhat generous. It was a few haphazard and poorly edited segments of my father reminiscing. The sound is awful, the picture is faded and grainy, but you can usually figure out what's going on. On the cardboard box, Vera had written in black marker: GILI—VARIOUS. I have no words to describe what that film does to me, and how my heart goes out to the girl I used to be, who looks—I'm not exaggerating—like the human version of a dodo, an animal that would have died of embarrassment had it not gone extinct. In other words, a creature profoundly out of whack in terms of what it is and where it's headed—everything was up for grabs.

Today, twenty-four years after I filmed that conversation, as I sit watching it with my dad at Vera's house on the kibbutz, I feel amazed by how exposed I was, even though I was only the interviewer and hardly ever appeared on-screen.

For quite a number of minutes I can't concentrate on what my father is saying about him and Nina, about how they met and how he loved her. Instead I sit here next to him, folding over and shrinking back beneath the force of that internal conflict, projected unfiltered, like a scream, from inside the girl I used to be. I can see the terror in her eyes *because* everything is so open, too open, even questions like: How much life force does she contain, or how much of a woman will she be and how much of a man. At fifteen she still does not know which fate will be decided for her in the dungeons of evolution.

If I could make a brief appearance—this is what I think—just for a moment, in her world, and show her pictures of myself today, like of me at work or me with Meir, even now, in our state, and if I could tell her: Don't worry, kid, in the end—with a couple of shoves, a few compromises, a little humor, some constructive self-destruction— you will find your place, a place that will be only yours, and you will even find love, because there will be someone who is looking for an ample woman with an air of the dodo about her.

I want to go back to the beginning, to the family's incubators. I'll squeeze in whatever I can before we take off for the island. Rafael's father, Tuvia Bruck, was an agronomist who oversaw all the agricultural lands between Haifa and Nazareth and held senior positions on the kibbutz. He was a handsome, serious man of many deeds and few words. He loved his wife, Dushinka, and cared for her through her years of illness as best he could. After she died, people on the kibbutz began mentioning Vera, Nina's mother, to him. Tuvia was hesitant. There was something foreign about her. Always, in any situation, she wore lipstick and earrings. Her accent was heavy, her Hebrew peculiar (it still is; no one else sounds like her), and even her voice sounded diasporic to him. An old friend from the Yugoslavian group put his arm on Tuvia's shoulder one evening as they walked out of the dining hall and said, "She's a woman of your caliber, Tuvia. You should know that she went through some things you would not believe, and there are things that still can't be spoken of."

Tuvia invited Vera to his apartment so they could get acquainted. To make things less awkward, she brought a friend, a woman from her hometown in Croatia who was an enthusiastic photographer. The two women sat quietly, with their legs crossed, in uncomfortable armchairs made of metal rods with a woven web of thin nylon cords that cut into their rear ends.

It took the self-control of a monk on a pillar for them to avoid laughing when Tuvia attempted to transport the refreshments his daughters had prepared out of the kitchen. Later, for thirty-two good years—happy years—together, Vera enjoyed impersonating him in those first moments, walking to the kitchen for a bowl of peanuts or pretzel sticks while regaling them with facts about Prodenia larvae and the leaf-miner moth, returning empty-handed, smiling apologetically with a charming dimple on his left cheek, then heading back to the kitchen for a vase of wildflowers.

While Rafael's father performed his convoluted mating dance, Vera looked around and tried to learn something about his late wife. There were no pictures on the walls, nor any bookshelves or rugs. The lampshade on the floor lamp was moth-eaten (she wondered if it was a leaf-miner moth), and strips of pale-yellow foam poked out of the sofa. Vera's friend thrust her chin at a folded-up wheelchair and an oxygen tank, which were wedged between the sofa and the wall. Vera sensed that the illness that had permeated the home for years had not yet fully retreated. Some part of it was still unfinished. The knowledge that she had an adversary made her sit up straighter, and she commanded Rafael's father to finally sit down and talk to them properly. He dropped to the sofa and sat erect, with his arms crossed over his chest.

Vera smiled at him from the depths of her womanhood, and his spine began to melt. The friend started to feel redundant and stood up to leave. She and Vera exchanged a few words in fluid Serbo-Croatian. Vera shrugged her shoulders and gave a dismissive wave that seemed to say, I don't actually mind that at all. Tuvia, whose entire existence was being swiftly assessed, was a firm and confident man, but he now felt undermined by this little woman with the sharp green eyes. So sharp that every so often one had to look away. Before she left, the friend asked for permission to photograph them with her Olympus. They were both embarrassed, but she said, "You look so lovely together," and they glanced at each other and for the first time saw the possibility of themselves as a couple.

Vera got up from the torture chair and sat down next to Tuvia on the narrow sofa. In the black-and-white photograph, she leans back on one arm, looking sideways at him with a certain remoteness, and smiles. She seems to be teasing him and enjoying it.

That was 1963, early winter: Vera is forty-five. A stray curl droops over her forehead, her lips are full and perfect. She has narrow eyebrows, Hedy Lamarr eyebrows, penciled on. Tuvia is fifty-four, wearing a white shirt with a broad collar and a handmade cable-knit sweater. He has a thick black forelock with a very straight part. His giant fists are crossed over his chest. He looks awkward, and his forehead glistens with excitement. His legs are crossed, and only now do I notice, looking at the picture, that under the table (a plank perched on two wooden crates, covered with a white cloth), Vera's right toe, in a strappy sandal, is slightly touching the sole of Tuvia's left shoe, almost tickling it.

The friend left, and Vera and Tuvia were stuck on the sofa on their own. When he raised his arm to scratch his forehead, Vera noticed the black hairs peeking out of his sleeve. Thick hair also sprouted from his chest, stopping at the red shaving line on his neck. This both repelled and attracted her. Her first and only lover, Milosz, had had smooth, fair skin that took on a honeyed hue in the sun. Vera's body suddenly remembered how she and Milosz used to cling to each other like kittens. She loved to burrow into his thin, sickly body, to inject it with warmth and strength and health, of which she had plenty, and to feel how the more she flowed into him, the fuller she became. Now her stomach contracted and her face fell, and she almost got up to leave. Tuvia, who had not noticed the commotion she was experiencing, stood up and said that he had to go to a secretariat meeting, but as far as he was concerned the matter was settled and they could give it a try. He held his hand out in a straight line, as though unfolding a carpenter's ruler.

His clumsy proposal elicited peals of laughter from Vera, despite her mournful thoughts of Milosz. Looking scolded, Tuvia stood there and made a characteristic effort to shrink his body. "So what do you say, Vera?" he asked pleadingly, and sat back down on the edge of the sofa, lost and completely pliable. Vera still hesitated. She liked him, he seemed manly and direct and readable—"I straight-away saw his potential"—but on the other hand, she knew almost nothing about him.

Just then, with the miserable timing that typified almost every important moment in his life, in came Rafael, Tuvia's youngest son, with a black eye, gashes on his face, and blood congealing around his mouth. He'd been in another fight, this time with some older boys at school. He lived, as was the kibbutz rule in those days, in a school dormitory with the other kids and had come home for the customary afternoon tea. He had on the hooded sweatshirt from his mother's funeral, which he wore every day no matter the weather. He opened the screen door and saw his father sitting shyly next to Vera, and he froze. Vera quickly stood up and went toward him, and he sounded a cautionary grunt. She was not frightened. She stood facing him and gave him a curious look.

Rafael, like his father, was confused by her gaze. He'd seen her before, of course, passing by on the kibbutz paths or in the dining hall, but she hadn't made any impression. A little woman, determined and fast, with pursed lips. That was more or less what he'd seen. It had never occurred to him that she was the mother of Nina, the girl who furnished his fantasies day and night. "You're Rafael," Vera said cheerfully, and it sounded as if she knew a lot more than that. Without taking her eyes off Rafael, Vera sent Tuvia to the bathroom for some iodine and gauze. Then she reached out to Rafael's bloody face and touched the corner of his mouth with her finger.

There came a sharp yell and a muffled curse in Serbo-Croatian, which brought Tuvia running from the bathroom. Rafael stood there startled, with a taste of foreign blood on his lips. Vera was trying to stanch the blood dripping from her finger onto the floor. Tuvia, who had never hit Rafael, lunged at him, but Vera pounced with her arms out and stood between them. As she did so, she let out a hoarse, deep, almost inhuman warning. Her movement and the terrifying sound she emitted made Rafael feel, deep in his gut, like a cub: "She was an animal fighting for its young," he told me.

And although it was incongruous with everything he felt toward her, he suddenly wanted very desperately to be this animal's cub.

Tuvia was not a violent man, and he was frightened by the force that had burst out of him. Ashamed, he kept mumbling, "I'm sorry, Rafi, forgive me." Vera leaned on the wall, slightly dizzied, though not from the blood—blood never scared her. She shut her eyes. Her eyelids trembled and concealed a quick conversation with Milosz. It had been almost twelve years since he'd committed suicide in the

UDBA's torture chambers in Belgrade. She told him she was going to live with a different man now, but that she was absolutely not saying goodbye to him or to their love.

She opened her eyes and looked at Rafael. She thought how much he looked like his father, and what a striking man he would become, but she also saw what it had done to him to have lost his mother at such a young age. Nina, her daughter, had also lost a parent, under indescribable circumstances, but Rafael's devastation and loneliness and neglect made Vera feel motherly in a way she never had before. She reiterated that sentiment to me several times over the years, with a broad spectrum of emphases. "How could you have never felt it before?" I once blurted. "You already had Nina! You had a daughter!" We were walking on our favorite path, in the fields around the kibbutz, arm in arm, which is still how she likes to walk with me, despite the difference in height. She, as is her wont, replied with dreadful candor: "It's like with Nina I had missed-carriage, and with Rafi it all of a sudden was everything right."

Rafael and Tuvia scarcely breathed under her gaze, and that was the moment when she knew without a doubt that she would marry Tuvia, and would have married him—she said this more than once—even if he'd been ugly and a scoundrel and a drummer in a brothel; this was one of her many peculiar idioms, the meaning of which was never entirely clear, and which Tuvia's family through the ages gleefully adopted. Because what are all your noble ideals worth—Vera asked herself at that moment—and what is the point of all the communism and the solidarity and the red star and the inspiring Pavel Korchagin in *How the Steel Was Tempered,* and what is the point of all the wars you fought for a better, more just world?

They're all worth zilch—she answered herself—if you abandon this child now.

For a moment or two they were each lost in their own world. I like to imagine them standing there with their heads bowed, as if listening to an emulsion beginning to fizz inside them. That was, in fact, the moment when my family was created. It was also the moment when, ultimately, I myself began to transpire.

Tuvia Bruck was my grandfather. Vera is my grandmother.

Rafael, Rafi, R, is, as we've said, my father. And Nina—

Nina isn't here.

She's gone, Nina.

But that was always her unique contribution to the family.

And me?

Dear notebook, with your seventy-two locally made tree-free pages: I've filled a quarter of you already and we haven't even been properly introduced.

Gili.

A problematic name whichever way you look at it, being not only derived from the Hebrew root for "rejoice," but phrased in the imperative.

Rafael retreated into his room, which was as tiny and dark as a lair. He shut the door and sat down on his bed. The little woman frightened him. He'd never seen his father so enfeebled. On the other side of his door, Vera walked Tuvia to the sofa and let him bandage her two bitten fingers. She delighted in how pale her hand looked between his. They shared a good silence. Tuvia fastened the bandage with a safety pin. He put his mouth to her fingers and bit off a stray thread, and her heart was dissolved by his potent masculinity.

He said, "The boy has been like that since his mother died. Or since she got ill, really." Vera put her bandaged hand on his. "I have Nina and you have Rafael." The quiet words brought them closer. She resisted running her fingers through his thick hair.

"So what do you say, Vera, maybe we should—"

"Together, we can try, why not."

Two days ago we celebrated Vera turning ninety (plus two months; she had pneumonia on the actual date and we postponed the party). The family gathered in the kibbutz clubhouse. "The family," of course, means Tuvia's family, which Vera had joined, but, over the course of four decades, she'd become its core. It's always amusing to think that most of the grandchildren and great-grandchildren who cling to her and compete for her attention don't even know that she is not their biological grandmother. Each child in our family goes through a little initiation rite when, usually around the age of ten, they learn the truth. And then, without exception, they ask a question or two, furrow their brows slightly, narrow their eyes, and finally give a quick flick of their head to shake off the bothersome new information.

Chana, Grandpa Tuvia's eldest daughter, my father's older sister, gave a short speech: "After thirty-two years of them being together, I think I can say from the bottom of my heart that not only is Vera a full member of the family, but that without her we probably would not be the family we are." Chana spoke simply and modestly, as usual, and Rafael was not the only one who wiped away a tear. Vera twisted her mouth—she has an automatic grimace of disdain when she senses things are getting sappy—and Rafael, who was taking pictures, as he does at all family events, whispered to me that every movement and gesture Vera makes are so hers.

She'd announced right from the start that today she was the only one who was allowed to say nice things about herself, so we could just go ahead and eat. But this time the family wouldn't let her off the hook. People from every generation and every age got up and sang her praises, a highly unusual occurrence because the Brucks are not known for being gregarious, and it would never have occurred to them to say such direct and intimate things to anyone, and in public moreover. But Vera was someone they wanted to say things to. Almost every person in the room had a story about how Vera had helped them, cared for them, saved them from something or from themselves. My story was the most sensational, featuring a touch of suicide at the age of twenty-three due to having my heart broken by a man whose name shall be expunged from my film-ography. But it was clear to both Vera and me that what I had to say I would tell her privately, as always, eye to eye. One especially stirring moment occurred when Tom, Esther's two-and-a-half-year-old grandson, needed his diaper changed and adamantly refused to have his mother or Grandma Esther do it, and when Esther asked whom he wanted, he shrieked, "Tata Vera!" and everyone laughed heartily.

Vera jumped up with remarkable speed, ran almost like a girl, except that her body was slightly bent to the left, and changed Tom's diaper on a side table, all while signaling for us to go on talking and "get it over with already." She focused on Tom's grinning face, speaking into his belly button with Serbo-Croatian murmurs in a Hungarian accent, while also listening intently to the things being said about her behind her back. When, unburdened by her ninety years of age, she waved the freshly changed Tom up in the air while he laughed and tried to grab her glasses, I felt a bite deep inside, the pain of what I will never be and never do, and I missed my man Meir so badly, and I realized I should have asked him to come with me: I knew, after all, how exposed and vulnerable I would be here, with Nina, my rarely seen mother, present.

Forty-five years earlier, in the winter of 1963, on the evening when Vera and Tuvia were about to start living together, Rafael was walking to the kibbutz gymnasium. Behind the gym was an empty sandy lot, where, in the year since his mother had died, he went to practice throwing shot put. The sun had set, but there was still a faint strip of light in the sky, and splinters of rain were in the air. Again and again, dozens of times, Rafael launched three- and four-kilo iron balls into the air. The fury and hatred did wonders for his distances. When he got cold and wanted to go to his room at the boarding school and bury his head under the pillow and not think about what his father was doing tonight, or perhaps at this very moment, with his Yugoslavian whore, suddenly there was Vera right before his eyes. She was holding a brown suitcase that was almost as big as her, fastened with leather straps and metal buckles (a beautiful accessory that I've been coveting for years). Vera put the suitcase down on the mud and stood facing Rafael with her arms spread out, as though she were offering herself up for trial. He had no choice. He kept putting shots without looking at her. In the two weeks that had passed since he bit her on their first meeting, Rafael had learned that Vera was the mother of his beloved. This fact was so horrifying that he tried with all his might to distract himself from it, but now Vera was right in front of him, a living reminder.

The rain had caught her by surprise. She was wearing a thin eggplant-colored sweater with a white muslin collar, and white shoes that were already muddy. A small purple hat was perched on her head at an angle that irritated Rafael no less than the hat itself.

She also had a thin gold chain and pearl earrings, things that only city girls wore.

In fact, now that I'm writing this, it occurs to me: that was Vera's bridal outfit.

It was her wedding night.

In her heavy Hungarian accent—at home in Croatia they'd spoken mostly Hungarian—she asked, "Rafael, will you talk to me for moment?" But he pulled his hood down over his eyes, turned his back, and put another iron shot into the dark. Vera hesitated, then walked forward, picked up a shot from the pile, and gauged its weight. Rafael stopped in midmotion, seeming to have forgotten what the next step was. Without any preparation, no circling around herself, only one deep groan, Vera put the iron shot to an absurd distance, perhaps a whole yard farther than his.

Rafael was a thin but strong young man, one of the strongest in his class. He picked up another shot and nestled it in the round of his shoulder, his eyes closed, in no hurry. He crammed all his loathing of her into that ball.

It was not enough, and he kept circling around himself, infusing the ball with his hatred of his father who was about to betray Mother with this stranger who was Nina's mother. Even that thought could not make him launch the ball, and he kept turning on his axis until he discharged a dark spurt of fury at his mother—at her, of all people—for having begun her retreat into her illness when he was only five years old.

The darkness thickened; the rain hardened. Vera rubbed her hands together, because of the cold or because of the competitive glee that had been sparked in her. In my film, Rafael gave a demonstration. I had seen that quality in her, and I did not like it. Incidentally, to this day she's the same way: something steely and determined emerges in her face, her eyes, even her skin, at the height of an argument or a conflict, usually over politics. If, say, she suspects someone in the family or the kibbutz of adopting a right-wing position or if they dare to say a kind word about the settlers or, God forbid, begin to find just a little bit of religion—then she'll unleash an ungodly terror, fire and brimstone.

Rafael the boy also sensed—he later explained—that this was "not the way a mother moves." Not that he knew exactly how a mother might move. He was utterly illiterate in motherhood when Vera burst into his life. She took off her necklace, bracelets, and earrings, placed them next to one another on the suitcase, and covered them with the ridiculous hat. When everything was in its place, she quickly rolled up the sleeves of her sweater and blouse. That was when Rafael saw her muscles and snarled tendons. He stared at them anxiously: With muscles like those, how could she dream of being someone's mother?

The world had gone dark now. Thunder rolled in from Mount Carmel. Vera and Rafael hardly saw the shots they were putting. Only their black metallic glimmer was briefly visible in the light shed by a path lamp, and sometimes by a distant flash of lightning. The shots fell closer and closer to them, and when they picked them up off the mud, they had almost no strength left to hurl them again. But they kept at it, the two of them, throwing and groaning and standing there panting with their hands on their hips. Every few minutes they walked side by side in silence to retrieve the balls that lolled about like fattened tadpoles in puddles.

A moment before Rafael admitted he was out of strength, she put her shot down, held up her hands, and walked to the suitcase. He had the feeling that she'd intentionally lost to him, and he liked that. That *was* what a mother did. ("You have to understand, Gili, in those days I divided all of humanity into two, and you'll laugh, but it included men: who is a mother and who isn't a mother.") Vera stood with her back to him and quickly put on her jewelry, then her hat, which she tilted at the angle that gave Rafael the urge to grab it off her head and throw it into the mud and jump up and down on it with both feet. Then she turned to him. Her body was trembling from the cold, her lips were frozen, but her gaze was steady.

"Listen for one minute. I came here to talk to you before I go into your home. I need you should know: I do not want to be your stepmother, God forbid. I could never mother you." She had decent Hebrew—back in Yugoslavia, while waiting for their exit permits, she and Nina had learned Hebrew from a Jewish journalist—but she had that accent, and it was raining, and for a moment Rafael thought she'd said *murder you.*

You'll never be my mother, he thought to himself. You'll never know how to be like my mother. In the last years of her illness, she had been confined to her bedroom and he'd hardly seen her. Sometimes, when he heard her calling him in the throaty, masculine voice she'd developed, he would jump out of his bedroom window and run away. He couldn't tolerate her face, which had puffed up like a balloon and rendered her a caricature of the lovely, refined mother he used to have, and he couldn't bear the sour smell she gave off, which filled the house and clung to his clothes and his soul. When he was little, five or six, there were nights when Tuvia carried him sleeping to his mother's bed, so that she could see him and touch him. When Rafael woke up the next morning, he always knew—by the smell of his pajamas—that he'd been taken to his mother at night, and then he would demand, sometimes with a tantrum, that his pajamas be sent immediately to the laundry.

Vera said to Rafael, "No one in the world can be like your mother, and it's your home and I am only guest, but I promise to try and do my best, and if you don't want me, you only must say one word, and I will at that moment take my things and leave."

A minute? Five minutes? How long did they stand out there in the rain? There are different versions. Vera swears—replete with a ceremonial dry sideways spit, her upper lip covering her lower—that it lasted at least ten minutes. Rafael, without the spitting, maintains that it was less than half a minute. I, as usual, tend to believe him.

In my old movie, which we're now watching on Vera's television, you can hear me quoting to Rafael something I once heard from his father, Tuvia, my agronomist grandfather: "Some seeds require nothing but a speck of earth to sprout." At fifteen, I found that line captivating. Ten minutes or half a minute, Vera caught hold of Rafael's hands, and he did not pull them away. She was still bandaged where he'd bitten her, but with her little thumbs she stroked his hands over and over again and waited until his sobs had subsided. It turned out that a speck of earth could provide for two, if they were desperate enough.

Then Vera said, in her Ben-Gurion-like domineering tone, "Rafael! Off we go!" She would not let him carry her suitcase. They walked silently to Tuvia's apartment. That walk, with the rain falling diagonally in the yellow beams of the path lamps, is something I'm dying to reconstruct one day, when I start making my own films, which will be any day now, fingers crossed. They did not meet anyone on the way. The whole kibbutz was indoors while the two of them, drenched and distraught, wordlessly confirmed their simple, unequivocal pact, a pact that has been upheld for forty-five years and never once violated.

They reached the apartment—"the room," in kibbutzish—and Vera put her suitcase down by the door. They heard Rafael's father inside, singing an aria from *Il Seraglio*, which he always sang when he was in a good mood. Vera looked at Rafael: "Will you come tomorrow for tea?" He stood there looking down, tortured. With two bandaged fingers, she lifted his chin. It would have occurred to no one else to do that to Rafael. "This is way of the world, Rafael," she said. He thought that after that night he would not be able to look his father in the eye, or her. "Good night," she said, and he repeated her words in a whisper.

Vera waited for him to disappear around the bend in the path. Then she took a little handbag out of one of the suitcase pockets, retrieved a compact mirror and a pencil, and proceeded to make up her face. Peering from behind a bougainvillea, Rafael watched her try unsuccessfully to puff up her wet hair—her hair was always sparse, which to me slightly belied the force of her mental and physical strength. When she looked up at the sky and her lips moved, he thought she was praying, but then he realized she was conversing with someone invisible, explaining things to him, listening, blowing a kiss up to the heavens. To Rafael she was "like a woman you see in the movies," but unlike in the movies, she was practical and utilitarian and, as she herself attested, "without drop of patience for scoundrels or fools."

Vera perked up her nose, her chin, her short stature. Rafael forced himself to think about his modest, quiet mother, but she faded, refusing to appear. Vera knocked once on the door with her hand clenched in a fist. Tuvia stopped singing. Rafael knew this was his last chance to do something. He feverishly searched himself for his mother, so that at least she would know that he was being loyal to her at this moment, or almost loyal, and so that she would finally free him from the punishments and deprivations he imposed upon himself for her sake. She gave no sign of response. Her absence inside him was frightening, as if part of his soul had been erased along with her. That was when he understood that his mother had withdrawn her forgiveness forever. "Like the mark of Cain," Rafael said to the camera in a dwindling voice. I was only fifteen, as I've said, but I was already starting to grasp something about families and missed opportunities and things you can't go back and repair, and mostly I wanted to stop filming and go over and hug him and comfort him, but of course I did not dare. He would not have forgiven me if I'd squandered a shot like that.

The rain fell softly. The globe lamp over the door cast a pale-yellow light on Vera. Tuvia opened the door and said her name, at first in astonishment, because of her drenched clothes, and then in a feverish murmur, over and over again, holding her in his arms.

The door was shut. Rafael stood there, empty. He had no idea what to do. He was afraid to be alone, afraid that now he would have to do something terrible to himself, something inevitable that was growing stronger inside him. A hand touched his shoulder and he jumped. It was Nina, who'd been driving him wild in his fantasies. Her beautiful, white, soulless face. The face of a raptor, he now thought. "Mommy and Daddy are having a good time," Nina said with a crooked smile, "we can, too."

Many years later, at the shiva after Tuvia's death, Vera told us what she'd said to him when she walked into his room on their wedding night. "Before we go in bed, I want you to know right now: I will always respect you and be your best friend and most faithful, but I will not lie. I am a woman who can in her life love only one man, and no more. I love Milosz, who was my husband and died by Tito, more than anything in world, more than my life. I will every night tell you about him, and also what I went through in camps because I so loved him. And also I cry very much." And Tuvia said: "It's good that you're saying everything directly, face-to-face, Vera. This way there are no illusions and no misunderstandings. Here, in our bedroom, there will be pictures of them both: your husband and my wife. You will tell me about him, and I will tell you about her, and they will be sacred to both of us."

And we, the younger members of the family—known collectively as the kindred—who worshipped the ground she walked on and stayed with her for the entire shiva, bowed our heads, as required by the gravity of the situation and out of respect for the dead, and also so that we would not encounter one another's eyes and burst out laughing. Vera wiped away a pearly tear with the edge of the purple lavender-scented handkerchief (such a thing does exist, I swear it does; up until a few years ago, Khaled, her Bedouin friend from the nearby village, used to bring her sacks full of lavender) and then, to the astonishment of us all, Vera noted in an utterly flat and horizontal voice, "But during the . . . you know . . . the business, Tuvia and I would used to turn around their photographs to the wall." She waited with a blank face until the kindred had finished shaking with laughter, and added, with perfect timing, "They got to know that wall very much well."

Since I'm already meandering off course in that dubious neighborhood, and since I've already desecrated the modesty of my grandparents, I must offer another anecdote for posterity: I don't recall exactly when it was, but Vera and I were standing in her tiny postage stamp of a kitchen, as we often did, when suddenly out of nowhere she said, "On our first night, the first time that me and Tuvia, you know . . . well, Tuvia put on 'head covering,' that is what we called it, even though he knew very well how old I was. And that is when I saw that he truly was gentleman!"

The next morning, while Rafael, stunned by happiness and awash in love, was lost in the deepest sleep he'd known for years, Nina packed up her belongings in a backpack and silently left her room in the leper colony, where the two of them had spent the night. She crossed the kibbutz in a straight line and barged into Tuvia and Vera's apartment without knocking while they were eating their first breakfast as a couple. Without any preambles, she relayed to them in minute detail what she'd done with Rafael. As she looked at Nina, it occurred to Vera that not even in the UDBA's torture chambers in Belgrade, and not even with the wardens on the barren island, had she been hated the way her daughter hated her. She put her knife and fork down. "Our whole lives, Nina?" she said. And Nina replied: "Even beyond."

Years later, Vera told me that she stood up that morning and said to Tuvia that if he asked her to leave now, she would. She would leave the kibbutz with Nina, and he would never have to see them again. He went over and put his arm around her shoulders and said, "Veraleh, you are not leaving anymore. This is home." Nina looked at them and nodded. Nina had—still has—a nod of bitter happiness every time an ominous prophecy of hers comes true. She picked up her small backpack and hugged it, but for some reason she couldn't walk out. Perhaps something in the way they stood there facing her drove her mad. Then there was a quick-fire skirmish in Serbo-Croatian. Nina hissed that Vera was betraying Milosz. Vera clapped her hands to her cheeks and yelled that she had never betrayed Milosz: on the contrary, she was madly faithful to him, no other woman would do for her man what she had done. Then it went quiet. Nina sniffed something in the air and bristled all over. Vera turned pale and pursed her lips, then sat down weakly.

Nina slung the backpack over her shoulder. Tuvia said, "But, Nina, we want to help you, we both do, let us help you." With tears in her eyes, she stomped her foot: "And don't go looking for me, d'you hear me? Don't you dare look for me!" She turned to leave but soon stopped. "Say hello to your boy from me," she said to Tuvia, "your boy is the kindest person I've ever met." Her face was briefly illumined by a note of childishness, of heartrending innocence. Sometimes, when I feel kindly toward her—I have those moments once in a while; a person isn't made of stone—I manage to remind myself that innocence was one of the things she was robbed of at a young age. "And tell him it's not because of him at all," she said, "tell him that women will love him a lot, a whole lot, and that he'll forget me. You'll tell him, right?"

And she left.

Jumping ahead again. I've been writing day and night. The flight is the day after tomorrow and I'm not getting out of this chair until then. Here is another memory that seems pertinent: It's years after Vera and Tuvia's wedding night. Tuvia, the sweetest of grandfathers, is still with us. Grandma Vera and I peel vegetables for a casserole in her kitchen. It's afternoon, one of the loveliest hours on the kibbutz and in the kitchen. A low-hanging sun sends golden rays through the jars of pickled cucumbers, onions, and eggplants on the windowsill. A pail full of pecans that Vera and I gathered that morning sits on the counter. Vera's big tape deck plays "Bésame Mucho" and other drooling tunes. It's a moment of perfection and great intimacy between us, when suddenly, out of the blue, she says, "When I married your grandfather Tuvia, it was twelve years after Milosz. Twelve years I was alone. No man ever touched me even this much! With fingernail! And I wanted Tuvia, how could I not, but mostly I wanted to live with Tuvia so that I could take care of your father, Rafi, which was for me like they say in Zionism—the dream come true. But I was also scared of the bed like fire! I was scared dead what would happen, how would I know which way is up, and if I would even get back the wanting. And Tuvia did not give up, after all he was a man, only fifty-four, and to tell truth he still doesn't give up today, even though I've been ready to close up shop for long time."

"Grandma!" I spluttered. I was barely fifteen: What were the grown-ups in this family thinking? Had they no instinct for preserving children's innocence? "Why are you telling me this?"

"Because I want you to know everything—everything! No secrets between us."

"What secrets? Who's keeping secrets?"

And here she let out a sigh that came from an inner crypt I was unfamiliar with. "Gili, in you I want to put everything I had in life. Everything."

"Why me?"

"Because you are like me."

I knew that this, coming from her, was a compliment, but something in her voice, and even more so in her look, made my skin crawl. "I don't understand, Grandma."

She put the peeler down and placed both hands on my shoulders. Her eyes were in mine, and I had nowhere to escape. "And I know, Gili, that you will never let anyone here twist my story against me."

I think I laughed. Or, rather, giggled. I tried to turn the conversation into a joke. At the time, I knew nothing about "her story."

Then her eyes gleamed with an inconceivable, almost animalistic ferocity. And I remember thinking, just for a moment, that I did not want to be this animal's cub.

They did look for Nina, of course. They turned over every stone, tried to get the police to help, unsuccessfully, then contacted a private investigator, who combed the country from north to south and finally announced: "The earth has swallowed her. Start getting used to the fact that she's not coming back." But after almost a year they began to receive signs of life. Once every four weeks, with strange punctuality, a blank postcard arrived. From Eilat, from Tiberias, from Mitzpeh Ramon, from Kiryat Shmoneh. Vera and Tuvia followed in the postcards' tracks, walked the streets, went into stores and hotels and nightclubs and synagogues, showing everyone they met a photo of Nina from when she'd immigrated to Israel. Vera grew very thin in those years, and her hair turned white. Tuvia was with her everywhere, driving her in a pickup truck the kibbutz let him use, making sure she ate and drank. When he realized she was deteriorating, he flew to Serbia with her, to the little village where Milosz was born and buried. There, in the village, Vera was like a queen. Milosz's relatives loved and admired her, and every evening they came to hear her tell the story of her love for Milosz. In the mornings Tuvia repaired the engines of tractors and old threshers, while Vera, wearing a wide-brimmed straw hat, sat on a rocking chair by Milosz's grave, in front of the mossy gray headstone. She lit long yellow candles and told him about the hardships she was suffering because of Nina, their daughter, and about their search for her, and about Tuvia, her angel, without whom she could not have borne all this.

Rafael conducted his own searches. At least once a week he ran away from the boarding school and roamed the streets of cities, kibbutzim, and Arab villages, simply looking around. He grew up quickly in those years, becoming even more handsome and anguished. Girls pursued him; they were crazy about him. A little over a decade ago, for his fiftieth birthday—Vera would not let such an occasion pass without a big production, of course; even at fifty he was still her beloved orphan—she pulled a treasure out from one of her jumbled drawers: an envelope full of photographs of Rafi from those years. Pictures of parties and field trips, races and basketball games, graduations. All the moist looks sent his way, the smiles, the lips, the young breasts surging at him—he neither saw nor felt any of it. "He sees Nina in his bowl of soup," said Vera, employing one of her typically enigmatic sayings. Even when he began his military service, he kept looking for her whenever he had a day off. With money she got from Yugoslavia—the president, Marshal Tito himself, had ordered that she be paid a lifelong pension—Vera bought Rafael a secondhand Leica, which she hoped would distract him from his anguish and perhaps put an end to his yearning. But instead he began to photograph his voyage.

He wandered the roads and described Nina to people he met, then asked permission to photograph them. Hundreds of times he told strangers, men and women, what little he knew about her. Over and over again he held up her picture and said, "Her name is Nina, we were together once, and she disappeared. Maybe you've seen her?" Sometimes when he heard himself, it sounded as though he were telling them a fairy tale.

But these random encounters began to work on him. His eyes opened up, he told me in my youthful movie when he talked about that era. He learned to observe. He was mainly drawn to the faces of hardworking people, whose features made them magnificent, sometimes even regal: "You could see that these people were trapped in a small, restrictive life." Vera and Tuvia tried to persuade him to stop wandering, to wake up, get his hair cut, go to university, take on a role at the kibbutz. After almost two years of searching he accepted that he would not find Nina and that he had essentially given up on her, but he could not give up on the photography. Moreover, I think—or I know, who better than me—that he could not abandon the search, could not stop watching the way a person who has lost something watches.

Thirty-two years after their first night together, Vera stood in the kitchen boiling water for afternoon tea. Tuvia was very sick by then. Vera refused to have him hospitalized or allow a paid caregiver into their home. For four years, day and night, she revived him, cheered his spirits, took him to concerts in Haifa and plays in Tel Aviv, solved crossword puzzles with him, changed his diapers, and read three newspapers out loud to him every day. It was widely believed among the kindred that due to Vera's war of attrition, death was considering making a special dispensation for Tuvia.

The kettle boiled, and she called Tuvia with their private whistle: the first few notes of "Tzena, Tzena." Tuvia came slowly, skin and bones, coughing heavily. He walked down the hallway—the same hallway he'd run down years ago when his son Rafael bit Vera (excuse me for sticking that in here, but a person likes to have her own little mythology). On his way, Tuvia held on to a coat hanging on a hook, then a chair back. He sat down and sighed. Vera looked at him and her heart sank. "Tuvia!" she thundered. "In pajamas? Is that any way to dress for five o'clock tea with a lady?" Tuvia gave a translucent smile, shuffled back to his room, put on his black polyester trousers, a light blue striped shirt that accentuated his blue eyes, and, to amuse Vera, the suede jacket that had served him for twenty-five years of formal events and was now several sizes too large. "Is this better, m'lady?" he asked and sat down, out of breath. Vera poured his tea. They both stared silently at the thin stream coming out of the spout, and Vera saw Tuvia's eyes roll back and his face turn ashen. She shouted, "Tuvia, don't leave me!" And he fell to the floor, dead.

I think I've already said that my dad and I are at Vera's, on the kib-butz, two days after her ninetieth birthday party and two days before we fly to Croatia. Where is Vera? Why aren't we hearing from her? We will, have no doubt. She's gone out, as she does every morning, to visit "her old folk," all of whom, incidentally, are several years younger than her. She will sprinkle them with her peevish dust of optimism ("I already told Rafi: fifteen minutes you're not to keep me alive if comes the day when I can't stand up for Women in Black protest on Fridays! Not fifteen minutes!"), and she'll walk thirty laps around the pool in her pink bathing cap, lips pursed, arms swinging vigorously. Then she'll straddle her mobility scooter—face glued to the front visor, bum up, a menace to anyone on the kibbutz paths—and ride to the cemetery. As is her daily cus-tom, she will place one rose from her garden on Tuvia's first wife Dushinka's grave, then proceed to Tuvia's, where she will lay two roses, one for him and one for Milosz, whose spirit she summons to make the subterranean voyage from his grave in a village in Serbia.

Perched on the edge of Tuvia's grave, she rocks her body back and forth and tells her two husbands what's new in the family and in Israel. She laments the sorry state of things: "The world wants to kill the humanity. Some of them it killed already, and now wants to kill what's left." She bemoans the occupation: "*Yoy!* And to think that it happened to us, to Jews, such tragedy of tragedy are we." She cries a little, off-loads things from her heart, and wonders, "Milosz and Tuvia, my dear husbands, where are you? I'm more than ninety already! When will you come to take me? Don't forget your Vera here!" Then she hurtles back on the scooter to her little clinic next to the doctor's office, where she sits for three hours without getting up, dispensing advice concerning diets, love, and varicose veins to all who seek it.

And then one day, by chance, he saw her. Rafael did. On Jaffa Road in Jerusalem, next to the Generali Building, at a bus stop. He quickly hid behind a noticeboard, snapped a picture of her getting on a bus, and did not follow her ("I was afraid she'd make a scene"). The next day at the same time she was there again, wearing a floral headscarf, large butterfly-shaped sunglasses, and a short, narrow green skirt. A delight to anyone seeing her for the first time, but lonely and wan to Rafael. Nina was working at the State Laboratory for Analytical Chemistry, near the Russian Compound downtown. For eight hours a day she analyzed food dyes to find out if they contained toxins.

(It sounds so strange to write that. Why would she be working in a place like that?)

Her duties at the lab included cleaning, and she always stayed after the other workers had left for the day. Out of boredom—or because she was in no hurry to get home, to the preposterous stranger waiting for her there—she began painting with food coloring on the thin glass microscope slides. She painted the street as viewed through the barred window. She painted her father, Milosz, and his beloved horse. She painted various parts of their little apartment on Kosmajska Street in Belgrade. Sometimes she painted Rafael. The beautiful lips that had kissed her, the bleak and demanding passion in his eyes, the devotedness that had terrified her.

Every afternoon Rafael darted around the streets and alleys leading to her bus stop. When he got lucky, he tracked down another section of the route she took from the lab to the bus. After a few days of this scuttling, he located the lab, and he walked in and stood opposite Nina while she mopped the floor. She gave a startled yelp, followed by her sardonic laugh, and leaned one arm on the table. From up close he thought she looked ill, anemic. There were black crescents under her eyes. They say rescue fantasies are a feminine thing. If that is true, then there is no one more feminine than my father: his mind told him to leave right then. To recuperate from her. Instead, he hugged her as hard as he could and heard himself ask if she would come to live with him.

She looked at him with her slow, faraway gaze. I can actually see her dipping him in some internal wasteland for a long moment. Then she ceremoniously handed him the mop and said, "But first you'll have to slay the dragon." He thought she was joking.

But there was a dragon.

"I ran away from the kibbutz and I was all over the country and I partied like crazy, and at some point I found myself here, in Jerusalem," Nina told my father's camera in a film I found a few months ago in his "archives"—four fruit crates from the kibbutz where he keeps souvenirs from his filmmaking years. It's a seven-and-a-half-minute clip from a sixteen-millimeter film about her, which he never finished. This year I digitized the clip, and I might use it in the film I make about them, if there's any good material from our journey to the island. There, I've said it explicitly, and the sky hasn't fallen off its chair.

In the clip, Nina is girlish and beautiful, and she's in a good mood, at least at the beginning of the conversation. "In Jerusalem I met a Korean man—yes, from Korea, can you imagine?" Her teeth are small and pure white, her amazingly dark eyebrows are almost straight, the thin crease beneath her eyes adds a hint of disdain to everything she says. "And he got me that job at the lab, he knew someone there, and on weekends he would take me to work for him. He was a strange sort of man . . ."

Vera told me about him once. The whole story is such a non sequitur, so disjointed and cold and foreign, that it almost hurts even me. This man was a biochemist who ran a private lab in his home, "a terrible man," Vera told me, "and he used to force Nina to give blood once in a week for his experiments." But Vera did not know everything.

Nina in the film takes a delighted drag on her cigarette and laughs slightly hysterically. "I usually like tall, handsome men, like Rafi, who's filming me now. Hello, Rafael, *amore*"—she blows him a kiss—"and this guy was small with big ears. Okay, I'm telling the story . . . He was Korean . . ."

Her face grows more rigid by the minute. I notice tiny changes in it, which I seem to be very aware of with her, and not only because of my professional instincts. From this point on she talks fast, in a dry, flat voice: "But he grew up in Japan, and later he ended up in America—"

It's as though a total stranger is speaking from inside her. The smoking gets frequent and irritable, almost mechanical. My response, when I saw the clip for the first time, was: What is this rubbish? Who cares about this? Why is she going on about some Korean?

"And then he fell in love with a Jewish girl—she's dead now, never mind—and followed her to Jerusalem, and that's how he met me on the street when I was looking for somewhere to stay, and he used to send me out to sleep with strangers and come back and tell him about it."

If there is any last remaining trace of evidence that might incriminate me as her daughter, it is that even today, at my age,

I seriously want to die when she talks about her sex life. "That's what he liked, and the crazier and more bizarre it was, the more he liked it. He always wanted details. Wanted me to notice every detail." Great, I tell her silently, you really could have been a fantastic script girl. Maybe that's where I get it from. I try to guess where, in what location, he filmed her for this clip. There are pine trees in the background, and it's a hilly area. A wood in the mountains outside Jerusalem?

"How did I feel?" She laughs, and her laughter is slow, disconnected. "You're not asking, Rafi? Of course you're not. You're always a little afraid of my answers, aren't you?"

"How . . . how was it for you?" Rafi's voice is also dry and flat. His camera is really honed in on her, on her face, her eyes. Her pretty mouth.

"Like drinking water from a plastic cup and throwing it away." Silence. Nina shrugs her shoulders impatiently, as if to say: Let's get this over with.

"And . . . how long did it go on with the Korean?"

"Two years."

"For two years you threw out cups of water?"

"A couple times a week."

"Tell me."

"What is there to tell. I would go out, walk the streets, hunt down a person, a man, sometimes a woman, do it, come back to tell him."

Rafi lets out a long, quiet exhalation. When that film was made, he did not yet know what she had in store for him.

"And in the end you found me, Rafi. You all know that already." Nina looks straight at the camera, suddenly smiling with all her beauty, erupting at us. It's all a game for her. "Life poseur"—a forgotten idiom from my youth heaves inside me like nausea. The term used to terrify me, even though I did not understand it. I found it in the book that was my secret bible in those days, *Ideal Marriage: Its Physiology and Technique* (whose Hebrew translation included a bonus treatise: "The Law of Marriage" by Prentice Mulford). I was eleven when I found it on Vera and Tuvia's bookshelf, and for a couple of years I used to read it every time I was alone in their home. Even the chapter names were titillating: "The Purpose of Human Eroticism," "Advances in Sexuology for Married Persons." I read feverishly. I memorized. "The preamble to one's choice of a lovemaking partner is the lovemaking disposition—a physiological condition in which the organism reaches a state of mental and physical arousal that requires release." I didn't understand it, but my organism quivered with a new sort of tension that required release. I read it over and over again. The language was peculiar, almost biblical. "Woman is not the 'weaker,' but the finer vessel, which contains the wine of spirituality. She is to man what the delicately adjusted magnetic needle of the compass is to the helm which steers the ship. Being the finer instrument, she does need to be shielded and protected . . ." I would walk down a street in Jerusalem, or on the kibbutz paths, and pick out beautiful people, but also others, men who looked like they could helm, and women who definitely contained the wine of spirituality. I would look deep into their eyes and, unbeknownst to them, force them to recite selected quotes for me: "It is sufficient for a creature of the opposite sex to appear, one who is blessed with the physical and emotional virtues suitable for the lovemaking conditions of a particular individual and his dreams, for love to be born!"

As I said, I was eleven, or slightly older, when we made each other's acquaintance—my guide to the jungle of matrimony and I. I did not tell anyone, I progressed through the chapters and deciphered every single word, sometimes with the help of a dictionary, and I learned how to speak like the book, but only under my covers. I liked to open it to a random page and put my finger on a passage, and I felt as if a prophecy were being thrown out at me. I remember the time when I read: "There are people who possess a feigned affectivity. People who are extremely impoverished in the realm of emotion and play the part of affectives. They are known as 'life poseurs.' Such individuals are only rarely qualified for sustained married life."

I wanted to die. Why did I, of all people, have to have a woman like that—

"Hey, Rafi, my darling," Nina chirrups in the film. Her Hebrew is impeccable, without the slightest accent. She speaks five or six languages just as fluently, the life poseur. "You combed the whole country for me until you found me, and you took me home, and you beat the living daylights out of that guy, you almost slayed the dragon. I want you to know, dear viewers, that Rafi always dreamed of rescuing a princess from a dragon. And ever since then we've been together, and not together, and meanwhile poor Gili was born, and now we're even more entangled, and Rafi is making a movie about us." She waves her hand at Rafael.

I rewind the film. Even on the hundredth time, she really does say it.

The camera holds steady on her face, as if giving her a chance to take it back, to say it was all a lie. But Nina has long ago erased any expression. She's gone. She is not. But where is she when she is not?

"And meanwhile poor Gili was born."

Rafael in the movie, as in life, cannot let go of her. He asks her if all that time she hadn't felt any living feeling for someone.

It takes her a while to come back from the place she was erased into. "There actually was one time . . . I went to the Old City, he often sent me to hang around there. He liked it when things happened to me with Arabs. It turned him on even more. Suddenly I heard Serbian, actual Serbian, with an accent from the villages in my father's region. Milosz's region. They were three sailors whose ship was docked in Haifa, and one of them was cute. I walked past him and threw out casually, in English, "Hey baby, come on, lose the others." I took him home, and he couldn't believe this was happening to him, that a girl who looked all right and spoke Serbian in his dialect would take him home and show him a good time, and even walk him to the bus afterward. With that guy I felt something."

Silence.

"Yeah, it wasn't a good situation," she says, and her face falls.

The camera is still on her.

"What's wrong with me, Rafi?"

Rafi does not answer.

The clip ends there.

I play it again.

They stayed in Jerusalem and lived together in a third-floor one-bedroom apartment in Kiryat Yovel. Nina worked at the lab, and Rafael took odd jobs. He loved her in all the ways she allowed him to, or imposed on him. Maybe she loved him, too—I'm not even getting into that, into what she felt for him; there are areas where every time I venture into them I experience suicidal nuttiness, and I can do without that—but her expressions did not return. On the contrary. Her beautiful face seemed to become even blander. He suspected that she was intentionally emptying it of meaning every time he looked at her with his kind eyes. "Like she was punishing me for something," he told my Sony in a perplexed tone, and the interviewer, a young expert on ideal marriage, its physiology and technique, remained tactfully quiet.

Time after time, Rafael told me, Nina would come back to him from her rambles, "dirty, smelly, defiled," he said softly, "sometimes actually injured, cut, with black-and-blue bruises." When she saw his look, she would flare up and fly at him, and not infrequently hit him, and he would defend himself, try to lock her in his arms so that she would calm down, but she was faster and wilder than him. And then there would come a moment when he lost his mind and started hitting her back, Rafael told the terrified young interviewer, who despite her rampant powers of imagination had never considered that possibility. "But you loved her!" the interviewer whispered in a choked-up voice. "How could you hit her if you loved her?" "I don't know, Gili, I don't know. These two"—and he raised his upper lip and showed the embarrassed camera his mouth and the gap where two molars should be—"these two, I lost in our wars." Silence. The camera is on him, but the drama is occurring in the camerawoman. Because suddenly, when I look at it now, it's painfully clear that the girl I was then, when we shot that film, was paying the price of her great deceit: posing as an adult.

By the way, in that horribly faded and pixelated film, you can see that Rafael also feels uncomfortable. He constantly shifts in his seat, doesn't look at me even once. He must know that he should stop the conversation here. That it's not appropriate. That the girl's emotional vessels cannot contain everything he is pouring into her. That it's practically criminal. But he also cannot stop. He cannot stop.

At least he spared me the descriptions of their sex when I filmed him, or kept them very concise. But again, he failed to grasp—how could he fail to grasp?—that it was the descriptions of their battles that distressed me and pained me far more.

We are both adults now. We sit in Vera's apartment on the kib-butz, just he and I, and we watch—what a sifted word—the conver-sation we filmed here, in this same room, twenty-four years ago.

And I never did anything with that film.

The two of us, Rafael and I, we did nothing with it. We shoved it into storage and forgot.

"I'm so sorry," Rafael says now, looking anguished, "I was such an idiot."

"Yes," I say, and I want to cry for me, but I don't, I never cry, and we both say nothing more.

What is there to say when there is nothing to be done.

At first, when he and Nina still had tender moments (almost always aided by marijuana and gallons of domestic cognac), he dared to hope—although of course he did not tell her, because how could you say something like this—that if they had a child, her expres-sions would return. But even after Nina gave birth to a five-pound baby just shy of being a preemie—who looked as if all she wanted to do was grow smaller and smaller until she vanished completely—even then Nina's missing expressions did not return, and perhaps even the opposite: her eyes were more hollow, always looking right through you, and seemed to hardly blink, as though they'd frozen in a distant moment on something she suddenly saw or understood. That was the face the baby saw once she began focusing her gaze and noticing details. Those were the eyes that looked through her when she breastfed (for three days, or it might have been four, there's a bit of vagueness around the issue; Rafi once said three, and another time four), and when her diaper was changed, and when she attempted cautiously and probably without much hope to examine the effect of her smile on the face before her, and perhaps that is why to this day her smile collapses slightly, retreating ahead of time.

And that's that? No memories? Not even bad ones? No moments of pampering, of cuddles in Mom and Dad's bed? No kisses showered on her babyish stomach? What about cheering her first step, her first words? *Where's the light? Say "papa."*

A large eraser runs back and forth over my consciousness.

And then Nina left. One morning we got up and she was gone. Probably heard a whistle from outside, on a frequency that only dogs like her can hear. Didn't even take a toothbrush, left and disappeared for years. She flew—as we later learned, from letters she began sending Vera—to New York and was absorbed by the city, and this time no one searched for her. Rafael and the little girl were on their own. Grandma Vera came to help, of course, at least twice a week, three buses each way, bringing baskets of food, coloring books, wooden animals carved by Tuvia. On the other mornings the girl was deposited, along with a few other younger children, in a day-care center at a neighbor's, a woman who hardly spoke, and her silence must have infected the children because she remembers the day care as a very quiet place (which doesn't make much sense, but that is how she recalls it). Devoted friends of Rafael came to watch her at night, when he worked. He was an aide at Bikur Cholim Hospital, a night guard at the Biblical Zoo, an attendant at a gas station. In the mornings he studied social work at the Hebrew University, and took a Ministry of Labor course in cinema. The girl was always waiting for him. That anticipation is her most solid memory of the period. Constant hunger. She cannot remember what she did while she waited, but even today she can reawaken that anticipation in herself, the stomach contracting upon hearing his heavy footsteps on the stairs. Apologies for the third person employed here, but the first person is too painful.

Vera begged them to come and live with her and Tuvia on the kibbutz, where a new life awaited. Everything Nina had robbed them of, Vera would give back. But Rafael, and perhaps the girl, too, in her own way—who knows, who knows what the world whispered to her animal instincts—seemed to need a complete consummation of the abandonment Nina had condemned them to.

But still, what does she remember of that time? Not much. Almost nothing. Meals eaten in silence. Rafael standing at the closet with his face weltering in Nina's dresses. A real puppy with long ears, which Rafael found and brought home for her and which, after a week of unimaginable joy, fled the moment someone accidently left the door open. A gray afternoon at the neighborhood playground. A young mother turns to Rafael and tells him the girl isn't dressed warmly enough for the weather, and the two of them, she and Rafael, get up and leave without a word.

There was the life she conducted under her covers. She lay there for hours on end, telling stories and staging plays. She did not speak Hebrew in there. She had a different language, one that existed only under the blanket, and of which she apparently did not remember a word when she was outside. But one evening the blanket was suddenly flung off, and there stood Dad in a fluster, claiming she was speaking Serbo-Croatian in complete sentences. He didn't understand the language, apart from the little Nina had taught him ("Mommy," "Daddy," "daughter," "family," and a few dirty words), and the girl, of course, had no idea what he was talking about.

"But remember that we were also really happy together," Rafael says in the film, almost pleading. "I used to put on shadow-puppet shows for you, and we had a whole family we made out of potatoes, and a gang of matchsticks and beer caps, and we played foosball, with nails for the players and a marble for the ball, and we saw lots of movies, don't you remember?" He leans over and suddenly pulls the camera out of my hand and aims it at me, and then you see me shouting and protesting, flailing my arms hysterically to try to erase myself. "Stop flipping out for a minute and see how cute you are," says movie-Rafael and laughs, and I put on an act of laughing with him like everything's cool: "You and Nina are so good-looking, how come I came out such a train wreck?" Movie-Rafael laughs even harder: "You're totally nuts, Gili, honestly!" And that is an unsatisfactory answer to an issue that tormented me in those years—I saw the grimace flicker over my face in the film—and it's another one of those moments when I hated Nina with all my heart, because you can see on me what I lacked, you can see the barrenness, because bottom line, no matter how crazy I am about my dad, and no matter how deeply *Ideal Marriage* delved into my secrets, a fifteen-year-old girl sometimes needs a mother, even a cuckoo-bird one, even a mother of all sins, but a mother who will look at her once in a while, woman-to-woman, who will hug her confused body, who will marvel and tell her how much of a woman she is.

And this is where the picture gets stuck, just when my face fills the entire screen. The magnetic emulsion must have peeled off, black-and-white spots flicker, and all at once my face fractures into twisted fragments and then freezes, and it somehow looks like a mirror that shattered after Nina looked into it, and it is concrete and terrifying, and we both sit and stare for a few seconds, until Rafi jumps up and unplugs the machine.

I remember: the magazine of the Bolex, my dad's first sixteen millimeter, held four hundred feet of film. Eleven minutes and eleven seconds waiting to be filled with moving images. To this day, the movements required to load and unload the film are fresh in my fingers. I was maybe seven as my hands and my dad's moved together in the lightproof black changing bag. The bag was made for one pair of hands, but we managed to both fit in. He guided me, leading my slender fingers. As he loaded and unloaded, he would shut his eyes and tilt his head back, and I did the same. With our eyes closed and our hands inside the bag, we would open the camera lid, gently grasp the edge of the new film, and thread it through the rollers. His thick fingers moved swiftly and delicately. Today, with video and digital, all this sounds ridiculous, but I have sweet memories of the way our hands moved, and also of how time felt back then, the eleven minutes and eleven seconds that galloped through the rollers.

Where was I?

Starting at age five, the girl breathed in chemicals. She got used to sleeping on a mattress in an editing room. Her father was apprenticed to a very important man. The important man had cat eyes, and sometimes he made funny faces so the girl would laugh, but most of the time he sat hunched over a Steenbeck, cutting film and taping it together, muttering to himself. The room filled up with drapes of film, which she rustled as she walked among them with her arms spread wide.

Rafael took her to see films at Lessin House in Tel Aviv, or at Lia van Leer's home in Haifa. From producers' trash cans, he fished out films whose distribution rights had expired. He swiped films from the workers' union library. He educated himself: Antonioni one week, Howard Hawks the next, Frank Capra, Wilder, Truffaut . . . She would fall asleep on him, with her head on his shoulder. Waking up in the dark, in unfamiliar rooms, she saw the movies reflected in double vision on his glasses lenses.

At the age of seven, halfway through the school year, the girl was brought to Gershon Agron School and introduced to the class as "a girl who needs help." On the other hand, almost that same day, writing was invented, the miracle of reading was discovered, and a new life began.

Well, I've worked hard this morning. I haven't written this much for ages, and I'm doing it by hand. Here is just one more little anecdote before R and I go have lunch in the kibbutz dining room, where we will meet people who knew me back when I was in a stroller, and who will very tactfully not ask me anything about myself.

When the girl was eleven, and to everyone's surprise and to her own horror she had sprung up to over five feet (she did a great job of growing, the almost preemie) and was secretly writing breathless poems and moving stories of orphans and had read almost all the grown-up books in the kibbutz library and in the Phillip Leon library at the community center in Kiryat Yovel, and had memorized *Ideal Marriage* and *The Perfumed Garden,* which had utterly discombobulated her, but in a different way—after all this, she stood up one morning in front of the whole school at the Remembrance Day ceremony, and instead of reciting Haim Gouri's war poem, as planned, she declaimed a mortally embarrassing private lamentation that began with the words, "Where do expressions go when a person freezes?"

Nina arrived the evening before the ninetieth birthday party. It took her three flights to get from her Arctic village all the way to the kibbutz—Rafael paid, of course, using money he doesn't have, and Vera chipped in, too, because Nina was broke, as usual. I'm told that despite her exhaustion, she outdid herself and stayed up late getting the clubhouse ready for the party, and only called a cab after midnight, having insisted on mopping and polishing the floor herself. She chose not to stay at Vera's, or in Akko with Rafael, a decision that hurt and angered him, and of course the unnerving idea of her staying with me and Meir in our one-and-a-half-bedroom on the moshav was never raised. Instead she rented an Airbnb in Haifa for three days. That was as much as she'd allotted for her visit to the hinterlands. From the Tromsø Airport in Norway, she called Rafael and promised to write a birthday toast for Vera and read it at the party. But on the day of the party she went up to Rafael twice and asked in a whisper if it was okay that she hadn't written anything. Rafael said something like, What matters is that you speak from your heart, just say something nice to Vera, and Nina agreed to do exactly that: she would simply look at Vera and speak to her. "After all, I have so many good things to tell her," she added with a vigorous nod. But every time Aunt Chana, who was emceeing the event, turned to her with a questioning look, Nina gave a "later" or "after this speech" wave, and in the end she did not say a word to Vera.

The longer her silence stretched on, the more we could all see the disappointment on Vera's face. And we all sensed that although Nina was agonizing, she couldn't do it, she simply could not sing Vera's praises. The whole family tightened around Vera in those moments, like a body protecting its own vulnerable organ. She was one of us, and Nina was not. We were willing to accept Nina only by virtue of Vera. And another thing: the family always knew that the border area between Vera and Nina was infected, perhaps even malignant, and it was best for us Brucks not to go near it. Besides— thought the thick-necked domestic Brucks to themselves—we'll never be able to understand the perplexity of what happened almost sixty years ago between Vera and Nina. And I should clarify: the Brucks, generally speaking, do not perceive such fine resolutions of the human soul, and I have no complaints: you don't choose your family.

What else did I want to write?

That it's a pleasure the way this notebook allows for things.

I haven't handwritten anything for years. I thought those muscles had atrophied long ago.

Putting pen to paper, as befitting the days when the events
occurred.

Come and find me, carpal tunnel syndrome!

We're at the party. In the clubhouse. God-awful furniture. Everything looks like it was slathered with mud some time back in the
fifties. Rafael and Nina haven't seen each other for five years, not
since her last visit to Israel. Nina and I also haven't met since then.
And on that visit we barely exchanged a few words, at the end of
which I let loose on her in front of everyone. I put on quite the
horror show and humiliated myself spectacularly. We undoubtedly
give new meaning to the term "family."

Before the event began, while everyone was standing around
chatting, catching up on family gossip, I shut my eyes and slowly
counted down from ten, and at zero she walked in. I have no explanation. Nina entered the room, and Rafael's heart grew very weak.
I saw it. And then there was a flurry of kissing and hugging around
her, while Nina just stood in the middle, smiling quietly and hugging herself as if even here she was cold. The family took advantage
of the occasion to get a little taste of abroad, namely to yell "Oh my
God" and various other American shrieks that signified excitement
and smacked of hypocrisy, and beneath all that, of course, were
the hasty appraising glances, the tallying of wrinkles and skin and
hair and teeth. The usual jamboree. I could tell straightaway, as
could everyone, that Nina was not in good shape. Not only had her
beauty faded (here was one fate that we fuglies were exempt from)
and not only was the skin on her forehead and her amazing long
cheeks and around her lips covered with crisscrossed lines, thin dry

creases, as if someone had lashed her with a bundle of little twigs, but also—and this was what shocked Rafael most, as he told me with his eyes—Nina had expressions.

I noticed it, too. It is the job of a script girl (also referred to, fittingly, as a "continuity girl") to notice these sorts of surprising changes, irrational skips in the frame or in the text. I looked at Nina, and an alarm went off inside me. Rafael stood up, heavy and flustered. I hurried over to him, linked my arm with his, and felt him lean on me, his pulse going crazy. I offered him a chewable aspirin and some nitroglycerin spray for angina, which I always have on hand for him. He rejected both, with an irritated and slightly unkind gesture, but he had extenuating circumstances.

How does one describe something like this phenomenon, where a person who did not have facial expressions suddenly does? Of course she'd always had slight expressions, Nina. Let's not—she wasn't a statue or an iceberg, and she wasn't really a sphinx, I only described her that way to uphold and foment my own aversion, and Rafi claims I'm exaggerating the whole thing. Still, she really was unbelievably different now. One might cautiously say, difficult as it was to admit, that she suddenly *was*.

That child from Victor Hugo's *The Man Who Laughs*? The one the Comprachicos kidnapped and disfigured so that he always looked like he was laughing, because it was good for the begging business? When I was little I was so scared of that book, terrified by the child's frozen expression on the cover illustration, yet I repeatedly read about his bitter fate and cried.

Here's a question: What makes an average, reasonable person, meaning not someone who was disfigured by Comprachicos as a child, look almost always indifferent or unmoved? Or scornful. Is it something in the eyes? Is it the thin little crease under her eye sockets? The distant, hollow, always slightly distracted look?

From the spindly, foal-like appearance she'd had up to a fairly late age, at least five years ago, when I last saw her, she seemed to have skipped straight into the wilting stage, without spending any time in mature, full womanhood.

In life.

Her face magnetizes my father and me, as if we're watching a film—another film—that has been shelved for decades. A film about our unlived life. The life we might have had. Ripples of affection and happiness and disappointment and sadness blow across her face. And smiles. Good God, how warm and quiet and simple her smile is: Where was all that when I needed it? Rafael beside me stares at her, with his pulse and the shortness of breath—I think I've said that—and I swear I will not let him fall because of her, not again; there's only so much a person can be tormented.

Nina saw Rafael's horrified look when she walked in. He couldn't hide it. Over all the people crowding around her, she shrugged her shoulders at him somewhat apologetically, and something in that movement reminded me of a scene in the film Rafael tried to make about her back in the seventies, before she ran away from us for good. "Do you think you'll still love me when I'm old and ugly?" she asks him on camera. They're in bed, where else, in tangled sheets, sharing a rare moment of warmth. "You know me," he replies, slightly puffed up with pathos, "if you were to suddenly turn into . . . I don't know . . . a hunchback, then I'd start loving hunchbacks." "Eh," she says, waving her thin bare hand, "I bet you've said that to a thousand hunchbacks."

—

Later, after the speeches that were delivered and Nina's that was not, and the talk that did not take place between Nina and me, our little tribe, which is not so little anymore, stormed the tables laden with delicacies. The women of the family, and a few of the men, had prepared dishes inspired by Vera's cuisine. Only the four of us—Vera, Nina, Rafael, and I—remained seated, each in our spot, slightly bruised even before we'd really connected. Nina and Vera looked at each other, and it was a look . . .

A dreadful smile suddenly came to Nina's lips. I could clearly see that it was almost involuntary, a sort of grimace that Vera arouses in Nina by her mere existence, a cranial grin that instantly mocked and dispelled all the praises that had been heaped on Vera, exposing a secret disgrace.

I was afraid. Abruptly invaded by the kind of fear you feel only when facing human darkness. And I knew that Nina's smile had no translation into any language spoken in the light. I saw my grandmother shrink into herself, as if Nina's smile were sapping the nectar that makes Vera who she is even at ninety.

At that moment Nina also looked at what she herself had caused, at the shell of Vera, and she was horrified. I saw it. She got up and walked over to Vera tentatively—

And she knelt in front of Vera's armchair in a strange but rather touching way—I was caught off guard, I admit it—and wrapped Vera in her arms and put her head on her lap, and Vera leaned over and stroked her daughter's thin, brittle neck.

With long, slow caresses.

A few of the relatives noticed and signaled to others, and there was silence. Vera and Nina were braided together. And I thought that for the rest of their lives those two would be encircled by a line that separated them from everyone else. From the whole world.

I thought that I, too, whether I wanted to be or not, was slightly surrounded by that line.

Nina stood up, and I could tell that it was hard for her. Her body had lost its youthful ease. She wiped her eyes with both hands—"Pfff! Don't know what came over"—and went back to her seat. Vera took a compact mirror out of her handbag and used a napkin to quickly wipe the smeared makeup from the corners of her eyes and moved her red-painted lips this way and that in the mirror. Nina watched, gulping her down with her eyes, and for a moment I could imagine her giving Vera that exact same look when she was a six-year-old girl in Belgrade, in their pretty apartment on Kosmajska Street, watching her mother put on makeup in front of—I'm guessing—an oval mirror adorned with bronze vines that hugged her figure, and perhaps a tiny photograph of Milosz, looking fair skinned and serious, tucked into the frame.

Esther, Dad's sister, who cannot tolerate even one moment of awkwardness or silence, clinked her teaspoon on a glass and declared that Orli and Adili, her granddaughters, had prepared a short piece based on "two or three humorous anecdotes" that Vera had told them for their roots project at school. Nina tensed up, apparently not finding much humor in her mother's recollections. The two vivacious girls, with curly black hair and red cheeks, said how lucky they were that Grandma Vera had chosen to fulfill her grandmotherly aspirations in their family, and how, with her wisdom and her giant heart, she had restored everyone's happiness after Grandma Dushinka, Grandpa Tuvia's dear first wife, had died. They spoke on top of one another, and interrupted, but with a synchronicity and amiability that only a healthy family—way to go with the oxymoron, Gili—knows how to instill.

They asked Vera to forgive them if they went a little overboard with their imitation: it was all from love. Vera waved her hand and said, "Go ahead," and the girls signaled to their cousin Evyatar, and the sounds of Sinatra's "My Way" filled the air with pink cotton candy. The two girls pulled a suitcase out from under a table, and the script girl skipped a heartbeat, because it was the very same suitcase that Vera had brought to Tuvia's on that evening when she and Rafael threw shot put together. From the suitcase they began to pull out colorful necklaces, large and small, which they draped around their necks, and they swayed to the music in a dance that was, if not salacious, then at least flirtatious—it was a little embarrassing, in my opinion. Then, like magicians, they pulled out all manner of hats in light blue and purple, Vera's colors: small and wide brimmed, respectable and bold, European and tropical, native and colonial. I can confidently declare that no other woman on the kibbutz, nor in the entire kibbutz movement, could carry off Vera's combination of hard labor in the dairies, in the coops, among brambles and thistles, with such a naturally aristocratic elegance.

(After she moved in with Tuvia, who had been known throughout the kibbutzim of Israel as a desirable widower, the ladies in charge of the work schedule assigned Vera to week after week of cleaning and mopping in the dining room. At the end of her shift she would come home to Tuvia and show him her hands, with their skin peeling off and eaten away by detergents, and her grimy, broken fingernails. Tuvia would soak her hands in warm water with chamomile, then apply nail polish—Vera used to imitate him, with his tongue between his lips. "Chin up," he would always say. And just like that, with her head held high and her nails held out like ten glistening drops of blood—"I am *proletariat* in my soul! No job is too low for me!"—she would return to the battlefield the next day.)

Then the girls sat down on the suitcase and held each other's hand and, in a perfect duet, parroting Vera's voice and her accent and her Hebrew mistakes, recited a story that most of the family knew: "When I was born, in town of Čakovec, in Croatia, in the year eighteen, it was still World War First, and when Austrian soldiers saw that Austria was losing, they quickly ran home, and my mother was afraid of what they do to us, so she took me on train to her parents in Belgrade. And me, because there was so little food, I was very ugly, skinny and pneumonic, with running nose and coughing, and Mother held me on train high up above people, and it was all crowded and stinky and drunks, and people shouted at her: Throw your ugly cat out the window! Soon army men will come home and you will make beautiful new babies!"

The little crowd in the clubhouse rolled about laughing. Vera called out "Bravo!" and clapped her hands. Nina, sitting opposite Rafael and me, shook her head with a strange blend of amusement and ridicule. Just look how she's enjoying all this, said her bitter smile, and Rafael and I yanked our eyes away from her as one, wary of joining her in any conspiracy against Vera.

"And my father," the twins stood up and kept recounting in Vera's voice, "was such army man! *Yoy!* And our mother all the time said to him: But, Bela, you have no soldiers at home, you have four daughters! But he did not know another way, how could he? In his soul he was sergeant major, even though he was never in the army for a single one day. And when he came home, we must stand up in his honor, even, excuse me, if we were sitting in toilet. Such Hungarian man, it set the fear of God!"

The two girls crouched down, stood back up, and clicked their heels together. The kindred overflowed with laughter and cheers.

"And my mother, she was very closed," the girls said, resting their chins wistfully on their fingertips. "She was dead scared of him. Everyone was! Not a person in town would dare say a word to him!" The twins stuck out their chins, and for a moment they both resembled the young Vera in a way that has no logical explanation, because they had none of her blood. "One time, I was maybe fifteen," Vera said through their mouths, "I heard Father raise his hand on Mother. I don't know how I found courage, and I went into their bedroom without knocking the door and I said to Father: That's it, no more! Last time! You never slap her again! You never shout at my mother again either! And Father stood like this, mouth open, and I for two years did not talk to him because of that . . ."

Already at fifteen—said the look Nina held on Rafael—already steel.

The girls flicked their heads up sharply, with Vera's strident expression, lips pouting, and the room frothed with applause and cheers. Vera jumped up from the armchair we'd decorated for her and went to stand between the girls, who were a head taller than her, and waved their arms up: "Wait, wait a minute, listen, children, another thing you forgot to tell about my father: there was one time that my older sister, Mira, she was nineteen, maybe twenty, and in little town next door they make dilettante theater, and there was one *very* famous play, which Mira she played part of some very important madam, with long cigarette, and my father jumps out of auditorium onto stage and in front of everyone he gives her one *pljuska* on her face—'You must not smoke!'"

"Vera, let the girls breathe, you're strangling their hands!" exclaimed Shleimaleh, Esther's husband, and Vera said, "One more minute listen well, girls, so that you'll have material for my hundred birthday. For me, since day I was seventeen, Father put every evening outside my door one new pack of cigarettes and wrote on it that he hopes snotnose with hard head will get a little more softer . . ."

But the snotnose never did soften up, Nina mouthed to Rafael from the other side of the table.

"What? What did you say?" Vera whipped her head back toward Nina. It's hard to understand how—on what frequency—she'd picked up Nina saying something about her silently. "Nothing, nothing," Nina mumbled. Vera let go of the girls' hands and went back to her seat with suddenly weary steps.

But she recovered quickly, straightened up, and crossed her legs—neither foot reached the floor, they dangled in the air: "My children, my dears, first of all I want to thank you from my heart's bottom for this lovely fete you held for me, and I very well know how all of you worked here until last night late, and you made efforts and cooked and put pictures on walls of me, so that everyone will see how much beautiful I used to be . . ." Vocal protests from the crowd: "You still are! You still are!" "And also you came all the way from such places—*yoy*! From end of world you came, and my Nina even came from Norway with three airplanes from her little snow village, and I know how hard it is for you, Nina, and how busy you are and how important and sacred your work is there, and still you found time for me and you came to be with me on my festivity." Nina shifted uncomfortably in her seat. "Well, okay," Vera hastened, "I just want to tell you how happy and joyful I am to have everyone here, apart from my dear Tuvia, who is not with us, and my beloved Milosz, who has not been for fifty-seven years, and how I thank you for taking me with whole heart into your beautiful family and letting me be part. And every morning all over again I say thank you—not to God, God forbid, and don't argue with me now, Shleimaleh! You are wrong and I will tell you why: because if there was God, he would commit suicide a long time ago. Okay,

okay, we know what you have to say, you clericalist! What are you all laughing? Why? I'm not right?"

Nina sat watching the buzzing family hive where Vera reigned supreme, and what she saw both enthralled and repulsed her. I could see it, I even recognized some of it in myself, and I found myself feeling sorry for her.

"But even without bringing Shleimaleh's God into this," Vera continued, "to my good fortune I do say thank you every day for meeting here my dear Tuvia, who gave me thirty-two good years together, and thank you, thank you, thank you for meeting here also Rafi and Chana and Esther, his children who agreed to take me, and Rafi was only a boy then, only just sixteen, think of what heart he must have for letting a stranger woman . . ." Tears appeared in her eyes, and others were tearing up, too. Rafael's eyes turned red, as did his big porous strawberry of a nose—

I took the camera from him, though it was hard to pry it out of his hand, as usual, and I slowly ran it over the whole room. The familiar faces, the young and faded and beloved and annoying faces in which I knew every wrinkle and mole. When I got to Nina she bowed her head a little, and I skipped over her slightly, and the synchronization of our movements alarmed me for some reason. I gave the Sony back to Rafael and sat down feeling weak in the knees.

The party slowly wound down. We had coffee and gobbled the cakes Vera had baked, and then we dispersed. Vera asked Rafael and Nina for one last coffee at her place before they left, she to her rented room in Haifa, he to his austere apartment in Akko. It's been a long time since he's had a woman in his life, and that worries me. Rafael without a woman always seems slightly less deciphered, and I like my Rafael deciphered. Of course Vera asked me to stay and spend the rest of the day with her, but I was anxious to get home, where there was a talk with Meir that I suddenly could not put off for even a second longer. A fateful, if not fatal, talk. And so everything I recount from this point onward is what I heard in retrospect from my father, my mentor, Rafael, although I did fill in a few gaps myself.

"So we've met again without talking," Rafael said to Nina as she walked him to his car. As usual, her head was down, and she was hugging herself. Rafael wondered if she was thinking, as he was, about what she'd told him in the final moments of their last meeting, five years earlier. She was living in New York at the time, and he wanted to ask if in her new place, on an island halfway between Lapland and the North Pole, she was still carrying on the way she had with her American lechers. That's what she'd called them. But he couldn't bring himself to talk about it. He remembered how he'd felt after she'd told him.

At some point she put her arm in his and they walked slowly, at a pace she dictated. "I found it strangely slow," he noted when he told me, "because always, my whole life, I've had to run after her." They reached his Hino Contessa 900, twenty-three years of age and, according to Rafael, "in the prime of her life." "Nice wheels," Nina said with a laugh, and scraped an imaginary spot off the windshield coated with mud and droppings. "I gather the social-work business is booming." "You've done well, too," Rafael said. "Why, what did I do now?" "Oh, nothing. It's just that you've been here for two days, and tomorrow morning you're flying away for who knows how long, and you've managed not to be alone with me for even a minute." Nina let out a forced laugh. "Why are you so afraid of me?" Rafael asked, the insult riling him up as it always did. "We're old now, Nina, and the world is a shitty place. Isn't it time we did some good for each other?" "I'm not 'good,' Rafi. I'm a major burden, I'm a

pain in the ass, get it into your head already, give up on me already."
"I gave up on you a long time ago," he said, trying to fake a laugh,
but the words came out heavy and crooked. He saw her lips clench.
He enjoyed hurting her a little, but it also pained him. It was their
age-old ritual, yet Rafael felt as if they were in a different place now.
There was a new, invisible partner to their conversation.

"Maybe you could try to like me a little after all? At least for
show?" she said. The words sounded fawning, but the melody did
not. Her voice was tense, almost desperate. Rafael remained cautiously quiet, trying to understand what he was hearing.

"So that's a no?" she murmured painfully. "You're right."

She let go of his arm and hugged herself again and shivered. The
unwritten rule of their mutual torture dictated that she desperately
needed his unrequited love. His stubborn, absolute adoration was
axiomatic, one of the few stable elements in her life. But this was
something different, Rafael told me, and he felt the earth slowly
dropping away beneath his feet. Yet he still tried to grasp at the
familiar, at their blithe way of talking: "You'll laugh, but sometimes
it feels like an ulcer, or like a wound I have to keep scratching so I
can keep feeling something for you."

"I've never been compared to an ulcer before," Nina hissed with
a bitter laugh, "come on, give me a hug and let's say goodbye." She
hugged him, noting, as usual, how plump he'd become, drumming
both her hands on his paunch. "It's like hugging a mountain," she
grumbled into his chest, but she did cling to him for a moment
longer than usual, said my father the erotic trivia fan. Oh well, I'll
be objective and throw her a bone: it's hard not to cling to him,
it's hard not to hug into him. Something about the contact with
that large, solid body works on me, too, I admit it—like a can of
Ensure hopefulness. And it's amazing ("Write down everything,"
he taught me when I was his script girl, when he was still a director,

"write down everything that goes through your mind; in the end everything belongs to everything, it's the law!"), it really is amazing how a fragile and frail and unhealthy man like him can give such a feeling of security and stability. He told me that he tried very hard not to make a single mistake at their moment of parting. He was careful not to abandon himself completely for her. Her body was virtually unchanged, he reported without being asked. In fact I explicitly asked him not to go into detail. I'd seen her myself, after all: the long, slender body, thinner and bonier than it had been, with the same itty-bitter breasts, as I used to call them. Nina gave him a quick peck on the cheek, and then, to his surprise, her fingers slid over his face with a tender motion he'd forgotten.

He tried, but he couldn't resist asking if he was going to have to wait another five years to see her again. Nina said, "Who knows, this time it might be much quicker than you think. My life is a mess." Her throaty laugh made him feel, again, that she was both hinting at something and obscuring it, as she always did, so that he would guess wrong. He realized how exhausting their meetings always were. He was too old to keep up with her moody pendulum swings. Nina felt him retreating and quickly pushed him into the Contessa, so that it would be clear who was getting rid of whom, and she made sure to shut the door after him, then leaned her arms on the open window. Her face was close to his, and for a long moment they looked into each other. "No other woman looks at me that way," Rafael told me. "What way?" I asked, bracing myself. "You know, with that mixture." "What mixture? Explain," I insisted. My voice sounded synthetic, like that woman who announces the elevator floors. "Of love and grief," Rafael said, refusing to collaborate with my tone. "Or passion and grief," he added, and I almost screamed, I could barely keep my mouth shut: What passion are you talking about? She doesn't give a crap about you! And as for "the business," as Vera calls it, Nina has her herd of lechers to ride, so do me a favor, okay?

But deep down I knew Rafael was right. And that she also had a mixture of mockery and grief, and of cruelty and grief. The grief was always there, the foundational color of her eyes. I vividly envisaged that scene between the two of them, so that I could reconstruct it if I ever, maybe, made my film about him and her (the victim's cut). Her face in front of his through the car's open window, they do not touch each other, but they are together in a tense, trembling severity, like an arrow before it's shot. Was that how they looked at each other when they made me? Did she stop him a moment before he came and force him to look into her eyes? Did she warn him then, with her gaze, that she couldn't do it, that she didn't have it in her? That he was making a child for himself?

And meanwhile poor Gili was born.

Nina ran her hand over Rafael's face again. Over the unkempt beard. It was strange. He felt she was having trouble saying good-bye this time. She touched his forehead, on the spot where she'd headbutted him forty-five years ago and given him that legendary goose egg, which had merely hinted at all the horns she was yet to grow on him. "See you later, half brother," she said with a sigh, and gave the Contessa a little pat. She walked away and Rafael mumbled his part of the ritual, and I thought for the thousandth time: Hey, I'm actually the product of marriage between relatives—is it any wonder I turned out this way?

Rafael was slowly coasting out of the little parking circle by the old-timers' neighborhood, when he heard a familiar two-fingered whistle, and in the side-view mirror he saw Nina running after him. There was something extraordinary about it: with all her restless flitting around the world, Nina always had a ladylike way of moving her body. She flung the door open and sat down next to him: "Drive." "Where to?" "Doesn't matter, just put me in motion." Rafael cheered inside and hit the gas and off they went.

"For maybe ten minutes we didn't say a word," Rafael told me on the phone, "your mother just sat there with her head back and her eyes shut." As I've mentioned, a script girl's job is to notice the little details. For example, the way Rafael switched from "Nina" to the slightly preposterous "your mother," which signaled imminent danger. Nina's long, sinewy hands sat limply on her lap. Exhausted, he thought they looked. He could barely overcome the urge to take her hand in his bear paw. Without opening her eyes, Nina asked if he had any music, and he told her to look in the glove compartment, a little embarrassed about her seeing his taste. He was stuck in the sixties in that regard, too, with the same old Moody Blues and New Seekers and Mungo Jerry tapes, but apparently she couldn't be bothered to open the compartment, or her eyes.

"And I drove," Rafael told me, "I flew, you've never seen me drive like that, and I felt like we were"—I could hear his disconsolate smile—"like those couples in the movies? Where the man snatches his beloved from under the wedding canopy just as she's about to marry someone else?" I listened, though I could not completely decode his voice. Why was he talking like an adolescent girl? Nina didn't look at him. Without opening her eyes, she said, "Rafi, I have to tell you something, are you sitting down?"

He laughed, but his mouth went dry.

"It looks like I have something."

"What kind of something?"

"A problem. An illness."

"No, you don't."

"It's that funny one," Nina went on, "where you forget things. Where you say the same thing a hundred times, ask the same question a hundred times."

Rafael slowed down at once. "This is a joke, right? You're not serious. You're too young for that."

She turned to look at him. "Amnesia. Dementia, Alzheimer's, wackiness, something in that family. It'll take time, probably, a few years, they said, so I'm just at the beginning of the beginning, with all the excitement of newness and discovery. But the train has left the station. Even right now I'm being a little bit erased, look"—she held her hand up before his eyes—"now I'm in color, but three or four years from now I'll be flat white, then transparent. No, don't stop!"

"But I can't talk about this without seeing your face."

"Everything will be erased, even you, even Gili, maybe even Vera, although I can't imagine that. Drive! Don't stop. If you stop I won't be able to talk." Then she laughed: "I'm like those dolls you have to move to make them talk. *Mu-mee, Mu-mee.*"

He asked how she'd found out, and she told him, without any wisecracks this time. Where she lived, in the north, on a tiny island in the archipelago between Lapland and the pole, you can't bury people. The layer of ice constricts and spits out the bodies, and the polar bears eat them, and that can cause contamination and disease. So once a year the residents have to undergo a physical, and anyone who has an incurable or life-threatening disease must leave the island and go back to the mainland.

"It's horrible, it's cruel," Rafael murmured, and Nina said, "Not at all. It's the law, and everyone who goes to live there knows that from the start." "That's not what I meant," my father said. He was driving slowly. Drivers honked and conveyed their opinion of him with hand and finger gestures. His head was swirling with arguments and reasons to disprove what she'd told him. She saw this and sighed. "Let it go, Rafi. Let me die. This life is kind of a lost cause anyway." Another high-pitched laugh that sounded to him like a whimper. "Maybe it really isn't for everyone."

At the first interchange they turned back to the kibbutz. Rafael thought, Here I am, taking her back to her black canopy. "Ultimately it defeated me, her 'Let me die.'" He asked if Vera knew. "Vera will know in a few minutes, but I wanted to tell you first, like with a pregnancy." He said nothing. "You really are the first, Rafi. This is the first time I've heard myself say these words out loud." He couldn't speak. "It's a little stressful, the way you're being so quiet," she said, and her hand sought out his paw and her fingers found their place among his. "It actually makes sense, though, doesn't it?" she observed.

"How does any of this make sense," he said, choking.

"It makes sense," she replied, "that if you spend fifty-some years investing humungous efforts to forget one particular fact—like, say, that your mother abandoned you and threw you to the dogs when you were six and a half—then in the end you forget the other facts, too."

"Your mother didn't abandon you," Rafael hastily recited his lines, "and she was thrown to the dogs, too, to prison, to forced labor. She had no choice."

"Try explaining that to a six-and-a-half-year-old girl." Nina had her lines, too.

"You're not six and a half anymore."

"Yes, I am."

Rafael drove into the parking area. He stilled the engine and turned to her. "Don't say anything now," she commanded and put her finger on his lips, "don't pity and don't comfort." He kissed her finger. He didn't dare ask where she would go if she wasn't allowed to live on the island. He was afraid she'd go back to New York, to those men, who'd drop her the minute they found out she was ill. He imagined her there, alone, drowning in the illness and forgetting how to get back, and he thought that if need be, he would overcome his fear of flying and go to be with her, or bring her back to Israel if she wanted that. "Everything's up in the air," Nina said, "I mean everything's coming down now. Slowly coming down. It's actually quite interesting to see how it happens. All the microscopic movements the body makes, and the mind. A whole bureaucracy of absorption into the disease, before I've even figured anything out."

In the little mirror he saw Vera marching toward them, one hand on her waist, her whole body slightly bent. "Why did you two leave me and disappear?" she grumbled. "Nina, didn't you say you were staying for dinner? I made a salad." She stuck her head into the car and sniffed. "What's going on?" she demanded. "What's wrong, children? You had another fight again? Why are you crying? What did you say to her, Rafi?" Nina suddenly caught Rafael's hand and kissed his fingers one by one. It was an odd gesture, which embarrassed all three of them. Vera quickly pulled her head out of the car and looked far away. Nina got out and went over to Vera and put her arm around her shoulders. "Come, Majka," she said with a sigh, "let's have a talk."

"And honestly?" said Rafael, who called me from the car right after he'd said goodbye to them, "everything she held back from me, your mother, all those years, is swelling up inside me now, blowing me up. I feel like I'm about to have a stroke, I'm telling you." When he called I was almost home, and I thought I was going to have a heart attack myself because of what he told me about Nina being ill. I felt as if someone had suddenly pulled the keystone out from an elaborate structure I'd been building my whole life. I pulled over on the side of the road. The first thought that popped into my mind was that I couldn't have the conversation I wanted to have with Meir in this state. Maybe I'd put it off for a while. A few days. "Look, Gili, let's talk frankly," Rafael said, or yelled. "I'm not a man of many talents—no, don't stop me. At my age I know what I'm worth. Making movies, that's something I know how to do, more or less. Or used to. I'm no Antonioni or Truffaut, definitely no Tarantino, but I knew the craft, and if someone in Israel had given me half a chance instead of tripping me up every step I took, I'd have made even better movies." I said nothing. I thought how awful it was that my father had ultimately internalized the critics' eye. "I was a craftsman. Not a genius, I know that, but every profession needs people like me, and that's totally fine. They can call me sentimental, they can call me the poor man's philosopher, they can call me—" and here, as usual, he went on a tangent and enumerated the clauses of his charge sheet, with which I was all too familiar, having heard them dozens of times from him, and from others. But this time he got ahold of himself quickly: "I closed the book on that chapter of my life a long time ago, Gili. I cut it off, I cleansed the wound, it didn't metastasize, I moved on, and now I have a job I like, one far better suited to me, a real world with real people—"

On this point he was right. The bitterness remains in him to this day, but when the filmmaking dream was shattered, he quickly rebooted. Six months after recovering from the heart attack he suffered on set, he started working with groups of at-risk youth in Akko and Ramleh. I'm jumping ahead. There are lots of things I want to relate, and it's important to me that I write as many of them as possible before we sail to the island. I've waited too long—a whole lifetime.

Where was I—

"Dad," I said. "Dad, listen—"

"Wait, let me talk. Are you with me?"

"Always."

"But there's one little talent I do know I have, and I might be the only person in the world who has it. Don't laugh."

"I'm not laughing, Dad." I knew exactly what he was going to say.

"I know how to love her. You may think that's pathetic, you may think she doesn't deserve love, but I simply know how to love her whatever state she's in. That's my thing in the world: loving one person who is not easy to love. Making her slightly more able to tolerate herself." I heard loud thuds. I guessed he was slamming his palm on the steering wheel. "And loving her is the one thing she's never let me do, your mother. That's the one thing she fled to the other side of the world to get away from. And I'm telling you, Gili, if she'd stayed with me, she would have had a life—" He choked up and pounded the wheel again. I imagined him exhaling and puffing his cheeks out and looking like a massive Poseidon, the way he used to. The way he did when I was a little girl riding on his shoulders while he lorded over a set, or when he decided—contrary to all the advice he received and despite all the pressure—that I would be his script girl. Who ever heard of such a thing, a seventeen-year-old script girl who'd never worked a single day in the business—

I don't know why this came back to me now, but from within his roaring, injured speech, I was flooded by the feeling I used to have in my body when I would clap the board and Rafael would yell "Action!" and the set would come to life and magnetize itself to him, and his will became the will of everyone on the set. It was a feeling like nothing else, to be entirely within his desire, the desire of Rafael, my father, who now let out a long, whimpering sigh, and was once again a fat, ragged man with thick drooping lips, driving an ancient Contessa and mumbling to himself, "I could have, I could have."

When I got home, I took a deep breath and walked inside. "You're back," said Meir. He always looks slightly surprised, and also grateful. And so we stood. He put his fingertip under my neck, on my collarbone. I closed my eyes and waited for the grounding process to end.

Rafael drove to Akko and was all turned inside out with worry for her, and the next day at 7:00 a.m. he woke up when she phoned and realized he'd fallen asleep at the computer after a night spent mostly on websites related to her disease. He thought Nina had taken off ages ago. He asked if her flight was delayed.

"A two- or three-day delay. I'm still at Vera's."

"I thought you rented a place in Haifa."

"Listen for a second," she said, cutting off his sleep threads, even though she knows full well that Rafael wakes up heavy and you have to give him time.

"Listen, Rafi, such a lousy night I had, you don't want to know the thoughts."

"I can imagine."

"Maybe because I told you. I suddenly heard myself and the penny dropped and I realized this is it, it's my turn now. Listen, I want to ask you for something."

Money. He ran his meager savings accounts through his mind and wondered which one he could liquidate without too high of a penalty.

"Yesterday after you left, and after I told Vera, I was thinking maybe we should do it after all."

"Do what?"

"Film Vera telling her story." When Rafi did not answer, Nina went on: "She's not young anymore, and I was thinking that for once we should hear from her in an organized way, from beginning to end, what really happened there."

"Where?"

"On the island. On Goli Otok. But also everything that came before that. Say—since she and Milosz met. They had such a special love story, and what do we know about it? Two or three stories, always the same ones, almost nothing."

Rafael swallowed. He didn't think Nina could even guess how unique the love story was. "The truth?" he said.

"Only."

"I'm not sure that would be good for her now. It was a good idea at the time, when she was younger." He kept on prattling, but he wasn't sure whom he was protecting from the truth—Vera or Nina. "She's not what she used to be, you saw so yourself."

"I'm not what I used to be either," Nina pointed out dryly, "but it's my right, and I told her that, it's my right to hear the whole story for once, from beginning to end, isn't it?"

"Yes, of course, everyone . . . it's just that . . . what do you actually want us to do?"

"Sit her down in front of the camera for a couple of hours, maybe a little more, and you ask her questions. That's all. And I'll ask, too, every so often."

"But what do you need me for? Wouldn't it make more sense for *you* to sit down with her and talk to her like a mother and daughter?"

Nina had enough self-control not to burst out laughing, or crying. "We'll *both* talk to her. You and me. You were slightly her child, too."

"Not slightly," Rafael blurted.

"That's true," she said quickly. "I'm sorry, Rafi, not slightly at all. The slightly was what I got." She paused, allowing the past to swell and flood over the two of them, and then retreat and seep back into its tolerable places. "And you'll film it."

Rafael hesitated, trying to digest the meaning of this proposal. "We'll have to rent gear," he mumbled, "you'll want it to be high quality." He quickly drew up a list in his mind: a better camera than his decade-old Sony, a tripod, cables, reflectors, headphones—

"No, no," Nina cut him off, "don't start being some Hollywood big shot. The simplest home camera. Nothing professional. That one you used at the party on Saturday will do."

"Great," Rafi said with a sigh of relief, "I prefer that one."

He asked how Vera had responded when Nina told her about the disease. "As expected," Nina said, "total denial. It must be a wrong diagnosis, or maybe they switched the tests around in the lab, or maybe it's just all in my head, which is unfortunately entirely true . . . Did you hear what I said? You're allowed to laugh, it would do me some good if you kept laughing at my jokes." He let out a little snort, which could be interpreted any way one wanted to. "Then she started with her expert medical opinions," Nina ranted, "which are based on absolutely nothing! Just because that's what Vera wants, and she'll twist the arm of any fact until it confesses. And of course: you can't tell anything, I look great, I'm glowing, it's all a matter of healthy habits and good nutrition, and I should drink wheatgrass every morning, and she has a wonderful Chinese doctor who lives in Afula and she'll give me two or three acupuncture sessions and that'll be that, 'no more Avremaleh.'" Nina quoted another of Vera's aphorisms, the origin of which I don't have time to explain because a cloud is starting to darken over my head.

"And me," Nina went on, "I had the nerve to tell her that when it comes to diseases the most important thing is probably making sure you have good genes. She was offended, of course. Well, at ninety? If only we could all have a mind like hers. No, it's not from her, this shit," she pondered out loud, "maybe from my dad, maybe from Milosz, except he died on me at thirty-six, so who knows how he would have developed? Or deteriorated. And then I could hear her clicking away all night, *click-click-click,* and I guarantee you, Rafi, that she's already read all the sites that have anything to do with—"

"So you spent the night at her place," he couldn't stop himself from observing.

"Yes, I couldn't leave her on her own after that."

And me—you could? he thought.

"So tell me . . . what . . . what does Vera say about your idea?"

"Of filming her? I won't pretend she's enthusiastic. After all, she is a little beat up by what I told her. A mother's heart . . ." Nina couldn't resist. "Also, she's tired after the big party you threw her and all the to-do, but you know what she's like, she can't say no, to me or to my request, which is, you have to admit, a death row inmate's request." She stopped, allowed Rafael time to protest. He said nothing. I imagine her heart sinking and shrinking with loneliness and fear. "But mainly, she can't say no to the chance for another minute in the spotlight, even though it's not like anyone's going to watch this film except me and you."

"And Gili," Rafael said.

"I wish. But I've released Gili, from everything."

Rafael said nothing. The wound of his life bled a little. Drops, no more.

"Rafi, there's something else."

"I'm listening."

"I'm not doing this just for Vera."

"You're not?"

"I'm telling you this in the clearest possible way, okay?"

Rafael replied quickly, "It's for you, too, of course. You don't know how happy it makes me that you've decided to . . . to document her seriously for once."

"And document me, too, right? I want to be on film as well. There are things I want to ask her."

He tensed up. I imagine him carefully treading backward. He once again asked why she really needed him to interview her mother.

"You know exactly why. It'll be easier with you."

"For you or for her?"

"Both."

Silence.

"But that's not my whole idea," Nina said.

"It isn't?"

"Listen."

"She totally surprised me," he tells me at this point on the phone. I'm sitting on the windowsill at home with my first cup of coffee. I'm watching Meir dig on the hillside opposite, and almost without realizing it, I have a pen in my hand, and I'm writing every word my dad says in my notebook, like we've gone back to the days of that production, when I was his script girl. But the pen suddenly goes limp in my hand.

"I was thinking," Nina said, "that maybe we could all go."

"Go where?" Rafael gawked.

"To Goli Otok," I tell him immediately.

Rafael was astonished. "How did you know, Gili?"

"I felt it coming," I murmur. Then I realize: since yesterday, since he told me she was sick. It's been falling on me like a slow-motion avalanche.

Nina asked, "Rafi, do you think Gili would be willing to come?"

"I don't think so."

"It'll be short," Nina said, as if the duration of the trip was the issue, "two or three days at most."

"Then why don't you suggest it to her?" Rafael said.

Gili—the subject of the conversation—quickly doodles the atomic mushroom over Hiroshima.

"Me?" Nina said with a bitter laugh. "She won't even listen to my voice. You saw how she avoided me the whole party. She can't look me in the eye for more than one second, she's so disgusted. But maybe you could ask her? She won't say no to you. Give it a try, what's the worst that could happen? She won't eat you up."

"You know what? I'll suggest it. Worst case, she says no."

At this point there was a long pause. I know Goli Otok as if I were born there. I could give guided tours of the place. For my roots project in seventh grade I made a card-stock model of the island. Anything else? My email address? Gili.otok@gmail.com.

I rest my case.

Rafael is quiet. I draw the cliff hanging over the gulf and the sea. There, at the highest point of the island, my Vera stood for fifty-seven days in the blazing, hot sun, and did not jump. If I ever make it to that island, I know exactly what I'll do: I will climb up to the cliff on the hilltop and stand there for an hour, two hours, and I'll shout at the waves and the rocks and the gulf, because they're still there, and they are part of the story.

"Gili looks good," Nina told him.

"She does," my father was happy to confirm, and to repeat to me.

"She's grown prettier over the years," Nina said.

"She's happy now, and on her you can always see everything."

"So tell me . . ."

"Yes?"

"Is she with someone?"

"Yeah, for a while now."

"How long?"

"A while. Almost six years."

"Six years and you didn't tell me."

"No."

A long pause. Rafael cleared his throat. "By the way, he's not . . . not her age."

"What does that mean?"

"A little older than her."

"Oh."

"Eleven or twelve years. He's a special person, very gentle, with a complicated story."

"I didn't imagine Gili would find someone with a simple story," Nina said.

This, incidentally, was a crude violation of a basic law. Usually, before their weekly talks, Rafael asks me for permission to tell her something about my life, a crumb. I always refuse. Rafael says that every time they talk, every single week, she asks about me, as if she enjoys hurting herself with my refusal.

"I'll talk to Gili, yes," Rafael said.

"Just don't tell her it was my idea."

"Of course not."

"Ask her to come with us. She doesn't even have to talk to me on the way. I'm willing to keep being air to her. But it'll be much better, from Vera's perspective, too, if Gili is with us when we shoot. And maybe . . . what would you say about suggesting that she write down some of what's happening?" He smiled and his cheeks turned red. (How do I know? I know him.) "She can be your script girl again," Nina said, and I have no doubt that she knew exactly which buttons she was pressing. "Suggest that she come on the trip and write 'what the camera picks up and mostly what it doesn't pick up'—wasn't that the motto?"

Rafael laughed. My naïve father. So easily bought. Then she asked him another couple of questions about me, about my job, about my plans for the future. Rafael didn't go into detail when he reported to me, and I didn't pressure him. This, as I said, was a clear violation of the law, but on the other hand, I would like to note that in those moments they were doing something together that had not happened for many years: in their limited and fucked-up way, they were being my parents.

"So what do you say, Gili?" Rafael asks cautiously.

"I'll come."

"Yes, obviously." He sighs. "I totally understand. That's what I told Nina. I didn't have any—"

"I'll come."

"I'm just saying, suggesting, you know . . . What did you say?"

"I said I'll come."

"To Goli Otok?"

"Yes."

"And you'll be with us when we film?"

"Yes."

Silence.

"But, Dad, listen, I have a condition."

"Whatever you want, Gilush, anything—"

"This is my film."

"What . . . What do you mean, yours? In what sense?"

"In the sense that you and I do everything together, but when it comes to editing, I have the last say." I'm amazed at what comes out of my mouth. At standing up to him like that. It's as if I've been preparing for this moment for years.

"Look, that would be . . . I don't know . . . It wouldn't be easy."

"That's true. Can you handle it?"

"I don't know. We'll give it a try."

"No. I need your promise, Dad. Otherwise I'm not coming."

"You're not going to give me time to think about it?"

"No."

Silence. For a long time.

I'm not backing down. I'm not backing down.

"I agree."

"That's it?"

"Are you leaving me any choice?"

Another silence. A very long one. His heavy breathing. I hope I haven't hurt him too badly.

"Then that's how it'll be," he said.

"Then I'm coming."

"Can I tell Nina?"

"Yes, but with my condition."

He makes that sound again, the exhalation that comes after puffing his cheeks out so far that they almost burst. Poseidon blowing wind into the sails of a ship. My heart pounds. There's going to be a voyage. We'll be on the road soon.

"Great. Good," he says, sounding suspiciously serene. "Very good. Excellent, thank you."

"Don't thank me. I'm doing it for me."

"Still."

"Just tell me where and when. Do you want me to take care of the tickets? What about a hotel? Car?"

"Wait, I need . . . Wow, this is something . . . But what about your work? Won't it be a problem?"

"There's a project on the horizon, but only in a few weeks."

He swallows down his bitter urge to ask what the project is, who's directing. It pains him most when it's someone from his generation. I've turned down two pretty good offers only for that reason.

"Okay, I'm calling Nina, I'll get back to you with the details." He chuckles. Maybe he actually feels relieved to know it'll be my film and not his. "This is unbelievable, Gilush, what you've given me here is . . ." He makes an inappropriate little yelp and hangs up.

I scribble a tall, large figure with a pile of black curls, head in hands, terrified eyes filling half the face. I look at the hillside across the way. A tall, slender man is out there working. The unhappy joy of my life. Ripped jeans, black T-shirt, shaved head glistening with sweat. Even with his back to me, he can feel me watching him. He stops digging, turns around, leans on his hoe. Maybe he also senses that I've made up my mind about us. Maybe yesterday, when we did our grounding ritual, he picked it up. He wipes the sweat off his forehead and smiles and waves at me awkwardly. I breathe a sigh of relief: he doesn't know. I wave back. When I get back from Goli Otok, I'll tell him he's free.

Free of me, I mean. Free to leave me.

I have no right to prevent you from being a father, I'll tell him.

There, it's in writing.

Rafael and Vera have an osmotic relationship. Every piece of information delivered to one immediately seeps into the other. No more than seven minutes after I finished talking with him, the phone rang. "Gili!" my grandmother thundered. "Rafi just this minute told me! And I want to tell you how much thankful I am for it!"

"You really don't need to thank me, Grandma, I'm doing it for myself, too."

"Still, it's very important also for your father and for me, and mostly for Nina."

"Well, all right, we'll get through it. How are you, Grans?"

"Well, since yesterday, from your celebration for me, which you took completely too far, and then Nina who told me what she thinks she has, you already heard, and I looked it up on the computer a little, and with all that I haven't had any rest. And when I started thinking of us going there, to Goli, and I didn't know it would be you, too, I lay in bed thinking, and I saw things running like movies, and some of the parts I've already told you, and some of the parts you don't know, and all the way to this morning I had this sort of tremble . . . And I know how much you, Gilush, always felt all my pain, all my sadness . . ."

Something in her voice, a certain shadowy little curve it took, reminded me of what she'd told me in her kitchen all those years ago, when she'd literally ordered me not to let anyone twist her story against her.

This was the moment when I should have asked her if what I remembered her telling me, or think I remembered, was right. It happened a long time ago, when I was lying almost dead in intensive care at Hadassah Hospital, after slicing my veins and, to be on the safe side, stuffing my body with a cocktail of pills, because of that fuck-him who walked out on me after three years. He just tired of me in the blink of an eye, got up one night out of my arms, and I saw him sitting on the bed looking down at the floor contemplatively, which was peculiar in and of itself, because this was not a man necessarily known for contemplation, and then he ran one hand slowly through his wonderful wheat hair and said, Listen, Gili, this isn't working for me. I looked where he was looking, in case the secret of life had revealed itself to him in that spot, and what I saw were my slippers, slightly larger than his, and I swear that was what brought down the empire. After three years of passionate togetherness and "kindred souls" and "You were born for me" and promises of a shared future. Grandma Vera stayed with me in the ICU for three nights and three days, demanding that I not die: Gili, don't die, Gili, you're not going to, Gili, chin up. Meanwhile, my father roamed the corridors and roared like a wounded lion; the whole floor could hear him, security guards asked him to leave, he kept promising to keep quiet, but the minute he got near my bed the roars erupted again. And all that time, Vera spoke to me constantly, she never slept, she fought to pull me out of wherever I was, for three days and three nights she barely ate—my father told me when I woke up—and she tore at the skin on her arms with her manicured fingernails to keep herself awake. Even though I was comatose, I could hear her, or I think I could, moaning to herself in a trance: Oy, how us Bauer women get crazy with love, we go all the way, we love our man more than ourselves, more than life. There was a strange sort of pride in her voice, something that even in my sorry state I could sense should not be there, that it was unbecoming for the situation. She seemed to be insinuating that I had now been accepted into an exclusive club of spider-women. And inside my fog, on the second or third night, during one of the dark hours when she fought for me, I heard her relay—or I somehow absorbed it the way knowledge sometimes seeps wordlessly between two people, or perhaps I merely hallucinated on an empty stomach just flushed clear of thirty clonazepams and twenty Tylenols, yes, more likely I hallucinated it—the uncensored version of what happened in the UDBA's interrogation room in Belgrade, which had screwed up Nina's life and continued to poison our family for three generations.

"And now Rafi tells me you'll come too with us, and you'll make it into your movie together . . ." Vera rejoiced on the phone, and I almost dared, it was on the tip of my tongue to ask her whether it had really happened or if I'd been dreaming, but I didn't. I was suddenly afraid that I wouldn't be able to prevent someone (but who?) from twisting her story against her. I was so afraid of no longer being able to love her. "And the fact that you will come, that shocked me even more so out of a coma, Gili, and it showed me that I really might be so old—like Methuselah!" She laughed. "I'm as old as the Bible! And for so many years I was like a bear hibernating all winter, and now—uh-oh!—it's springtime, and I must again fight for the life, for the truth of what happened."

My ninety-year-old grandmother's first stage in preparing for battle was to climb up on a chair perched on top of a table, crawl into the attic, and pull out an enormous suitcase: not the one from her wedding night, but the one Tuvia and she had taken on their travels, all the way to Japan and Patagonia and Greenland. As she maneuvered herself backward out of the attic—I shudder to think of her doing that, at her age, alone, propping a chair on the table, climbing up, climbing down; I imagine her stuck with her head in the attic, her spindly jean-clad legs sticking out; it brings to mind Luigi Galvani's experiments electrocuting frogs—she hit the dusty cardboard box on which she'd once written in black marker GILI—VARIOUS, which contained my ancient Sony and a few crumbling videotapes, and one dusty but intact tape, my first and last film, from age fifteen, which had never been shown, and which might now be resurrected thanks to whatever we film in Goli Otok.

Thursday, October 23, 2008. Six a.m. Duty-free shopping area, Ben-Gurion Airport. Waiting for a table to free up. Vera and Rafael stand to one side speaking quietly. They throw us the occasional glance. Nina and I stand facing each other like two scolded children who won't look each other in the eye. Rafael pulls the Sony out of his backpack; Nina and I move away from each other in perfect synchrony. He records, and I turn my back on him. Filming my morning face is totally unacceptable, and sharing a frame with Nina makes me claustrophobic. He zooms in on Vera. Strong, small face, pursed lips, red lipstick, irritated wave: "Really, Rafi, stop that, there are prettier girls around here!" He leaves her and moves over to Nina. She can't be bothered to shoo him away as he circles around her. She huddles deep in a blue parka that used to belong to Tuvia, which also gets on my nerves. I mean, just think how you made his and Vera's life a misery, and now you're wrapping him around yourself? On the other hand, I can't stop looking at her. Her pallor. Her face without a drop of blood. Transparent lips. Almost no chest. "The most feminine she ever looked," Rafi told me once, "was in the weeks after she gave birth to you."

"Well, obviously," I said at the time, flipping my hair back gracefully, "it was the contact with me."

What he saw in her, as a man, and what he still sees in her—God only knows. Almost all the women he was with after her were real women. Not always paragons of wisdom, but within a reasonable margin of error. So why is it that he's been soldered to her skinny ass for forty-five years?

He constantly circles around her with the camera, and she suffers silently, understanding that it is a sort of travel tax that she must pay. She is lost in herself, but not impervious to him. I observe them. There is undeniably something between them. What makes two people a couple? Longing? Belonging? Suspending a fraction of the pupil during a seemingly meaningless look? All of the above. And most important—feeling at home. Something like homeland. Now you're getting carried away, Gili. Define "homeland." Maybe: the place where you know in your body when the traffic lights are supposed to change? Not bad, but when it comes to two, Gili, two human beings—what makes two a couple? Maybe it's the same thing with the lights?

We've been together for six years, Meir and I, and it's the first time in my life I've really been a couple. But now he wants a child. He's been wanting one for quite a while. He's stopped talking about it, delicate man that he is, but it constantly hovers between us, and I can't do it. Me having a child is not possible. I'm child-accursed.

Deflecting my wistful momentum, I flick away Meir, and myself. We're not the story now. I'm erasing him for the next few days. He is not on this voyage. There's no Meir, no Meir and Gili.

I think about my father's idea from when he was a boy, that if he slept with Nina she would regain her expressions, and about how what began as a romantic childish folly determined his fate and hers, as well as mine. And how a stupid, arrogant notion ultimately turned into such total love that it hardly depended on anything Nina did or did not do, on what she was or was not. Paradoxically, that love makes me respect my father, who is currently somewhat demeaning himself by badgering her with his camera. Because honestly, how many people at his age continue to sustain such an active, devoted, dogged love, something truly slavish, sometimes pathetic, and, on top of it all, so one-sided?

Nina says quietly: Rafi, stop. And he stops, as if coming out of a seizure, and he stands aside and wipes his forehead with a handkerchief. I've been begging him for years to upgrade to tissues, but what we have here is a particularly stubborn retro stylist.

With an argyle sweater, knitted by Vera.

He stands alone, parting the flow of people. They're all moving toward a target, while he is stuck, a man without a purpose. He does have his street gangs, four tough groups in Akko and Ramleh, and he treats those kids as if they're his children, I'm not exaggerating, and they see him as a father. But what will truly invigorate him, what will kick his life up a notch, if he gives up the heart flutters caused by his love for her?

He turns to me and nods, as if having heard the question.

Put in some work now, G, so R doesn't accuse you of being a freeloader.

Nina—puffy blue parka, light gray jeans, thin blue belt with a small silver buckle, light blue shirt as anemic as her, blue sweater with round collar. Hair tied back, undyed, gray on the verge of silver. Glasses with a delicate green frame. No rings. No earrings. No bracelets, no watch. Thin silver chain around her neck. Flats. No makeup. Ever. Why am I even making this list, which is completely unnecessary for the minor family movie we're making? Because Rafael and I, as always, are taking our film very seriously.

Because maybe, who knows, something else might come of it? Something bigger?

That is why I adhere to the total school of thought advocated by Rafael, my father and mentor, who demanded that his young script girl take responsibility for the entire experience, including the one outside the frame: "Even things that only almost happen are part of reality." I think I mentioned that I was seventeen when he took me under his large wing and taught me cinematography and directing, in his strict way, and above all insisted that I write: You have a good eye and a good hand, and it's possible that writing is your thing, he told me more than once. He wanted me to write down the elements that don't explicitly appear in the film: thoughts, associations, even the random memories of crew members, but also my own. He valued the ideas and memories of a chaotic girl, and he wasn't afraid of abundance like some directors I work with now, who seem to regard abundance as simply bad taste.

He taught me to overflow—with ideas, sparks, "thought-bastards," as he called them, that's how he spoke, he had his own vocabulary, and I liked to think that I myself was in some way his thought-bastard. Once I even made the mistake of saying in front of other people that I'd leaped into the world from his head like, and I do apologize, Athena from Zeus's head, and his face fell, I saw it, he really didn't like that, and he quickly joked about how, at most, I'd leaped out of the goose egg Nina gave him when he was a boy. So once again he managed to bring Nina in, and once again I lost out to her. Never mind.

To achieve the totality demanded by R, I stand in the middle of Ben-Gurion Airport forcing myself to wonder, for instance, what Nina has gone through since the birthday party on Saturday. I try to imagine how she told Vera about her illness, what it was really like, moment by moment. Was there or was there not or could there have been on Vera's face a slight spasm of disapproval, or even contempt, for Nina who had taken ill, been defeated, surrendered? ("Nina is spoiled," she'd often told me, "she doesn't have strength for life like I do and you do, Gilush. With us, it can't be helped, inheritance skipped generation.")

Nina stares at me and suddenly everything in her sharpens, she gives me a terrified glare, and I panic: What has she seen? Which of my thoughts has she picked up? I push her away with a vigorous blink. Hey there! What's up with you? Software stuck? Need a reboot?

She shuts her eyes, and her face turns yellow. I shout for Rafi, but before he can move she takes a step forward and falls—falls? More like collapses onto me. "Sorry," she mumbles, "I'm sorry, Gili." I'm petrified, and the woman will not let go. "Sorry, I don't know what happened . . ." Still apologizing into my neck, she moves even closer, and even under normal circumstances I don't like being touched by anyone except Meir, or my father, who won't stop filming us together. That's what really pisses me off: that instead of flinging her off me, he's immortalizing a false moment of kitsch. And I completely lose my sense of reality, because suddenly there's skin, and it's warm skin, delicate skin, and then the smell of Dove shampoo, which I also happen to use, and there's a body, and her chest, I feel it pressing against me, and it's soft—where does she hide it? And the tenderness of a cheek, and delicate wrists.

She clutches me, this woman who thirty-six years ago cut me out of her life, had an abortion, for real aborted me, even if she did so a fashionable three and a half years late, because by then I already existed—poor Gili had been born, and she was a pretty cute girl judging by the pictures and some accounts, and this woman went and scraped me out of her, and now she's shoving her head into my neck, and me, instead of throwing her the hell off me, I don't move. And by the way, I discover that she is horribly light. Turns out, not only does she have no heart, but other internal organs seem to be missing, too.

And to think how many tons she weighed when she was gone.

My father keeps filming madly, surrounding us from all angles, stitching us together. His face glistens. His fleshy, droopy lips fill out. The man has waited a whole lifetime for this shot. I watch him betray me and I know he has no control over it. This is my father, who stuck foam onto the corners of shelves and tables when I was learning to walk, and now here he is in a frenzy, deserting me. I swear I'm going to throw up.

And then I grab her waist. There's no flesh there whatsoever. Right now, in front of the camera, I could give one hard squeeze and chop Nina in half—two wasp halves would fall to the floor. Except that my hand suddenly reaches up and strokes the back of her head. Is there any way I can stop from losing my cool? Can I rationally accept that my hand, flesh of my flesh, is sneaking a caress like the last of the beggars? Her hair is smooth and thin, my fingers swiftly run through it to the place where it's tied back, and I touch the little elastic holding her ponytail—yes, this cuckoo bird does have a tail. But then I pull myself together and cut her away from me with both hands. Don't you dare, I say pleasantly, quietly, straight into her ear that is tender as a leaf, how strange, it's like a little girl's ear. Don't you dare touch me anymore, do you hear me? You lost your chance to touch me when I was three and a half and there's no do-over for motherhood—

I'm not sure I managed to convey the whole speech. My heart was pounding and I could barely breathe. I said maybe just a word or two of all that. And by the way, I never talk to anyone like that, under any circumstances. Not even in the toughest moments on set, when the film is getting insane and falling apart along with the director right in front of my eyes. So how did that garbage spill out of me instead of everything I'd practiced at home? We did rehearsals, me and Meir; I drove him crazy. He didn't complain. He's an adapter. It was like a press release, what I formulated in my head before I left the house, five or six levelheaded lines, the declarations it was important for me to make before we set off, and I wanted Rafael and Vera to bear witness: I have nothing with you, either good or bad. You stopped hurting me a long time ago. You were nonexistent my whole life, and you'll continue to not exist now, and I'm taking this trip only to preserve Grandma Vera's memories, capiche?

I have reason to suspect that I didn't say any of that.

She opens her giant eyes at me. Amazing eyes, she has, there's no denying it, the most living part of her. Vera's eyes. Sharp emerald green. In this case "inheritance" did not skip a single generation. She undoes herself from me and hisses at Rafael to stop filming, and he obeys. People are watching. She straightens her clothes and hair, which are in disarray from her little pogrom. Her hands are shaking. She seems truly shocked by what has happened. Even she can't fake that kind of pallor. And then I get it: Is she afraid it's a sign? A symptom of her illness?

I read up on it last night. I couldn't care less about Nina herself, but I do have a certain interest in the genetic diseases that course through her toward the future. And there was a lot of stuff about the patient's need, especially in the early stages, to touch and stroke, even to hug total strangers. (Aha! Maybe that explains the lechers? Could I have been unjustly castigating a sick, helpless woman all these years?)

I signal to Rafael: Maybe we should drop this? Look at the state she's in. How can we travel this way? Vera walks over to Nina, puts two hands on her shoulders, and rubs her arms, over and over again. Somehow the motion calms us all, even slightly hypnotizes us. We stand staring at it, at that movement, which seems to flow into me from the hands of Vera, who betrayed Nina, who abandoned *me,* and there's a hole at the bottom of the sea.

It's our boarding call. Rafael starts filming again, around the terminal this time: a pair of Indian flight attendants, a despondent puppy in a crate, an airport employee pushing a long snake of trolleys. Footage that will come in handy when we edit. Standing in line behind us, a family with a pair of angelic blond twins asks questions. Rafael explains that we're going on a roots journey. First we'll go to the town where Vera was born—"Granny," he calls her, as if she were a cute little Mrs. Pepperpot—and then we'll sail to the island where she was sentenced to hard labor for almost three years. Rafael likes talking to strangers, eager to turn them into nonstrangers. If he could, he would turn the whole world into nonstrangers. A quality he definitely did not get from me.

—

Outside the airplane window there are forested mountains. Heavy clouds, lower than the mountains. The cabin is almost dark. If this weather keeps up tomorrow, we won't be able to sail to Goli Otok.

At some point during the flight my father and I meet in the line for the bathroom. He looks pale and sweaty. His fear of flying is taking its toll. I ask if he has any idea what Nina is planning for us. What sort of film does she want us to produce for her—a film about Vera? About Vera and Nina and what happened between them? Where is the focal point?

He has no answers. He simply doesn't know. In one of their phone calls, she told him that she had an idea, but she wasn't capable of articulating it. "It's not fully baked yet," she'd said, and when Rafael pressed, she said that only when we were in the actual place, on the island, would she know if she was ready for it. Our dialogue is occurring, as I mentioned, outside the bathroom door, and it ends when my father goes in.

He spends a fair amount of time in there. In recent years he's been a little slow in that department, and now I, having interacted with him in public, am perceived by the other people in line as his representative and suffer their radiating bitterness.

Rafael comes out. Gili goes in.

Clean up quickly, destroy the evidence, even though no one would suspect I am the one responsible for this spillage. He is my father, besides everything else, and I do have some responsibility for him.

Zagreb: a pretty town from above. Rain on the windows. A soft landing. I learn that Croatians, just like Israelis, eagerly applaud the pilot.

Passport control. Everything goes smoothly. We split up: Vera and Nina stay with the luggage; Rafael and I go to pick up the rental car. Rafael speaks again, on camera this time, about that moment at the birthday party—the moment that stirred me, too—when Vera waved little Tom up in the air and, for one instant, seemed to be drawing the arc of an entire lifetime. Then comes the banal thought that Vera will probably not be here much longer—says Rafael while we wait for the Avis clerk with the Mohawk to bring our Mazda—and the thought causes him intolerable pain, as if it were the death of a very young person in the prime of her life, but also, he adds wondrously (Rafael, such a sweetheart, sometimes he's an accidental tourist in his own mind), he feels as if he himself were still a little boy about to lose his mother. "A pretty ridiculous thought for a man my age, especially a man who's already lost his mother once," he says with genuine surprise to the camera I hold up, and at that moment I see what I've already seen more than once when shooting documentaries: something ordinary, prosaic, which someone says on camera—an attentive, supportive camera—hits them as if they were hearing it for the first time, and the story they've been telling themselves for years shatters.

Rafael distractedly runs his hand over his large face, the disheveled beard and the high, furrowed brow, granting me a heartrending human landscape, then pulls himself together: "Stop it, Gili, the movie isn't about me, it's about Vera. Remember that." But I'm starting to think otherwise. It's about all of us: you and Nina and maybe me, too. No one gets out alive. And it occurrs to me that this is going to be a classic disaster film, except in slow motion: the ordinary disaster of life, which eats out of the palm of our hand.

"Go on, turn it off, you're wasting the battery," Rafael says, "there's our Mustang." I turn around with the camera, making a good smooth rotation—today there are cameras that move just as smoothly as nature; one day, when I'm rich . . . I see a little lime-green vehicle coasting cheerfully toward us, and my face falls. What a moron I was, honestly, why did I cheap out? Rafael explicitly told me not to pinch pennies on the car, but as usual, I was worried about the production budget, which in this case was my father's private budget, which came out of the crumbs he was thrown every week for being the oldest social worker in Israel, a street-gang tycoon, as I think I've mentioned.

The lime pulls up in front of us and spits out the agent like a seed. Rafael gives me a "what were you thinking" look, then stands scratching his forehead. The only way the four of us are going to cram ourselves in there is with a shoehorn, and we will suffocate. This really is going to be a team-building experience, military-style. We will simply be bonded into one entity. It soon turns out, however, that the lime is small but mighty. The suitcases and the backpacks and my father find space, and I sit down next to him, and there's even room for my ample legs. Apparently things are bearable in the back, too. Vera and Nina sit in stony silence, perhaps still stunned by the flight, or because they've finally grasped that we are all in this together—dead or alive.

"The Bermuda Quadrangle," I write in my notebook, and Vera leans forward: "What are you writing in there?" "Nothing, just stuff for myself. Notes. So we'll remember for the editing." Nina, from inside all her layers, takes an interest: "What kind of notes?" When I don't answer, Vera scolds, "Gili, your mother asked you something." And I say, "She's not my mother."

We're on the road. I struggle with the marvelously sophisticated GPS, which insists on giving us directions in Croatian. Vera complains that it reminds her of the commands that used to come over the loudspeakers in the camp. Nina is rolled up in her coat like a pupa in a cocoon.

Noon. Vera hands out sandwiches. More than sixty miles to

Čakovec, Vera's hometown. The direction is northwest. Soft hills. Lots of green. Abundance. Vera starts making choked-up sounds of enthusiasm. Claps both hands to her cheeks, points with her finger: "*Yoy!* Such forests! Such mountains! So beautiful, my homeland!"

Soft rain. Pretty games of light and clouds. I shoot some stills.

Rafael is driving surprisingly well (the man was a film director, and now he handles the toughest kids, but still, it always surprises me when he demonstrates any competency in the practical world).

I manage to Judaize the GPS. I suspect that Israelis were in this car before us, because the Hebrew directions are voiced by Shimon Peres.

Čakovec. The metropolis. Fifty thousand residents.

The rain has stopped.

Now I start getting excited. This is where Vera was born. This is where she was a girl. My whole life I've been hearing about this town, about the house, the shop—"the *kompanija*"—and my great-grandfather's exploits. I wish I'd had time for preparations and excitement. Everything happened so fast. The party for Vera, Nina's visit, finding out about her illness.

And there's also the ordinary civic excitement—I'm in a foreign country!

I haven't left Israel for seven years.

From one moment to the next, I can feel the Israeli stressors falling away (which immediately stresses me out).

A city parking lot. Row 3, column B. We walk to the center of town. It's starting. It really is happening. Notebook in hand. Rafael ahead of us. He films us, signaling for me to write down impressions, thoughts. I write. Flower beds, cafés, umbrellas with Coca-Cola logos, memorials. Tiled rooftops. Pigeons. "Write it down." Who knows what I might need when I edit the film that could be anything.

The main street in Čakovec. A serene pedestrian mall. Quiet. Only a barrel organ jangling away somewhere. No high-rises. There are maple trees (I think; I take stills on my cell phone to identify later). Red-and-white brick houses. A bright church. Almost empty cafés. Couples walking with strollers. "Write it down." Large dogs snoozing on the street, projecting something babyish and trusting. Vera runs ahead, wobbling on her spindly cavalier legs. This used to be that, and that used to be something else. She walks up to an older woman with a nano-dog adorned with a ribbon: "Excuse me, madam, would you happen to know me?"

And all this time Nina does not say a word. Straggles behind. Head down. As if looking for something she's lost.

That's the woman who darkened my life?

At every moment, at every second, even without looking, my body knows exactly where she is.

On the way to Vera's childhood home.

She seems slightly apprehensive about the encounter. She asks to stop for a reviving cup of coffee first. Declares that there is only one café worth its salt in all of the Balkans. Leads us swiftly down narrow lanes, navigating without a map to a café named Kavana Royal, which she knew as a child. Incredible how she has no doubt that it still exists and is waiting for her obediently after more than eighty years. "Can you help envying her?" Rafi whispers in my ear as he rushes past me with the camera.

Surprisingly, the café does still exist. Vera is all aflutter. "Here! *Yoy!* Here is where we used to sit. Here Father played *preferans* with his friends, and I ate strawberry ice cream!" A sign hanging over the bar announces a hypnotist's show. A silver star glints from the corner of his mouth. The headwaiter—or, rather, the only waiter, but he is mustachioed like Emperor Franz Joseph and has therefore been promoted—points to a glass box on the wall, which contains a gorgeous china tea set with delicate teapots and ornamental cups, and declares in Croatian, which Vera translates for us: "A tea set just like that, ladies and gentlemen, was owned by King George in Buckingham Palace! In London!"

He doesn't know whether there's a synagogue in Čakovec. "But there is a memorial statue for the city's Jews who died in the war. They took them to Auschwitz."

"My father and mother went there," says Vera.

"It was a terrible thing," the man says, "to this day it's impossible to understand that it happened." He says this simply and genuinely. Tears appear in his eyes.

A man of a certain age sits next to us reading a newspaper attached to a wooden dowel. Hearing us speak Hebrew, he comes over, bows, and asks permission to join us. Goatee, glasses. Brown suede jacket, elbow patches, shipshape. A professor of Slavic literature. He sorts out the Balkan mess for us. Tells us about the war that raged here in the nineties. "No!" he fumes when I make the mistake. "It was not a civil war!" His face turns red. "It was a barbaric military assault by Serbian soldiers with Serbian tanks!" And now he can't be stopped. He lectures furiously about rivers of blood and massacres and rape. Four members of his family were murdered by their neighbors and good friends.

I feel bad. Very bad. To the point of dizziness. All that bloodshed, that hatred, that humanity.

The professor continues his lecture, and I try to write, both to honor the man and for my own edification. But I grow tired pretty quickly and start skipping things, superficial being that I am. Rafi and I exchange casual glances on our internal wavelength. These Balkans are a real jumble, and I've only landed here three hours ago, and back in Israel I have my own charming conflict, which I don't fully understand anymore either.

The house where Vera was born is on the main street, not far from the café. We hurry over there. Vera is a few steps ahead of us all the time. By the time we get there, she's already standing outside, arm outstretched: "It's here, children, here I was born." He doesn't give it up easily, but I take the camera from Rafi and film Vera with the house in the background. I know its history by heart. On the first floor was Bauer General Store, owned by Vera's father, my great-grandfather, and the family lived upstairs. Father, mother, and four daughters. Now there is a large branch of Zagrebačka Banka on the first floor, and a private residence on the second. We can glimpse a large, neglected yard through the locked gate. I record, constantly switching between video and stills. The camera on my cell phone is lousy, the pictures come out with white spots and long cracks. I ask Vera if she wants us to try to enter the living quarters on the second floor.

"Nothing here is like it was and there's nothing for me to see here." But she happily tells us: "We had a good, rich life here, all on all. We had a cook at home, and my governess, like a nanny, until I was ten, and girl who cleaned rooms, and gardener, and one person who took care of trees in garden behind, and there was stove which took wood, three-level ceramic stove . . ."

She describes an enormous, well-lit sitting room, thick rugs, curved staircase to the second floor. Next to the kitchen was the špajz, the pantry, with sausages hanging and large sacks full of rice and flour and sugar, jars of goose fat, barrels of pickled cucumbers and sauerkraut. And in the cellar, on the straw, potatoes for the whole year . . .

Rafi, flushed with excitement, asks for the camera. His eyes are laughing. The trip is starting to hook him. He focuses on me. Leave me alone! But he insists, asking me to say a few words for the beginning of our voyage. I'm not good at these proclamations, but then I think of something: "There's a line from a poem by Moti Baharav: 'Before you are reborn, take a close look at where you are.'"

Rafi asks me where I would like to be reborn.

"What makes you think I want to be reborn?"

He moves away, looking for a more pliable collaborator. "Vera, over here, look at me. Tell us something about your parents. Was there love?" If that's where he's searching for the inspiration for Vera and Milosz's absolute love, he's looking in the wrong place.

"Love?" Vera laughs. "No, no. I suppose she got used to him in the end. But my mother was very restrained woman, and there were big differences between them. He liked to have fun, for example, to have good time, and she did not. He used to go every winter at Christmas to Budapest. Took with him something like fifty thousand dinar and went from café to café, to theater, to whose-know-what-else. And he did parties! He danced! That's how it is with Hungarians, Rafi, they hear tzigane music and they smash glasses! That was how my Milosz was, also. Much as he was shy and delicate, he danced like the devil. You wouldn't believe it of him. When he and his peasant mother danced, their feet did not touch the ground! My mother-in-law, she was like this, with handkerchief . . ." And she twirls around on the street, doing a clumsy tap dance in her bright purple sneakers. What a fantastic shot—Rafael grins at me.

But where is Nina? The script girl is also the sheepdog of the herd, and Nina, by any parameter, is both a lost lamb and a black sheep. She stands with her back to us, eyes on the ground, looking slightly crazy.

Vera goes on: "When I was twelve, for first time I had this serious thought: while I was still sleeping in bed under blankets, there came already the servant to the home, and she lit fires in rooms and in bathroom, so that when I get up, when the masters get up, they will be warm. And that was the first time this idea started to work in me."

"Which idea?" Rafi asks.

"Idea of responsibility for human beings, and idea of money and poverty. Because I went to high school on the train, and from all villages around came children who walked on foot in the dark, next to train tracks. And in school there was a stove and they put their socks on to dry. And I went home and asked Mother: Could I maybe bring two or three such children back to us? My three big sisters got angry at me: Those smelly kids with lice? What a little idiot you are, girl!

"Mother actually said yes, but she had no say in the home. And she sat down and read to me from the book *Mother,* by Gorky, and I then understood that Mother was with me, and here in my stomach started to work something about rich and poor people, and about injustice which there is in the world." She turns to me. "What are you all the time writing, Gili?"

"I'm writing down what you say, Grans. And what we're filming, and what's around us." And what is not said, and what is not visible.

"Really? What is that good for?"

"That's how Rafi and I work, it'll help us later when we edit."

The partisan in her is ill at ease. The woman who worked in Tito's counterespionage for two years after the war is ill at ease. She squints at me. The fact that I've been her granddaughter for almost forty years does not currently count in my favor. Her right eye moves in on me at a close-up. "And what, for example, are you writing at this second?"

I read out: "'Vera is a Communist at heart.' Is that right to say?"

"No! No, no, no! You see, it's good thing I asked! Socialist at heart, that is right! And only after that I came into communism, but God forbid not Stalin's communism . . . Not the murderers' kind!" She runs a puzzled look over me again. Her intuition is not flawed. Ever since we left, and on the days leading up to the trip, I've been a little distant from her. Every time our eyes meet, I send her warnings along the lines of: You're my grandmother and I'm crazy about you, and you saved my life when I was a little girl, you took care of me and Dad after Nina left, you raised me like a daughter—more than a daughter, because you didn't raise your own daughter like that—and you saved my life again when I committed suicide, and for a whole year you resuscitated me with casseroles and soups and cakes, you cooked me and baked me, and I will not forget that, Grandma, but if at some point on this trip you don't tell your daughter what you told me that night in the ICU, I swear I don't know what I might do.

Actually I do know.

I'll tell her.

But why would I tell her? Good question. On the one hand I say: Let Nina spend the rest of her life without knowing what really screwed it up. That's the punishment I've meted out—that to her dying day she will feel like one big dissonance. A chicken with its head cut off that spends an entire lifetime running around without understanding what's happened to it. But on the other hand—

Is there even another hand?

And even though in the name of the baby I was, and in the name of the girl I was, I should not make any concessions to her, ever, that's what I swore, I took an oath, I must not betray that baby and that girl, because there is no one else to seek their vengeance except me. Still, when she straggles behind us like that—

I don't know. Since this morning, since she fell on me at Ben-Gurion, I've been feeling down about what she brings out in me.

The meanness she brings out in me is bringing me down.

On the street outside Vera's childhood home: "When I was five, I had tonsils removed in private sanatorium, and Mother said: Because you behaved well and didn't cry and didn't get scared, you will have gift. And what was the gift? Five-year-old girl will go for first time in her life to opera! I don't remember what opera they made, but at intermission there was a singer with *perika* on his head like a judge, and he sang 'Funiculì, Funiculà.'"

And she stands there in the middle of the street, singing in Neapolitan. A little circle gathers around, a few people sing along with her, two wave their hats to the rhythm, one bangs his walking cane on the asphalt. Vera conducts them, her white plastic handbag with its gilded clasp hanging from the crook of her arm, and she's in seventh heaven. Glowing. People applaud her. But for me, somehow . . . Ever since Nina arrived for the birthday on Saturday, she's been slightly ruining the grandmother I used to have. Without any effort, just with that look of hers, she makes Vera seem a little—how should I put this—on the narcissistic spectrum.

"We're in Čakovec," Vera explains to the camera in a tour guide's cadence, "near to Hungary border, near also to Austria border. We went to see theater and opera in Budapest and in Vienna. That was our culture, and Hungarian was our first language. So I am not Balkan Jew, and not Ghetto-Jude. I am Jew of central Europe, is what I am! The most real Europe! There is no Europe like me left!"

Her little audience of locals does not understand Hebrew, of course, but her pathos captures their hearts. At their applause she bows her head magnanimously. We're going to have to hurry her up. The sun will set soon, and we still have a long drive ahead of us. It's a real shame that I didn't have enough time to organize this trip properly. We should have stayed here for at least another day. Allowed Vera to take in more. It hurts to think that this is the last time in her life she will be back here.

A quick walk takes us to the school. At this time of day it's empty and shuttered. A dreary, unremarkable building. Tiled roof, chimneys. I imagine little Vera running around here, a flash of light. Vera: "I was the smallest girl in class, in age and in shortness. I look like six, and they look like eight, and there is a girl in class, Jagoda, which means 'strawberry,' and she from my first day in school made herself like a bodyguard to me. And one week after that, I was already her commander in everything. Every time I make excursions in the snow and the forest, I take Jagoda by her hand and say where we go and what we do and when we go back—"

Nina, nodding to herself with a crestfallen face, on the fringe of the little group, has all the cheerfulness of a gallbladder. She forces herself into the role of a mangy, injured stray dog who straggles after us but knows we'll pick up a stone and throw it at her any minute.

I can see that Vera is torn between her excitement about being here and the pain she feels for Nina. I've had enough of it. "Look," I go over and tell Nina, "are you with us or not? Are we doing this whole thing for you, or am I wrong?"

She looks up at me with an utterly wiped-out face. Good God, she's barely alive. I feel suddenly scared. She holds on to a tree trunk. Perhaps we've underestimated how bad her condition is. Perhaps she wasn't telling us the whole truth. "It's all a little too much for me," she says, almost inaudibly. Her lips are white. "I didn't imagine this. Let's take it slowly, okay?"

"What's too much for you? We haven't even started anything. You haven't even been born yet." I cut away from her.

"Gili."

"What now?"

"I thought of something—"

I stand facing her with demonstratively impatient body language. This woman is going to keep me forever young, or at least forever three.

"I had an idea, Gili, and I think maybe—"

"Ideas are Rafael. Take it up with him," I blurt out and walk away. And then back. "Would you like some water?"

"No. I just need to talk."

"Rafael will be happy to."

"Gili-"

Freeze! That word I just wrote, "Gili" with a hyphen—

This is how it happened: The girl I was at sixteen, and to my great misfortune also at five foot six, with the jawline of a good-natured boxer and masses of acne, traveled to the Ministry of Interior's Haifa office to amend the national identity card she'd just been issued. But the stone-faced Gorgon at the counter refused to leave the MOTHER'S NAME box blank. The girl, who, due to her height and size was prevented from causing scenes or drawing any attention whatsoever to herself, was about to leave, shamefaced, but a moment before surrendering she astonished herself by asking if she could, perhaps, please, add "Nina" to her own name.

She threw the request into space, almost yelling, and immediately eradicated it from her memory because it was impossible to believe that such a request could have a hold in reality. And when, two weeks later, the new identity card arrived by mail, bearing the name Gili-Nina, the girl felt as if someone had cast a spell on her—

At age eighteen, by which time she was five-eight (God, she thought in those days, what if it simply never stops? What if she keeps going, like a bad joke, and where is the red line at which she will put an end to it?), the girl went back to the Ministry of Interior in Haifa. This time she was served by a smiling redhead who was working there over her summer break, and with great ease and no anesthetic she cut Nina off from Gili. And then Gili asked, with the submissiveness of those who cannot defeat their lust, if it might be possible, perhaps, for a while longer, to retain the hyphen, just for the hell of it. The girl asked, "What do you mean?" and Gili quietly pronounced her name with a hyphen at the end, like an open call into the void. The girl scanned her slowly, perhaps sensing something, and she looked around and whispered that it was really not done, to have a name with a hyphen, but let's give it a try, what's the worst that could happen, and if anyone asks we'll say it was human error.

Exterior. Day. Again outside the family home. Slightly chaotic and circuitous, our route around Čakovec. The little crowd of admirers has scattered, and we are four again. Vera: "My mother and father, a good marriage they did not have. That I already told you, children. She even at first did not love him, and he, I told you also, he was always cheating on her. And I was like, say, her couple. With me she spoke everything, to me she poured out her heart. Not with him and not with my three big sisters.

"Twenty years ago, you remember, Rafi, on my seventy birthday that you made so lovely for me, by surprise, my three sisters came from Yugoslavia to kibbutz, to see with their own eyes how silly Vera lives and is giving up private capital. And we sat together for a few days, and so what do we do? We talk about what passed. And my sisters asked me, 'How did you get close to that sphinx, our mother? She never laughed and never cried.'"

Nina looks up. I remember: on the kibbutz, when they arrived from Yugoslavia, my father said, the kids called her Sphinx.

"And I asked my sisters, 'Did you ever ask Mother something? Did you know something of her pains? Did you give her opening of your heart?' 'No!' 'Why not? Did you not have feelings to her?' 'Maybe our mother wasn't to us such an interesting person.' 'But to me every person is interesting! There is no person without meaning! Do you know, for example, that Father made her pregnant eight times, and she got abortions on the table?' 'No . . . we didn't know . . . But how did you know?' 'Because with me she talked, and to me she told, and me she took every time she went to the woman who does it!' 'She took you?' 'Well, who else did she have?' 'But you were just a girl, Vera!' 'What matters, just a girl? I was a girl and I was with her! I saw her! She would go inside, maybe half an hour, no more, and I would play in the yard.'"

Rafael and I, and Nina, stare at her and scarcely breathe. She sounds oddly lighthearted, detached, as though she's talking about someone else and not about her and her mother. "There were in that yard iron shelves, with boxes of screws and nails, probably belonging to husband of the woman who took away babies, and I would play with those nails like they were mother and father and girls, and talk with them and reassure, until Mother came out and we would put hands together and walk slowly, carefully home."

Her speech grows heavy and her gaze thickens, as if the story is only now beginning to percolate in her, for the first time since the events occurred more than eighty years ago. "And all the way home she would cry, and I would tell her about family of nails . . ." She stops. Licks her upper lip. "Well, this is surely not interesting for you. Let's keep going."

We are still recovering from the story when a heavyset man with a shaved head, walking a beautiful blue-eyed husky on a leash, stops to look at us. He asks what language Vera is speaking, and when I tell him, he spits on the road and walks away. Vera notices of course. She yells after him in Croatian and waves her fist. Rafael films her. Her face ignites all at once. Any minute now she'll run after the man and attack him. Rafael physically bars her, and she slams into the camera (great shot!). The man spits again, without turning around. I'm not sure what it is, but something about him, perhaps the folds in the back of his neck, makes me envision Vera's father crushing her mother, my great-grandmother, whom I did not know but to whom my heart goes out. The blue-eyed dog does turn to glance at us. He looks noble and somehow superior, which makes the whole affair even more depressing.

Our mood has blackened. It'll be dark soon, and we have almost two hundred miles before we reach the hotel on the coast, from which we will sail to the island tomorrow.

But the high point of our Čakovec visit is still to come. We quickly walk back to Kavana Royal, where, opposite the café, stands a building of yellowing stone. Wide door. "Here, this," says Vera, and suddenly everything slows down and there is quiet, and gravity.

A shroud seems to descend on us.

Rafael: "So this is where you met? What was this place?"

"It was for dancing, for balls. Now it's—" Vera puts on her reading glasses and gets so close to the building that her nose practically touches the posters on the wall. "Now it's a place for art shows."

Rafael: "And how was it that you happened to meet here?"

"It was my high school graduation party. I was a girl, seventeen and something, and I'm dancing with everyone and I'm happy, I'm the belle in the ball, and here comes this young man, asks me to dance, and I—"

She stops talking at once. I look up from my notebook and see that Nina has suddenly entered the story.

Meaning, the frame.

She took three or four steps and walked into the frame, on her own initiative. And now she's standing next to Vera, shoulder to shoulder, in front of the camera. She is rigid, her face pulled taut. Something's happening to her. Vera rolls her eyes at her. Looks at Rafi. Tries to understand what's going on.

"Please, go on," says Nina in a strange voice.

"Go on?"

"Yes."

Vera gives Rafi a questioning look. He nods. Vera takes a deep breath. "Well, all right. All right. Where was I?"

"A young man came up to you," Nina says.

"Yes. Well. And he is young soldier fellow, officer, very thin, tall, with big ears and forehead like some philosopher—"

Vera's eyes dart between Rafael and Nina. The words are like gravel in her mouth.

"Go on," Nina says, practically pleading.

"Yes, fine. And he comes to me, asks me for dance. And while we dance he says to me that he does not know anyone here in our town." She swallows. A dim sense of deceit hangs menacingly in the air. As though a crack is widening in the picture of reality. "And we dance and not talk, and slowly the not talking turns into talking more than before. Should I go on?"

"Yes."

"And I feel delight dancing like that, and for the first time I think maybe this is what people say is love."

Silence.

It might have been the word "love" that did it. Nina says out loud to the camera: "Hello, Nina."

Silence. Rafi slowly lowers the camera. "Nina, honey, you're a little confused."

"Why are you stopping me?"

He strains out a smile. "You got mixed up."

"About what?"

"Nothing, something small, probably from all the excitement. You didn't notice that you said, 'Hello, Nina.'"

"Don't—stop—me—Rafi."

"Okay. I won't. What now?"

"Just record."

"Okay. Tape's running."

"Hello, Nina," says Nina, looking into the camera. "Look at me. Please raise your head and look at me." Nina waves at the camera. "Yes, like that. Great. You can see me. Do you know me?"

Her voice is tense and choked up. It's starting, this is how it starts, with this kind of weird little nonsense. We hadn't realized how bad her condition was. On the other hand—no. This isn't really happening. It can't be that in such a short time . . . When was she actually diagnosed?

"I'm Nina. Look at me. I'm you. But you the way you were a while ago, years ago even." Vera cannot move her head to look at her daughter. She stands by her side and stares into the camera. I see beads of sweat on Rafael's forehead.

"Don't be afraid of me, Nina," says Nina to the camera. "I want you to be happy. Just be happy. Look at me, don't shut your eyes. Can you see? We're actually the same one. We're the same woman, the same person. Look at me: this is how you were three or four years ago, or five. I am you."

Rafael films. Judging by his face, the Sony weighs a ton.

"Hey, Nina, do you like me? Do you think I look nice?" A long pause. In my mouth, or between my mouth and my nose, a frost of disaster starts to spread. It occurs to me that what's happening to Nina might be a little stroke. I try to remember if we saw a sign for a hospital in town.

And yet her appeal sounds so honest and so convincing that for a moment I expect a human voice to answer her from inside the camera.

"Look at me, honey," she says, unzipping the parka that encases her. "See the sweater I'm wearing? Remember how happy you were when you found this sweater at that little market in Provence? Do you remember that you were in Provence?" She smiles at the camera, and I see that all this—but what is it? what is this thing that is happening?—is costing her dearly, but she won't give up. "It's a beautiful place in France, in the French people's country. Remember that there's such a country, France?" She smiles at the camera again. "You were in Provence years ago, with Rafi—remember Rafi? You were young. You were both young, and at least one of you was beautiful, as Rafi always says. And Rafi loved you very much. Do you remember Rafi who loved you so much?"

I look at my father. Amid all this madness he looks as if his entire fate hangs on the answer to Nina's question. More than that: her answer will determine whether he even existed for all those years.

"And you loved him, too," Nina whispers, "maybe you never told him properly, but you loved him."

Rafael makes a strange gasping sound.

"I hope you're being taken good care of, where you are," says Nina and takes a step forward. My father, perhaps in alarm, takes a step back. She makes another move toward him and he steadies himself, solid again. And he films. And she smiles at him gratefully.

She says, "I hope, Nina, that you're warm enough, and that you're well dressed, that they give you nice clothes to wear, tasteful, and that they cook food you like, and bathe you once a day, gently, and put on good moisturizer, on your elbows, too, Nina, because you always have dry skin on your elbows . . ."

What is happening here, I do not understand. Beyond my comprehension.

"And that they're taking care of your hair and your nails. Don't let them get away with not doing your nails, remember what your mother, Vera, always says: Fingernails are a lady's calling card . . ."

Now it's Vera who lets out a muffled moan.

"No background noises, please," Nina whispers to her and looks back at the camera with a proficiency that surprises me. "I want to tell you a story, Nina," she continues in that strange voice, floaty and slightly saccharine, "and it's a story about you, Nina, about your childhood, and about your mother and father, Vera and Milosz."

She is not crazy.

No.

She's doing something I have no words to describe.

Right at that moment Nina crosses her arms over her chest and says, in a completely different voice, her ordinary voice, "That's it, Rafi, you can stop filming. That's what I'm asking from you all."

Silence.

"But what is it?" Rafi carefully probes.

"That's my request."

"Request?"

"I can only ask it of the three of you."

Vera takes a few steps and stumbles, then sits down heavily on the sidewalk with her head in her hands.

"Are you okay, Mom?"

"You frightened me so badly, my girl."

Rafael swallows. "And when are you thinking of . . . I mean, where will you . . . Where will she see it?"

"Wherever she is."

"Where is that?"

"I don't know yet. When we get back from the island I'll start looking. Someplace where people in her condition live."

"In Israel?" Rafi asks voicelessly.

"Yes?" she replies forlornly.

A very old man walks down the alleyway. All hunched over. Supported by two walking canes. We say nothing. He stops and looks at us for a long time. The cogs in his brain turn slowly as he tries to understand what our story is.

"I'll find her somewhere good, a place where they'll agree to show this to her at least once a week," says Nina after the old man walks away.

"To who?" Vera asks, confused.

"To the woman I'll be in a while."

"And what will they show her?" Vera whispers.

"The film we're making now, and what we shoot tomorrow on the island."

"And she'll sit in front of a screen, or a computer," my father mumbles, and I know his head is somewhere else: Nina is really coming back. Nina will live in Israel.

"I don't know how much of it she'll be able to understand," Nina says, "but every so often, let's say once a week, or once a month, she'll sit and watch and listen to the story about herself, the way she once was."

"Like a bedtime story?" Now it's me whispering.

"Yes." Nina, surprised, thanks me with a nod. "Exactly. A bedtime story before she—" She clears her throat, swallows. "Before she goes into the dark."

The pain is like a punch. I never imagined how much.

"She'll sit and listen to the story about herself," Nina repeats wondrously, as if just beginning to understand what she's proposing. "Maybe it'll bring her back to herself for a few minutes. Maybe even give her the feeling that she's someone. She'll have a story, finally."

Silence.

"We'll do it," says Vera. She gets up and stretches out her tiny stature. "Won't we, children?"

Rafi says, "Yes, of course we will." And he goes over and hugs Nina. "We'll simply talk to her. Only to her."

"But it's not 'her,' it's you," Vera haggles.

"It's me when I've become very ill. By that time I'll be 'her.'"

The signs, the looks between us. Everything is slow and stark. We still do not completely understand what we've become partners to, but a quiet awe fills us.

"So you want—" asks Rafael.

"Yes."

"Where should we start?"

"Maybe here, where Vera and Milosz met," says Nina. "That's the most logical thing, isn't it?"

"Logical in what sense?" he questions.

"In the sense that it was how she came into the world."

"You."

"She. Me. She." Nina stretches her lips uncomfortably. "Could you just accept that this is what's going to happen to me in the coming years? Me, she."

"So should I tell it again from beginning?" asks Vera, looking very sad. "Should I start from how I met him?"

"Yes, but now just tell *her,* talk to her," says Nina.

Rafael adds, "Pretend the camera lens is her eyes."

"All right."

"And try to smile, Majka, don't put her in a bad mood."

They sound very businesslike. With pauses in between the sentences. They sound like people walking through a fog, navigating toward one another.

"And what do you say, Gili?" asks Rafael. "You're so quiet."

I say nothing. They've made up their minds anyway. They've already given up in the blink of an eye on the movie we were going to make, my movie. I've been thrown abruptly into a bad place. I feel my throat tighten. I'm too old for sudden creative reversals like this. And honestly? It drives me crazy that in one second she charmed Rafael and Vera into doing exactly what she wanted. She is such a master manipulator. On the other hand, well, yes, okay, on the other hand—

But that baby, and the girl from long ago, they leap at my jugular, claws out: Don't you dare let her soften you, there's no "other hand," don't forget for a moment what she did to you. I walk away and sit down on the curb, and I look up with swollen eyes at my father, who comes and strokes my head and peers into me sadly and reads me like an open book.

"Write it down, Gili. Write everything down, including you."

—

But it takes a while longer until we start. "Nina," says Vera, "don't be angry, but I can't go on with anything until I know one thing: Are you really positive you have it?"

"I'm sick, Vera. And I will lose my mind if you keep doubting that. *I am sick!*"

"Okay, okay, there's no need to—"

"How long?" Rafael asks.

"How long have I known, or how long do I have left?"

"Both."

"Really knowing, I mean knowing it's this, for certain, I've known for six months. Maybe more. Eight or nine months. Since January or so." She sighs. "For the time being I'm in pretty good shape and, as you can see, fairly lucid. But . . ." She chuckles. "Would you kindly remind me who you are?"

Rafael laughs, but he remembers, as I do, that at Vera's party, on Saturday, Nina couldn't remember the names of Orli and Adili, Esther's granddaughters, and she'd also asked Shleimaleh, Esther's husband, "And how is your wife?" and had quickly tried to make a joke out of it.

"And the doctors?" Vera asks.

"Very well, thank you. Fit as a fiddle."

"Nina," Vera groans.

"It depends which doctor I ask. If I average out the prognoses I've been given, I have between three and five years until I completely lose my memory and stop being me, but there certainly is a fear that I'll keep living for several years after that. Oh my, how we'll laugh at me."

Now it's my turn to groan. A strange sound escapes my lips, half shout, half whimper. Something shrill and ridiculous.

"You took the words right out of my mouth," Nina says to me.

She goes over to Rafael and puts both hands on his shoulders. "Do you understand what you're getting into?"

"I told you, I'll take care of you."

"And you realize that includes helping me end it, when the time comes."

He nods.

"You and Vera and Gili."

"Me?" I splutter. "Why me? What am I in this?"

"Because Rafi will soften at the last minute."

"And what about me?"

"You're a hardheaded snotnose."

She's not joking. She's completely serious. She looks at me. There is another conversation constantly occurring between us on a secret channel. So secret that we don't know what is being said.

"Gili," she says after the moment has been drained of all its juices, "it makes it easier for me to know you're around."

"Thank you."

"Shall we continue?" Nina asks.

But Rafael isn't up for it yet. He asks for a break. Hands me the camera. Walks back and forth down the little alley and clasps his massive head. That was how he paced the hospital corridors, roaring, after I committed suicide. Then he comes back and bombards Nina with all the questions he forgot to ask since she told him. As usual, when he's scared, he has unhelpful outbursts.

Nina is her callous self again, which offers some relief. Her answers to his questions are curt and acerbic. Dementia and amnesia and dying and death appear in them as frequently as punctuation. And she articulates them with a strange glee. She enjoys hurting us and—even more so—herself. I film her with a medium shot and move in for a close-up. I know what twinge lurks in this twisting, turning intestine of the soul.

But Vera, with one last surge of resistance, persists. "I'm not still a hundred percent that you're—that you have what you say. You don't! Look how fine you are! Where would you get this thing? This is something that's hereditary, and I have fantastic memory—"

Nina—I can see that Vera's stubborn skepticism is costing her in health. She holds herself back. "But maybe it's from Dad?"

"How could it be from your father? Milosz knew maybe a hundred poems by heart!"

"But he died young, and we couldn't know."

Then suddenly Vera's hand flies up to her mouth. "*Oy*, his father, Milosz's father . . . Your grandfather . . . When I got back from Goli . . ."

"What happened to him?"

"It happened. Never mind. It's nothing." Vera gives a dry spit, this time to her left side. One day I'll write up a whole dictionary of her spitting.

"Mom, what happened to him?"

"Well, that's just it, he used to get a little lost, but not very far, and only in the village . . ."

"Bingo," says Nina, and her face falls.

"And his wife tied a bell around him . . ."

"Do me a favor."

Vera leans against the wall. Rafael goes into Kavana Royal to pee. Washes his hands, washes his face. Looks in the mirror. The door is slightly ajar, so we can see him in the rectangle of light, leaning on the sink with both hands. His head drops, as if he's been beheaded. He's crying. He is doing what Vera and Nina and I are incapable of doing at this moment, each because of her own private defect.

"Shall we?" Nina asks when he comes back. She suddenly has a new power over us. Not only the knife effect of the disease that separates her from us, but also this thing she's doing here. It's as though she's put on something else, a thin layer of a different existence.

Something ghostly.

If I'm going to make a film about her—

Am I going to make a film about her?

Rafael takes the camera from me. "Nina, I'm ready when you are." Nina has her back to the wall again, shoulders drooping. Now, G, this is work; now the professionalism will talk. I stand before her rearranging her collar. It was twisted to the right before, and the twist should be the same. The little pedantries of a script girl. Nonsense—it's my hand's need to run over her cheek.

She constantly looks me in the eye.

Evening falls. A streetlamp lights up above us. It's a little town in Croatia, where I will certainly never be again. A peculiar sense of being unmoored. Of drifting in no-place. Perhaps this is similar to what awaits Nina not long from now. I have a momentary grasp of the terror she is living in: every wrong sentence, every mistake, every little confusion and forgetfulness, might be used as evidence against her.

Who am I without hating Nina?

"Intro, Nina, take three," Rafi mumbles to himself.

Nina takes a deep breath. Shuts her eyes. The vertical wrinkle on her forehead deepens, then softens. She opens her eyes. "Hello, Nina," she says to the camera, "today we're going to tell you a story. It's a beautiful and moving story, and it's about you, and about the great love that brought you into this world, and also about what—"

But we are doomed not to make this movie, because Vera suddenly pivots in a semicircle, like a puppet in a clock tower, and faces Nina with her back to the camera. "Why are you talking to her like that?" she asks in a whisper, as if the woman in the camera can hear her.

Nina is taken aback by the interruption. "Like what?"

"Like she's a bit dumb."

"She really is dumb," Nina says, so quietly that it's bloodcurdling. "I told you. She'll be totally erased by the time she sees this. Pause for a second," she orders Rafi, who keeps filming, "and do me a favor, Vera, don't direct me. You've directed enough!"

Like a whip the words lash out of her mouth.

"Gili, write it down," Rafi mutters.

"But that's how you talk to little child," Vera insists, "someone who doesn't have children, that's how they talk to little child."

"Maybe I didn't have enough experience with children?" Nina suggests. "Maybe you could give me some private tutoring?"

Vera goes back to her position. They stand beside each other.

It later turned out that I did still have some gray matter somewhere, because I found the following line in my notebook: "Something in the way they both stand with their backs to the wall, like they're facing a firing squad."

"My Nina, hello, hi, sweetheart," Nina says to the camera, and with these words I feel she is in fact responding to Vera's (appropriate) stage direction. "I want to tell you a story today, and it's a story that is connected to you, and it's a good story, don't be afraid, it's a love story. You know, Nina, there was a lot of love around you, and you were made with great love." She breathes deeply. "Here is your mother next to me. Her name is Vera, she's waving hello at you . . ." Vera waves a rigid hand at the camera. "And she will now tell you, together with me, the story of your life, from the beginning." There is relief in Nina's voice, as if she's found the right tone. "And if by any chance you don't remember me, or Vera, that's okay, it happens. Just know that the woman standing next to me is your mother, Vera, who loves you very much. Who always watches over you. And now she will tell you how she met her beloved Milosz, who was your father. Go ahead, Mom."

Vera rubs her cheeks with both hands. She stands up straight. In my body I remember those awakening movements of hers. That old lioness fought for me once, and she won.

"I'm ready, children."

"Take four," Rafi whispers to himself, "action."

"It was at the party for end of high school here in Croatia, in my city of Čakovec, which was once belonged to Hungary and was called Csáktornya . . ."

"Talk to *her*," Nina whispers out of the corner of her mouth, "and smile at her, keep smiling at her, keep thinking how much she needs you."

"I'm trying, Nina, but it's confusing a little, all this."

"I know. But think about her, how confused she is."

"I was a young girl, seventeen and something, and I dance with everyone, I'm the belle in the ball, and this and that, and then along comes this young man who asks me to dance."

"Talk a little slower. So she'll understand. No rush. We have time."

"And he says to me, this man, 'Listen, *gospođica*'—that's like when they say 'miss,'" she explains to the camera, "'there's something I want you to know about me right from the start: I was born in a small village, in a stable, on straw, together with pig and chicken and sheep. My parents are farmers, but with no land, and we are very much poor, and every month I send them half my salary."

From one word to the next, her voice opens up. Nina, beside her, listens with her head bowed. Sometimes she looks up and gives the camera a big grin. I ask myself what that other Nina, the future one, will grasp out of all this information. Out of these two women.

She's not going to get any of it.

"And he sees that I don't get scared at all by his poverty, and he tells me they had the muster, and commander general told him: 'Mr. First Lieutenant, your collar is ripped.' And this young man says to him: 'This is my collar also for going to church and also for dying! I have no other collar! I am the son of a farmer without land!'"

Nina confirms to Vera with a nod and a smile: Yes, go on that way. Talk to her, to her . . .

"And we dance, and I see that dancing he does know, and I also like very much to dance, to this day, and you know, Nina, when they play music at lunchtime on 'Magical Moments'? Radio show? I dance around with transistor in my hand . . ."

She demonstrates for the camera how she dances with the radio, as if she were born in a disco, shimmying with unbelievable ease (she's ninety!), humming "Bella Ciao," the song of her youth that was sung by Italian and Yugoslavian partisans. "And while we dance he speaks almost nothing to me, Milosz. Only holds me nicely, like a gentleman, doesn't take advantage, and only if I ask, then he talks. So he tells me that he finished military academy, and he was outstanding pupil, and they put him in our town, and he doesn't know anyone here, and he's alone . . ." She stops, embarrassed. "Is this okay?" she whispers to Nina and Rafi. "Are you recording me well?"

"It's great, Mom, don't worry about the filming, Rafi and Gili will edit everything later, so it'll be even easier for her to understand." My stomach still turns every time Nina says "her" or "she" about her future self. As if there really are two people whom she cut away from each other, and they each doffed their hat and walked off in opposite directions.

But why should that surprise me? Cutting away is her forte.

—

I forgot to write this before: ever since Rafi called to tell me about her disease, I've been spending every free moment digging up information. I read mostly at night, when I can't fall asleep, and then I can't fall asleep because I've been reading. I read research about how fast the mind gets erased and which regions of the brain decline. Language goes. Memory, of course. The capacity to recognize faces. To orient oneself in space and time, to comprehend situations. To draw conclusions. Perception of self becomes vague.

I look at Nina's head, that pretty little box. Such drama is occurring in there now. A fight to the death.

In all my searches I did not find any studies showing how fast or in what order feelings like remorse, shame, and guilt disappear.

"So talk about what you thought when you saw him, when you saw Dad, for the first time. What impression did he make?"

"I had no impression from him!"

"No impression?" Nina laughs. "Just like that?"

"Your father, Nina, was not a man who made impression. Not a handsome man at all—I mean, yes, handsome, in fact very handsome, like his entire family—all Novak men are handsome, women not so much, but men—yes! Very! And manly! But he was not a specially manly Novak, and not specially handsome, and that was what I also liked in him, that he was both tough and soft, and strong and weak, like lots of men in one man. And he was very thin, like *Windhund*. He was maybe one hundred twenty pounds with five feet eight. So in body and figure, almost nothing was there. Just there was character—so much!"

"More, tell her more."

Vera looks straight at the camera: "I am in general not a person who thinks much of impressions, Nina, but I *felt* him, do you understand? I felt him, and that made the impression on me. I didn't think: Oh, what a handsome man! Oh, what muscles!"

I sit on the sidewalk, writing. Of the four of us, Vera speaks the fastest. (Rafi slurs the most, and his beard muffles things, too.) I keep wondering what the other Nina, the future one, will be able to understand of the things Vera is recounting. We'll have to add subtitles, to make it easier for her. If she can even read.

But maybe that's not what will be important to her, in the film we make.

Not the words, not the facts, but rather something that cannot be put into words.

". . . I right away saw he has open mind and he is a free soul. In his seriousness I saw that he is a man who no one in the world will tell what to think. And how he talked about injustice, and how he talked about his parents! And I thought: This man is a goy, he is Serbian, he is a soldier—how can I be with him? If you look at us based on politesse, nothing connects to anything else. But there he was, a soul that came into the world for me."

A tenderness lights up Nina's face. A childish tenderness I've never seen in her. For an instant, the child she used to be stands opposite the child I used to be, and in my eyes a thought slowly passes: our thin skin.

But then, like a slap on the cheek, I am hit by what she told my father when they last met, five years ago. About her boyfriends. She was living in New York at the time. "Penelope's suitors," she called them, and also, with peculiar affection, "my lechers." "And it happened just when she started feeling something for me again,"

Rafael told me that morning, five years ago, after Nina had flown back to New York. He was sitting in my kitchen, in our house on the moshav, needing to talk with me even though we both knew it was a mistake that would pollute us. He held his head in his hands as if what he had found out was too heavy to bear. "She and I were so close at that moment, before she told me about them," he said, and held two fingers up with a tiny gap between them, "and then, like a punch."

"Like punches," I corrected him, as affable as only a toxic and loving daughter can be. "To be precise, Daddy, one-two-three-four punches."

He hadn't even heard what I said. "You know, Gili, when we were together, Nina and I, in those years in Jerusalem, I never called her 'my love,' always 'my beloved.' I had a few other loves after her, but she was my only beloved."

"So like that, one dance and one more," Vera continues, "and suddenly it's a little frightening to me. Frightening but I want more, more, more. And I keep looking at him and thinking: Who is this person? Who is this that came from nothing and takes my heart in one moment?"

Nina, on her tiptoes, moves out of the frame.

"Milosz's father," she goes on, "when Milosz was at high school in town, even before he was in the army, twice a week his father walked almost ten miles each side, so that Milosz will eat bread from their home, and corn from their field, and a piece of cheese his mother made. You understand, Ninaleh?" she asks the camera.

Ninaleh. I've never heard her call Nina that. I see that Nina also freezes.

"I looked at him while he talked, and I thought: How much

courage. He was twenty-two and looked so young! I asked what his mother's name was, and he said: Nina. I said: Such a pretty name. If I have a daughter one day, I will name her Nina."

Nina shudders, hunched over with her back arched, holding her hands between her knees.

"And he asked me: What are you doing tomorrow, *gospođica*? I said: Tomorrow is Sunday, I take the train to my friend and come back home by the train.

"He asked: When will you be home?

"In evening.

"And that's it, goodbye, thank you, *gospođica*. He bowed over like knight, walked backward out of the party place, here, he left from this door. And I already knew."

With those words she falls silent, dives into herself.

"That's that. Yes. That is how it was. What were we saying?"

"That you knew," Nina whispered.

"Yes." She sighs. "Milosz. Correct. I went home from the party and I said to Mother: 'Mama, today I met a young man who came to this world for me and I came for him.' And Mother said: 'What is so special in him?' I said: 'Mama, he is so proud of his poverty! People want to hide their poverty and lie about it, and he gets every month one *kvadrat* of wood for heat, and he sells half so he can send money to his parents, and he's so cold, Mama.'

"The next evening I come back on the train from my friend Jagoda, and my mother is suddenly there at the station. 'Mama, what are you doing here?' And Mother: 'I knew he would come here!' So I look around, and there on the side stands, next to a bicycle, sort of looking out, this Milosz . . ."

Nina smiles. Seeing her smile, and the way her parched face drinks in the story, I suspect this must be the first time she's heard it.

Dozens of times—I'm not exaggerating—Vera has told me this

story about the first time she met Milosz. And who knows how many more times she told it at all sorts of events with Tuvia's family. Plus at least ten times for each of Tuvia's grandchildren and great-grandchildren when they reached their bar and bat mitzvahs and did their family-tree projects. How can you deprive your own daughter of such a story? I seriously almost yell at Vera: If I had a story like that, I'd have kids just so I could tell it to them!

Nina looks stricken, bereaved. "A thousand times you told me about Goli, about the beatings and the torture, about the bedbugs and the swamps and the rocks. And I never heard how you and Dad met."

"It is possible." Vera's mouth twists into a scythe. "You were little, there was Goli. There was war."

"Well then," Nina whispers with a crestfallen face, "tell me now. Tell her. Me too, actually."

"That's it, that's how I met Milosz, here in this house. And from then until he died—"

"Wait," Nina calls out, "not so fast, there's still time before he dies."

"Since then until he died," Vera insists, "we almost were never apart. I waited nearly five years for him until army gave permission for him to get married. In '36 we met, in '41 we married, and in '51 he died. Altogether fifteen years we had."

Nina flutters her fingers at Rafi, draws the camera and cameraman to her, laughing desperately. "Did you notice how I'm not included in the important family dates?"

"Oh really, Nina," Vera grumbles, "will you always look for just my mistakes? I'm telling you now there are many, you don't have to try so hard."

Rafi and I exchange looks. We both think Vera is wrong: there are not many mistakes, not at all, but there is one that suffices for a whole lifetime. And what choice did I have? Vera retorts in a sharp look at me and Rafi.

Nina's eyes—the three of us notice now—dart back and forth between us. She's like a fearful animal sensing that its masters are sealing its fate.

"Break," Rafi declares and puts the camera back in its case. He takes out an apple and slices it with a pocketknife. The refreshing taste fills our mouths. We all feel easier the minute the camera shuts its eye. We'll be on our way soon, and tomorrow we sail.

"But did I speak well to the cinematographer?" asks Vera, glancing in her little round mirror and smoothing down a curl on her forehead with saliva.

"You spoke perfectly," I say, "you're a natural-born storyteller."

"Yes, well." She sighs. "Just brush the mothballs off Grandma."

At 8:00 p.m., with a thunderstorm raging, we set off. We drove south to Crikvenica, a town on the Adriatic coast where we planned to spend the night before sailing to the island in the morning. Vera and Nina were huddled in the back seat, very close together but each in her own world. I was filling in gaps in my notebook. I deciphered the notes I'd scribbled throughout the day, and wrote down some ideas. Then I checked my messages and texted Meir that it had been an exhausting day and the journey was, in every respect, a lot more than I'd bargained for. "It's ripping me to shreds," I wrote, but deleted that before hitting SEND. I mustn't overburden him, he's allergic to hyperbole. I waited a few moments. He's capable of going a whole day without checking messages. But this time the reply came quickly: "Take care of yourself."

There's no doubt: the man misses me like crazy.

The fog closed in on us. The rain grew more violent, and sudden gales rocked the lime. The heating started to waver. We huddled in coats and gloves, and in various and sundry wool hats that each of us had brought (and which, we discovered, had all been knitted by Vera), until we looked like the village fools' annual field trip. Rafi drove slowly, his head practically butting the windshield. Again and again he asked me to wipe his steamed-up glasses. Twice we drove into a pit the size of a mass grave and were convinced that it was over, the car had given up, but three cheers for the feisty lime, which forged ahead through any obstruction.

"Almost from first days that we met," I suddenly hear Vera murmur to herself in the back seat, and I dive into Rafi's equipment bag, which sits between my feet, and fish out the Sony. I switch it on as I unbuckle my seat belt so I can turn around, dismantle my headrest so it isn't in the way, and from the corner of my eye I can see that Rafi is pleased with me. I've already got Vera in a wide-angle, and Nina beside her rolls her eyes, confused. "I wasn't asleep!" she blurts, as if anyone had claimed otherwise.

So that's how she looks when she wakes up.

Terror-darkness on her face. How ugly fear makes us. A terrified little girl, bracing for the blow, for the catastrophe.

And then quickly—erasure.

I saw it.

No expression.

A six-year-old sphinx.

"From our first days," Vera says to the camera, "Milosz would walk every day at exactly one past our house, where you saw, with his officer's sword *thwack-thwack* on the sidewalk, and I was quickly at the window. And he looks at me and I look at him, without words.

"In evenings, Father was with friends at that café, where we went, playing *preferans,* and Mother was alone, and me and Milosz were walking, talking. After about a week I say to Milosz, 'I cannot leave my mother alone. From tomorrow she comes with us!' And Milosz says, 'I even more love you because you think about your mother!'"

Rafi wants to know if you can see anything on the camera screen in this darkness. He suggests we turn on the dome light above Vera and Nina. I also improvise a little reflector out of the tinfoil that wrapped some cookies Vera brought. Not optimal lighting, but I quite like the reddish, grainy picture.

"Just remember—" Nina warns.

"Nina!" Vera scolds. "I am not forgetting her even for minute."

"Thank you, Mom."

"And for three years, we three walk like that. We walk from factory of wool and knitting that belongs to Granner brothers, and sit on benches outside talking, and walk to railway station and back, and always talking. And don't forget, Ninotchka, you must not forget"—Vera wags her finger at the camera—"that my mother was from Hungary and did not speak one word in Serbian, and Milosz was Serbian and spoke only Serbian. So I walk between those two, translating. 'What did she say?' 'What did he say?' Turning this way, turning that way."

Nina smiles delightedly. "Three years?" she asks.

"Hard to believe, yes?"

They laugh. On the little Sony screen you can see two blurred characters, round and puffy in their coats, and so close to each other that it's hard to tell where one ends and the other begins. Their faces are a patchwork of pale red splotches and dark shadows. And again—I actually like the way it's sometimes difficult to know which of them is talking and which is listening. The story flows between them as if it's being redistributed.

"Mother kept from Father that I have a non-Jewish fellow, and no one in town either had the courage to tell Father that his Vera has a non-Jewish fellow, or that she has a fellow at all, and Mother and us all the time said what would happen if he knew, what would he do and what would we do, and if we would run away or stay, and if we would take Mother with us. You understand me, Nina, everything I say, yes?"

She's completely on it, Vera, as if that other Nina really is watching her right now from within the depths of the camera. The current Nina gives her a sideways look, amused but also a little embarrassed, and then she leans on Vera, very touchingly, as if to attract her attention.

"But on Milosz's family side it was actually fine. He came to his father and said: 'I am in love with a Jewish girl, and if you won't let me marry her, I will leave and you will never see me again.' And his father said, 'If you go with a black gypsy or with a little Jew, it is *you* will live with her, not me.'

"In February of the year forty, some Jewish woman told my father, 'Listen, Bauer, do you even see how your daughter looks? She'll come down with tuberculosis. They're so thin, she and her boyfriend, that Serbian officer, walking around town like two trench coats with no humans inside!' And that, Nina honey, was how the first time my father heard about my boyfriend Milosz, and he almost fainted!" She slams her knee. "Ran home and asked Mother if it's true. She told him: Ask your daughter. And he shouts at me to come immediately in his room. I run and see his face and I understand."

Rafi is driving slower than thirty now. We have the road to ourselves, and the rain, left with no other audience, puts on the show of its life for us. I wonder if the camera mic is picking up Vera's voice over the screeching windshield wipers and the din of the storm. Rafi has the same thought at the same time, and he slows down the wipers, but that turns out to be perilous, and we agree that we'll have to compromise on the sound, too.

"So my father stands next to the big stove, and his foot jumps like it's on electricity, and he asks me: 'Is it true you have a fellow?' 'Yes.' 'And is it true your fellow is an army officer?' And I say: 'Yes!' And he says: 'Only once I ask, Vera, so think carefully, because this is your last chance: Is it true your fellow is a Serbian officer, a goy?' And I hold my head up most high: 'Yes! Yes! Yes!'

"He turns white: 'First you'll have to kill me.' I say: 'Father, let me marry him.' He says: 'Before you bring that shame on me, I will jump out the window.' So I said: 'Here, I'll open the window for you.'

"Next morning, Father goes to see the rabbi. He was a Neolith rabbi, very liberal, and he says: 'Mr. Bauer, we are for three years seeing your daughter and her fellow, and how they walk respectably with Mrs. Bauer. We know him now in town, and he is excellent young man. Hitler is already in Austria, and who knows—perhaps thanks to this fellow it will only be your daughter left alive of all of us. We did not dare tell you, we were afraid you would kill the poor girl. Ask him to come see you, get to know him, see who he is.'

"My father thought he was going crazy, but he said, 'Bring the fellow to me.'

"And I never in my life forget that picture, Ninaleh: in our living room, next to the big stove, my father stands straight up like a soldier. And in comes Milosz, gets down on one knee, takes my father's hand, and kisses.

"Father shouts: '*Mein Gott!* Before old Jew an officer on his knee? Vera, tell him to get up now!'

"And ever since then my father loved him more than all his sons-in-law. '*Oy*, my lovely goy son-in-law,' he would say, 'there is no other in the world like Vera's husband!'"

She leans back, tired out. Gives a nod to the person who seems to be watching her from inside the camera, tying a thin thread between them that I do not completely understand.

"Want to hear some more, Ninotchka?" she softly asks the camera.

"Yes, tell us more," says Nina beside her, and she also sounds weak and faded.

A picture of Nina in two or three or five years flashes in my mind. Sitting in a wheelchair in an empty room in an institution. On the wall opposite her, between two hanging pots with plastic plants, there is a television showing this voyage of ours. Her head droops on her chest.

"One year after we met, because of a law that officers cannot marry until age twenty-six, Milosz went and bought a gold ring." Vera pulls the ring off her finger. They are thin and gnarled, her fingers, and shiny as if made of wax. She holds the ring up to the camera, and I focus on it. Her mouth looks like a hoop in the background.

"You see, Ninaleh?" she says tenderly to the camera, "this is the ring that your father gave your mother."

Rafi drums urgently on my thigh. Nina. He senses that I've abandoned her. He knows where the drama is really occurring: Nina's eyes are two throbbing embers. Look how Vera completely forgets us, her eyes say.

"And Milosz said to me: 'You are now my wife before God and before me.' And I said: 'There is nothing that will come between us. Such a thing has not been created.' And I did not show anyone the ring he gave me, not to Mother or to my sisters or my friends. I covered it with a bigger ring, and we kept living like before . . . And we had our life, yes . . ."

Vera puts one hand over her chest and shuts her eyes. At first I think it's another one of her gestures. She leans back with her mouth open, mumbling that she's hot, her heart is pounding. I keep filming. I'm a little alarmed, but I won't abandon the shot. Nina massages Vera's shoulders with one hand, and gives her some water. Vera chokes. Dry heaves. Scary. Rafi gives panicked glances over his shoulder, but drums on me with his hand to keep filming. (He once summed everything up for me in a golden rule: Photographers don't stand during the national anthem.) Vera motions for us to open a window. The storm pounces on us through the crack. A freezing-cold wind bursts inside with a strange, almost human whimper. It makes me want to jump into my mommy's lap. Nina, who technically is my mother, looks as if she's wishing the same thing. The car veers all over the road, drifting this way and that, and Rafi shakes his head, and amid all the chaos and fear (perhaps it's the storm that addles my brain) a thought jumps into my mind about how there are a few staples—a certain type of humor, for example, and a fairly high tolerance for loneliness, and generally speaking a cactuslike personality when it comes to relationships with human beings—regarding which it is Nina, more than anyone, who can understand me.

"You know, Mom," Nina says later, after we shut the window and Vera has recovered, "you never, really never, told me any of this."

She's already pointed this out. It's still eating at her.

"I didn't tell you? I actually did tell lots of it."

"No. You only told me about Goli, over and over again."

"That's not possible," says Vera, "maybe you forgot."

That was a cheap blow, even if an unintentional one.

"Do you think I would forget something like that?"

Vera doesn't answer. She crosses her arms over her chest. Her eyes roam far away, her lips pout innocently. She's a fox, the lioness.

"Honestly, Mom," Nina whispers, "do you know how helpful

that could have been for me? To give me some solid ground beneath my feet?"

"Come on, Vera, tell us some more," Rafael intervenes, hoping to douse the fire before it gets out of hand. "Do you have the strength?"

Vera: "Do *you* have strength?"

"It keeps me awake," Rafi says with a laugh, and pounds on the steering wheel.

"But Nina must say. What do you say, Nina? Should I tell more? Don't you want to sleep a little?"

"I've slept enough."

"You should also know, Ninotchka," Vera says, turning sharply to my camera, "that your father, Milosz, was not a very healthy man. He had serious illnesses, because he was a child of mountains and hills and countryside, and clean air and skies, and then suddenly he is in the city, the army, the smoke, the spoiled food, all the poisons. So he got tuberculosis." She sighs. "He coughed at night; like a dog, he coughed. He would put hot compress with onion and honey on his chest. Doctors told him he was the national champion in Koch's test, because, listen carefully, Ninaleh, he was the sickest person with tuberculosis in all Yugoslavia! Two *cavernas* in his lung! And six months after I met him and after we danced at the party, he got sick also with jaundice. Well, they put him in military hospital in Zagreb, and from then Milosz was never again well. And that had many consequences. Should I tell?" she asks us out of the corner of her mouth, and Nina snaps again, "Tell us everything, every detail, I have almost nothing, do you really not understand?" "Okay, okay, you don't have to shout. I'm telling. I'm telling everything." Vera looks down, for a long time. Forehead creased, face severe, lips moving soundlessly.

"*Oy*, Ninotchka," she says softly, and it seems to me that she's pulling herself up by the hairs on her head to look at the camera, "nothing worked with him properly anymore. Tummy aches and diarrhea all the time, and blood all the time, and fever, and weak and special diet and he ate like a bird. 'But I'm fine, Miko,' that's how he said. 'Miko,' he called me, which means for us like 'my little friend.' He generally spoke to me like I was a boy, a fellow. We liked to talk that way and I got used to it. He said: 'If you and me are fine, Miko, then the whole world is fine. We are two of us, in our togetherness, holding the whole world!' "

"Miko?" Nina laughs. "That's true, he did call you that . . . I remember . . ." She moves in closer to Vera again, slowly, sneakily, lowering her head onto Vera's shoulder.

Meanwhile, Rafi and I develop a language: his hand is on my knee, and he signals which way to aim the camera by pressing his pinkie or middle finger or thumb. To be honest, it's irritating. This is my film, as we know, but he's incapable of giving up control. On the other hand, in the nutty situation evolving here, it's good to have another pair of eyes.

Either way, very soon I will have to remind him of our agreement and which way is up.

"My mother, she did not care at all that he's not Jewish, it meant nothing to her! I told you. We were modern, atheist Jews, specially Mother. But she could absolutely not understand how a young healthy girl like me thought to live with such a sick man. And I said to Mother: Sick? So he's sick! When I met him half a year ago, he wasn't sick, and when I danced with him, he wasn't sick, and when I saw him at train station with bicycle, he wasn't sick, so now I should leave him because he's sick? In the contrary: the more he got weak, I was even more closer to him!

"And my sister from Zagreb, your aunt Rozi, she didn't talk to me for ten years. She called Milosz 'rotten Serb'"—Vera spits out the *S*—"and her husband asked Milosz to Zagreb, to talk to him." Vera leans forward, talking secretively to Nina deep in the camera. "Listen to this: that brother-in-law of mine, like he was all friendly, told Milosz, 'I will pay you a big amount of money if you ask army to send you to another town far away, and forget that there is any Vera in the world.' And Milosz told him: 'I am very poor, but I am not a cow for sale!'

"And they made him miserable!" she exclaims, presenting the facts for future-Nina's judgment. It drives me crazy how, within minutes, she completely internalized the strange plan hatched by Nina, about how we should talk to future-Nina, and translated it into simple, purposeful practicalities, just as she did five years ago, at eighty-five, when she decided she had to learn how to use a computer. "I will not be left behind!" she'd frothed at the kibbutz committee, stomping her feet, and twisted their arms into paying two fourteen-year-old computer geeks. Twice a week they sat with her, and of course they fell head over heels in love, and within a day or two she was sending them chat messages and emails roughly twice an hour, pounding the keyboard with her iron claws, surfing online forums, forwarding links to *New Yorker* cartoons, sharing her recipes for jam and *povidla* cake ("Milosz used to lick his fingers!"). A few weeks later she had an empire of contacts, corresponding with old friends in Belgrade and Zagreb, as well as new soulmates who popped up every day in Prague or Montevideo. They were all quickly brought into the family, knew exactly who Aunt Chana was, where Esther's granddaughters were doing their pre–military service, and the status of Shleimaleh's prostate. She achieved this with speed and technical acumen, and with a wonderful capacity to understand the inner world of objects and instruments, as if she were one of them. Exactly the same way that she grasps—without even glancing at instruction manuals—how to operate vacuum cleaners, microwaves, cell phones, and any other device Rafi buys her without a second thought because it's his way of keeping her young. While I, on the other hand, can spend hours just figuring out how to unbox similar machines. (My beloved has two left hands when it comes to anything requiring manual dexterity.)

(Correction: almost anything.)

"Eighty to go," Rafi reads out from a road sign, and we wonder if it's miles or kilometers. We conduct a quick debate about whether to keep driving or have a bathroom break, because the cold is destroying us. Only Vera, who has a bladder like the late president Hafez Assad's, is prepared to keep going straight to the hotel. But she's in the minority, and Rafi glides the car into a giant, brightly lit roadside rest area, which at this hour contains only a few employees manning food and drink stalls—pizza, pasta, burgers, coffee—and there's heavy metal shocking our ears, and it's very hard for the four of us to readapt to the external world and its screeching cogwheels.

We wander around in a daze, through long aisles of shelves packed with bright stuffed animals and electrical appliances and old-fashioned chocolate boxes. We keep turning to one another as if wishing to hold on to something we held before, which has quickly faded in the light. Nina and I find ourselves face-to-face in the maze, and we cannot avoid each other. Sounding oddly calm, she says, "Remind me what we were just dreaming?"

She says it with exactly the right measure of dryness for me to respond to, and I notice something nice on her face: her eyebrows seem to shrug their shoulders. Without thinking, I reach out and touch her thin collarbone, and it works. Unbelievable. She knows what to do with it. She listens to my trembling finger, nodding.

This goes on for a long time, and a lot of information is relayed. There is a moment when it seems she would like to reverse the direction, to touch me with her finger, but she is smart enough to understand that it won't fly. Then we turn away from each other and go back to roving the evergreen forest of capitalism, and my heart pounds.

Out there in the distance, my father perches on a stool, sipping a double espresso. Drawn to him like a baby tilapia to its father's mouth, I sit down next to him and find that he's already ordered me a latte with extra foam and a cinnamon-raisin Danish, heated for fifteen seconds.

In the enormous mirror on the wall above our heads, we can see Vera and Nina pass each other down parallel aisles.

"Do we have a film?" Rafi asks.

"Maybe. It looks that way."

"Don't get mad when I give you bits of advice. This movie is completely yours."

"Of course. But I'm glad you said that."

"Oh," he says after a brief pause, "I didn't think it was that bad."

"Just pay attention," I say.

"After they heard in army that Milosz and me are engaged," Vera continues the minute Rafi starts the engine, "Milosz was transferred one thousand kilometers, the most distance, to Skopje, in Macedonia, and that was punishment for him marrying a Jew, because in the government there were already pro-Germans, and there were laws against Jews, and in schools there was quota. And then my father said: 'Exactly because they sent Milosz to the end of the world, you should marry him.' So Mother and I—off we march! Quickly we went to Macedonia to meet Milosz and marry him.

"But on the way we said we'd stop at Milosz's village so that Mother should meet his parents and all his family. And it was a very tiny village in Serbia. First we went by train, and Milosz's father waited for us at the station with horse and carriage. Mother got on and sat up high, and she wore a suit that her tailor in Vienna made, with hat and veil, and blue parasol and high-heel shoes. After about thirty kilometers we came to a stream, and my father-in-law said: Come, *snaja*—come, daughter-in-law. I will pull the rope on one side and you on other side. And Mother sits up there and whispers to me: Where are you taking me, Vera? To hell?

"So like that we pull for six kilometers. There is no path, no electricity, no pipes, only mountains and rocks and the little stream, and that is why Germans did not reach there either.

"We arrive, and the whole village comes out to see the wonder: ladies from the city! They bring me gifts as Milosz's fiancée—three nuts, one egg, two sugar cubes, one chick . . . They wanted to give my mother one chick, and she shook with fear, she thought it was disgusting.

"From there we went to Macedonia, me and Mother, and there Milosz was waiting, and hugs and kisses, and he had already arranged with a priest, and we only needed someone to walk the groom. The priest gave us horse and carriage so we could find drunk officer to do it, and we took them, and there on the side of road is a man named Simo Mirković, and he was drunkest officer Milosz knew there, so we put him up on carriage and took him and that was how we got married.

"But most important thing I forgot: when we met Milosz, we saw he had a new problem, they'd given him an operation for his ulcer—oh, silly me, I forgot to show!" She dives into her white handbag and fishes out a dirty old plastic bag with a few photographs, including one of Milosz after the surgery. I zoom in on it. I thought I'd seen all the pictures of Milosz, and I wonder why Vera has hidden this one up to now.

Milosz. Chest bared, large square bandage on his stomach. He looks thin and brittle, but definitely not weak. Vera says this is her favorite picture of him.

That half-naked Serbian officer with his ribs sticking out—the pair of enormous eyes and the almost embarrassingly penetrating look—is my grandfather.

That skinny man with the high forehead and the authoritative nose, Milosz Novak, Nina's father, a commander on the Yugoslavian riding team, an officer of General Tito's cavalry, and a partisan in World War II—a war hero. My grandfather.

He is very fair and very thin. The thinness gives his face a spiritual aura. His cheeks are sunken, which makes his ears look comically large. But the main thing, without a doubt, is the eyes. There is something ageless in them. Like the wide-open eyes of a blind man, or of a profoundly complex and piercing soul. The more I look at them, the more I feel we could have been good friends. He's my people.

He's about thirty years old here, nine years younger than I am today. He reminds me a little of my father when he was a boy. I can even speculate that something in Rafael as a boy looked familiar—and beloved—to Nina when she met him in the avocado orchard. Maybe that was why she headbutted him as hard as she could.

And me—do I look like him?

If in some alternate reality our looks happened to meet on the street, would we guess that the same blood flowed in our veins? That I was his only grandchild? Would we slow our footsteps for a moment?

The thought saddens me. (I have an issue with the sorrow of randomness. But that's for another time.)

"He loved you so much," Vera says to Nina. "Did you know he wouldn't let me bathe you? Said I wasn't gentle enough with you. And he did everything—bathed, dried, changed diapers."

Nina asks to hold the photograph. She looks at him and then at me for a long time. I don't kick her away from my face. *In the contrary:* I want her to see me, to see who ran through her. To see whom she lost out on.

"It amazes me all over again every time," Nina whispers. The photo is passed around to everyone once more, including the driver, and judging by the silence I understand they are all seeing something I cannot see.

"That is why I love so much to look at Gili's face," Vera comments.

Nina says, "The eyes."

"Eyes like that only one person in the world had," Vera says. "Milosz is dead, and now they are Gili's."

"Hey," I say, "enough with the organ trade!"

Vera turns to the camera. "Now we tell happy things: it was once a Sunday, I think you had your birthday, Nina—five? Six? And after the horse-riding-school parade, all the riders on horses came down our street with swords, and they all sang together 'Nina! Nina!' and you did like this with your hands for them . . ."

Vera pulls out another photograph: she is standing in front of the tiny house that Milosz and his family built in their village for the new couple. The house looks like a children's drawing, with two square windows, a door, and a tiled roof with a chimney. Vera is about twenty-two here, wearing a thin wool sweater with a white collar showing beneath, very respectable looking, but her gaze is defiant, provocative, life-thirsty. She is beautiful. Arched brows, thinly penciled, full and glossy lower lip. The single curl falling perfectly on her forehead.

"Already when I was eighteen, Milosz used to send me the most loveliest letters, you couldn't believe it, Nina, that such a young person wrote them. But I also saw in him something that scared me. Sort of sadness in his soul." Vera leans in. "Because he felt despair, yes, and he did not at all believe in people. And that is a strange thing, because he was a Communist and an idealist, and most of all a humanist, but only I knew the truth, that already at young age he stopped believing in kindness of human beings."

Nina, upset by what she hears, gives herself a lonely hug.

"He always would say, 'To do even some little good in the world, Vera, you have to really make an effort. But evil, you just have to keep it going, just join in with it.'

"And he also would say: 'You brought me light, Vera, you gave me happiness, you gave me a path. Alone I had no path and I had nothing.' Because you see, Ninotchka, I always had lots of friends, and always there was noise around me, that is how I am in my personality, it can't be helped, there are some who like it and some who don't. But Milosz, he did not have one single friend. Never. Even when he was a child. Even in the village. He did not believe very much in human beings. He believed only in me."

Those words raise Nina's eyes to Rafi's in the mirror. The two of them conduct a constant conversation. Things Vera says arouse echoes in which I have no part.

For the thousandth time I realize that I probably don't have the courage to comprehend how powerful and deep—despite everything—their togetherness was.

"We were set for two," Rafi once explained to me.

—

"I opened eyes for your father. He was not at all revolutionary man. He was not! Sometimes, because of what he did in the war, in the forests, people think he was big revolutionary, big hero, brave partisan, ideologue. But no, no, that was all from me. I taught him from the beginning that whole language."

"See, this is what drives me crazy," Nina suddenly intervenes. You can feel her claws coming out. "Because if anyone else talked about themselves like that, people would say they were an arrogant egomaniac. But somehow, when it's you . . . I really don't understand how, but it works . . . it's part of . . . do you see what I'm saying?"

"No." Vera licks her upper lip. "Please explain to me."

"With you, people accept it. Everyone does. Everywhere. In the family, on the kibbutz, your friends in Yugoslavia. And more than accepting it—they admire it. How is that possible? No, seriously, Mom, explain it to me, teach me . . ."

Vera shrugs her shoulders. It is a cruel and terrible movement.

I was fifteen or sixteen, we were in her kitchen, cooking and talking, and as usual she was talking about Nina, her open wound, when she blurted out something: Nina has no charisma. That's what she said. I don't think I even knew exactly what that word meant, but of course I enthusiastically agreed with her: she has no charisma, she was always spoiled, and weak, and a princess, and with Vera and me, the "inheritance" had skipped a generation.

How could I have been seduced like that? What an idiot I was, to let her program me with her version.

"You should understand, Nina, honey," Vera continues, ignoring Nina's outburst, circumventing the trap without blinking an eye and aiming at the more submissive Nina, the one in the camera, "you should understand that Novak men have no revolution in their blood at all. They are quiet. No initiative. And I was always revolutionary. I was a fighter, from very small age and all my life."

"A fighter for what?" Nina agitates, but she's out of focus.

"For what, Nina? Don't you know yet?"

"I want to hear. I want it on record."

"I wanted more justice for humanity!"

The determined line between Vera's eyes. The exclamation point that juts her jaw out, straightens her nose. My cute, funny grandmother, my generous, warm, endlessly devoted, fanatical, tough, cruel grandmother. Grandma and the wolf under the same skin. How can it be tolerated? How can one tolerate what she did to Nina?

And how to keep being me and yet still love her?

"In that case," says Nina, "explain to me how a revolutionary like you fell in love with a man who was actually, from the way you describe him, an obedient soldier?"

"First of all," says Vera, "there was his head, and we had a very lot to talk about. For half a year after our wedding we only talked. Did not touch."

My father hits the brakes, the tires screech, and we all lurch forward.

Nina splutters: "You didn't touch?"

"What you heard." Vera crosses her arms over her chest and looks far ahead.

Nina asks her to explain.

"We had agreement from the beginning, that half a year after the wedding we will not touch. It was a platonic thing, Nina, that you cannot imagine . . . Like a magnet we were, and sleeping in the same bed and burning on fire—and no!"

"But why?" Nina practically yells.

"That is how Milosz said, right at the start. Half a year. Like a sacrifice. Where you give up something most precious of yours. That's what he created, and I liked his head and I went with it, and we were proud of it."

Nina blinks in the background. "So what did you talk about, you and my father, when you weren't touching?"

"Ah! Lots we talked about what was happening in world. There was already Hitler, and Mussolini, there were things to think about. Ideas, plans, discussions, new roads to search, and there was Zionism. There was where you feel at home and where you feel a stranger."

She keeps talking, but I, and perhaps Rafi and Nina, too, are not with her now. This notion of the young couple holding back, so determined, seems to shine an unflattering light on them.

"For example, in '42 we got from Moscow that the slogan now is 'For Homeland and for Stalin!' And I said, Milosz, I'm done with all that. Where do I have a homeland? Where there is proletariat— that is where my homeland is! I am an internationalist! Milosz got scared: 'Oh, Miko, you're Trotskyite! You're Nihilist! Don't say such things!' He was miserable over me being like that, it might God forbid tear us apart. And to me it was clear that with Stalin there was a lie. That Stalin did not settle my problems as a Jew, because I wanted socialism like there was later with Dubček. Humane socialism."

She stops and sighs. Perhaps she picks up the cool breeze and distance coming from us. "You cannot understand all this, can you? This is for you like the world of dinosaurs . . ."

"Why do you think so? It wasn't that long ago," my father mumbles, and Nina and I produce a noncommittal hum.

"No, no, you cannot understand my world. And my wars, and the air I breathed." She wrinkles her face and shrinks back. Her loneliness flutters, exposed, the loneliness of a ninety-year-old woman whose world is gone and whose friends have all died. "You won't understand anything," she murmurs, "you say 'war,' but war in the Balkan is not like with us in Israel. In the Balkan, war has different logic. War in the Balkan is first of all rape. Here they rape. Not because a man wants a woman. They rape with a gun at her head so that she will carry his seed, and then her husband doesn't want her. That is the logic of war. And here the Chetnik Serbs slaughtered children of Communists with knives and then licked the blood off the knife. And Ustaše Croatians who were servants of Nazis—I don't even want to say what they did. The Balkans enjoyed it. Something was left from what the Turks did to them. Something abnormal was left here. And you saw also their cruelty in the war that happened here recently, there was no other such thing in the world, maybe only in the Mid-ages there were such things."

Silence. Vera allows her words to seep in. Something evasive has slipped by.

"But you want to hear other things . . . Love stories . . . Hollywood . . ." She sighs.

"Tell us whatever you want to," my father says softly.

She shuts her eyes. "I want to tell you about Milosz and me."

"We want to hear," my father reassures her.

"For instance, we also had a lot of interest about books. Oh, Ninotchka, your father used to read! I never met another man who read like that." Her face slowly goes back to itself, shining at Nina in the camera lens. The way she turns her back—physically—on Nina sitting next to her starts to bother me.

"And you were little, sweet, and your father read to me every evening out loud, and once, you were maybe four, I sat in his bed knitting, and you played next to the bed with dolls, and we thought: She is a little girl, she doesn't understand. He read me a book about Momyshuly, who was the hero of Kazakhs in World War Second. So, after a few weeks later you had a high fever, and you started hallucinating and you shouted: 'I am Momyshuly! Give me shooting machine to kill all the Germans!'"

Laughter in the car. And laughter is an opportunity to breathe. Nina wipes her eyes. I hope it's just from laughter: "You see, Gili, they even nationalized my nightmares."

"Do you know when childhood ends?" my father once asked me after one of my rants about Nina. "Do you know when people really start to mature? When they can accept that their parents have a right to their own psychology."

"Your father and I, Nina, we had kind of a game, to see how together we think of all sorts of ideas. Thoughts. Him a sentence, me a sentence. To see how the logic of us together works. Everything we thought together. Everything we aimed together to the same point. One head, one soul. And don't think, Nina, even after half a year of not touching, it wasn't with us just sex and bed," she explains gravely to the camera, "it was a pact between our minds. In our brain, here, we had internal agreement and we had no need to talk much.

"Before we married, Milosz said to me: 'Listen, we are very young. No one has insurance that for our whole life we will be in love to one person. But I promise you that if something in my head will attract me to another person, I will very soon tell you, and you will also tell me, and we will separate like human beings. Chin up.

And everything we do, foolishness, mistakes, we come and tell the other. That way you never betray me and I never betray you. There is no such thing between us as betrayal."

Rafi drums madly on my knee. Good God—he's saying on our internal Morse code—she really did never betray him.

You could die from how much she didn't betray him.

"Yes, he was something special, Ninotchka." Her stark look into the depths of my lens embarrasses me, as if someone had touched me inside. In the close air of the car she is giving away something precious and profound, but she gives it to future-Nina, and has probably never given it to this Nina, who leans on her now without holding back, and I can finally see in real time what it looks like—that stripped need, that howl.

"Your father, Ninaleh, *mila moja,* my sweet, he was not handsome man or healthy man, I told you, but he was so much man, so human . . . Our minds talked together even when we slept. Lots of times I knew what he will say in a moment. I know what you want, Milosz—" Her voice suddenly changes. She shuts her eyes, and her hands come together as in prayer. "To this day I know to think together with you, and so deep I am with you that even after fifty-seven years I am all the time with tears shut up inside because you're gone." She is barely audible. "I lost something. Such happiness does not exist in the world. Few women, I think, have been blessed with such happiness with a man. A man who talks and thinks and loves and is weak and strong."

Nina draws away from her. Her entire being says: What chance did I have against that?

"But then there was already war and there was Hitler, and I suddenly don't know where is Milosz, and where are my poor parents, and only later I knew they took them to Auschwitz." Vera hesitates, then whispers out of the corner of her mouth to Nina next to her: "Can I tell her about Auschwitz?"

"Tell . . . that Nina?"

"Yes. What does she know, what doesn't she . . ."

"Try. I have no idea."

"Just imagine," Rafi murmurs to me, "forgetting Auschwitz. What a gift."

"Anyway, I'm in village at Milosz's family, and it's terribly cold, and there's no food. There is only two kilos of goose fat left, and maybe twenty kilos of corn, for everyone. And they start with lists of who was killed and who was taken hostage by the Germans. They hang them on school noticeboard, and Milosz is not on lists, and so I say to his father: 'Svekar—that is what I called him, father-in-law—I am going to look for him.' And he says: 'You are crazy, snaja, how will you go? Where will you go? There is a war!' But one more day, and one more, and he sees that I insist, and he says: 'I promised my son to take care of you and I will go with you.'

"So, with pistol that Milosz gave me once, wearing clothes of Serbian farmer woman, with pointy opanci shoes, and my father-in-law walks with me in his village clothes, thick embroidered socks, trousers puffed up in back, and big belt. Very handsome, he was. A handsome Novak. We walk on foot, and it's a hundred kilometers, because you always have to go around. We walk through mountains, we pass sheep huts. When night comes, my father-in-law says: Lie down here! And he stands in the doorway, stands straight, protecting me with gun in his hand. Every hour at night that I open my eye—I see him standing there."

I rotate the camera to capture Rafi. His large, bearded, wrinkled face. I wonder if he's thinking about his journeys in search of Nina.

"And all the way we talked. All the time he wanted to know

more and more, about the world, cafés, theaters, cinema . . . He was very smart. I told you, all Novak men are smart. Milosz's father, he was illiterate farmer, but such conversations, Nina! Such philoso- phizing! When evening came we would light a small fire and hide it with stones, so no one sees, and roast potatoes or corn, and talk. He asked me: Tell me, my *snaja,* about the big world, tell me about Jews, about your faith. He never as a boy heard there was even such nation as Jews. He thought we were Tsintsari, that is a sort of people mixed with Greeks and Serbians who lived in Macedonia.

"And all the time he says to me, 'You're crazy, *snaja,* what will happen if they catch us?'—'They won't!'—'But how far do you want to go searching?'—'As far as Germany! As far as Hitler! I will find him!'

"So we walked like that, from morning to evening. Eating a little bread with fat, drinking from streams, not seeing any person. If we see someone from far, we hide.

"He was a pure man and I had trust in him. Big blue eyes he had, like a child." Vera giggles. "His wife, Milosz's mother, was not beautiful, but she was stronger than him. She was a devil, oh yes! Listen to this, Nina honey—"

Vera shifts into a more comfortable position, leans into the camera, and rubs her hands together gleefully. "I once asked my mother-in-law if in World War First, while he was in the army, she cheated on him. So she said to me, 'You know how it is, Vera, when we danced, I had here on my head a red flower, and so-and-so took the flower from my hair in his teeth . . . ' Well, from this I under- stood that she had an affair with this so-and-so.

"In general, I told you and I will tell you again: Novak men are quiet, very handsome, very smart, but not sexy. The girls—devils. Not pretty at all, but they are sexy in their root. And Milosz's sis- ters—oh boy! Lots of trouble with them, lots of stories . . ."

Nina and Rafi's glances meet again in the rearview mirror. You can almost hear their sabers clanging. Because of the angle I'm sitting at, I have to contort myself to see in the mirror. Rafael sends Nina a slightly crooked smile, she sends one back, and I see everything. I keep every muscle in my face so perfectly still that Nina asks him, with her eyes, whether he's told me. He nods.

I asked you not to tell, say her insulted eyes.

I have no secrets from Gili, say my father's shoulders.

Vera furrows her brow: "Wait, wait, what's all that about?"

"Nothing, Grans," I say, "just survivors sharing a moment." Nina bursts out laughing, which fills me with foolish pride: I managed to make the sad princess laugh.

"You look a little stunned," Nina said to him. It was five years ago, in August 2003, after Vera's eighty-fifth birthday party. She'd dragged Rafi on an evening stroll where the avocado orchard they'd met in used to be. Now it's a phone-screen factory, which generates a decent income for the kibbutz. "I can see this is hard for you, Rafi sweetheart. Your eyes . . . You can't believe that what I'm telling you is true. And maybe it really isn't true . . . Listen," she said with a gravelly laugh, "sometimes in the morning, before I'm fully awake, I lie for a few minutes and think: This can't be my life, this can't be what it looks like, with this crazy thing going on—

"I don't even know why I'm telling you. I mean the whole thing, the whole point, is that each of them only knows a part of me, each one only knows his girl, and now here I am, giving everything away, of my own free will, giving the whole package to one person—and it's a person holding a camera, and it's the person I trust more than anyone in the world, there's no one I trust more than you, you know that, don't you, Rafi?"

Rafi said yes. He's allergic to alcohol, and her breath was giving him a migraine.

"But you're also the worst person to tell this to," Nina said with a laugh, "and the person who will be most hurt by it . . . You can still change your mind."

"I'm listening," he said dryly. It amazed him that she'd offered, and even demanded, to have him film what she wanted to tell him—a confession? A will? Another indictment of Vera? He couldn't make up his mind, but a coldness had begun spreading through him, and he already sensed that this was one of those moments after which many things would be irredeemable.

"Also because when I'm in those waking-up moments, when my brain is, how to put it, restarting me, I can't grasp that it's for real. That I've messed up my life like this, and now I can't see a way back to the life of a normal person, an ordinary, honest person. In here"—she rapped hard on the back of her skull—"I have so many secrets and lies, so how can I not lose my mind? Tell me that. How can I hold that whole knotty mess inside this little box?"

Rafi told himself he was only the cameraman. That he'd try to understand this later.

"When you and I were together, in Jerusalem, being with you was what held me together a little. Drew a line around me. I had a border. I knew where right was, I knew where light ended and darkness started. It's true that most of the time I wanted to run away from it, and I did, but I came back. Listen, Rafi . . ."

"I'm listening," he mumbled.

"I'm going wilder now than I ever have before."

Rafi told himself that none of what she was going to tell him would break him.

"And you should know that I haven't . . . to anyone, not any person in the world . . . not like this . . . And that's why I wanted you to film me saying it, do you understand?"

He shook his head.

"You don't, huh?" There was dark desperation in her eyes. "So that for once, in one place in the world, all these things will be together, all the lies, and then for a few moments they'll be the truth—"

"Nina," he said softly, "why don't you stop? Let's go back to Vera's?"

"—and I look at myself now, I look at myself through your eyes, and I can't believe it's me, that this is happening to me, that my life got so messed up. And my love—I'm not talking about love for someone, I don't have that now. I'm talking about the place of love that was inside me, the place where I could love simply, faithfully, the way you love Mom and Dad when you're three . . .

"And to grasp that it's become this depraven—is that how you say it? I'm losing my words, I've had a little too much to drink . . . My love is depraven, and I am, too, and it wasn't supposed to be this way!" She shouted those last words, and Rafi pulled back, and she laughed. "I'm scaring you, hey? This is not what was in my cards, Rafi, and I think it's also not in my character . . . My real character was taken away when I was six and a half, and they gave it back to me three years later ruined, destroyed . . . Because I still remember who I was, what kind of girl I was . . ." She shouted from the depths of her heart: "I remember her, I remember her, because I was a happy child, serious but happy, and she is the most precious thing I have, and from her I draw my strength to this day, I have no other strength. Just think: a woman of my age drawing everything she has from a six-and-a-half-year-old girl . . ."

"You're lucky to have her," he said, "now let's go back. Vera will be worried."

"I suddenly remember, this is just something unconnected, I was six, and Dad went to Rome with the cavalry, and he brought me back a beautiful pair of white sandals. And another time he brought me a shirt made of—what's the word—silk, shantung silk, and he said it would bring out the color of my eyes. But I wanted to tell you something else. My thoughts are running away . . . I've been a little forgetful lately, it's funny, with all this complexity, all the secrecy, the double life—if only it was double, but it's triple, quadruple . . . But we were talking about something else . . . What was I going to . . . Wait, just a minute, I remembered. About the difference between what you see from the outside and what is really . . . Look at me, for example, forget for a minute that you sort of love me, make the effort, for my sake, and tell me what you see. A pretty ordinary girl, right? Not in her prime. Not someone who, how to put it, turns heads, except for your head, luckily for me, but that has more to do with your screwed-upness, I'm not taking responsibility for that . . . So anyway, a pretty ordinary girl, at first glance. At her job in Brooklyn, where she's been working for seven years, maybe five people out of a thousand know her first name, or that she even has a first name. She's just Ms. Novak, a slightly anemic woman, not enough flesh on her, even though sometimes, in a certain light, she's quite attractive, almost pretty, but obviously not in her prime. Would you agree to that description?"

"I'll tell you later." He suddenly realized how important it was to her that he film her now, right after the family party, with the same camera he'd used to capture all the moments she'd exiled herself from.

"Now imagine that inside Ms. Novak, the pale blonde from the Hebrew desk in the Business, Finance and Technical Translation Department's Middle East branch, beneath her thin skin, there is something constantly darting around, a demon, but a real one, with a tail and demented red eyes, and Rafi—what is that demon inside me? Where did it come from? Tell me, if you even know, if you've ever felt how it burns your brain and your guts on its way down to your dick, and how it grabs you by the balls and turns you inside out like a glove, and it doesn't care about you, you see, it doesn't care about me at all, and I accept that, I'm okay with that, it suits me well, and I know the demon is just using me to survive. Using me for *its* pleasure, far more than for *mine,* and it rubs me up against any dick it comes across, that's what it needs, my demon, and I struck a deal with it, and it's good for me, because what it's looking for is the motion, the friction, you see? The speed, the movement, the friction, that's how it gets its electricity, and that's also what I need, you know that, the speed and the friction and the constant switching, the switching around of my innocent lechers, who never stop to imagine that they might not be the one and only name on my dance card, but now you know, and you're the only one in the world who knows, Rafi, that there are four of them, as of today, four that switch around, *flip-flap-flip-flap!*" She flicked her hands back and forth like a card sharp. Her eyelids fluttered shut, and there was a peculiar drunken quality, yet also an alertness, to her choked-up speech. "And four of them may not be enough for me soon, I'm warning you, Rafi, four might not be enough, because I've already learned how it is with four, see? I've learned to juggle four and none of them ever falls, none of them collide, and it's certainly conceivable that I'll need to up my dose soon, to juggle five, no, wait, six, why not six, and maybe after a while six won't be enough either, and I'll need seven, why not—"

She breathed heavily. Her cheeks were flushed. Seeing her like that—my father told me—seeing the look in her eyes, he understood the meaning of the phrase "strange fire."

In the end, by the way, he showed me everything he'd filmed, all the footage, nothing spared. He showed me after my endless pleas. I kept praying that he wouldn't, that he'd be a responsible adult and protect me, that he'd be my *father*. But in the end he gave in, which, he says, he regretted every single day of his life. And so did I.

Where was I.

"The way you're looking at me now, Rafi . . . I know what you're thinking, but I want you to hear everything and only make up your mind afterward, okay? When I'm done, you can give me a decent, cautious, sane man's verdict." She spat out the words. "Maybe you'll decide I need to be exiled, sent away for reeducation, maybe to a prison on an island. Islands seem to work out well for my family, especially a naked island like Goli, but remember, Rafi, remember that you can't scare me with that, because I've been there on that island for ages, I've been there since I was six and a half, and I'm alone there, I was put on the island without sentencing, just like that, no one could come to court to testify for me, and you're the only one in the world who might be able to say something good about me, the only person who still believes I might be acquitted, aren't you, Rafi?"

She puts her hands up before him, fingers spread, like a drowning person. "Acquitted not only when it comes to them, the lechers, but acquitted in general . . . If I could just for once be dipped in some kind of substance and pulled out clean and pure and, most of all, *simple*—that's what I miss most, forget about all the rest, just simple, the way I used to be, you know, for even five minutes, before what happened on that morning in Belgrade, when Mom sent me to Jovanka's and I walked away, and it was cold outside, it was October, and there was a half-erased hopscotch chalked on the sidewalk, and I jumped and skipped, and there were fall leaves, I remember it so well." She puts her head back, eyes closed. "Big yellow and red leaves, and the roasted-chestnuts man was just setting up his cart on the street corner, and I remember looking back at the house, I could tell that Mom was worried and distracted all morning . . . You know Vera, she's never distracted, but that morning she put my sweater on back to front, and twice she tried to braid my hair, but her hands wouldn't seem to . . . And when I looked back I saw a tall, large man in a black coat at our door, and he looked at me and it frightened me, so I walked quickly to Jovanka's house, and I didn't run back home, not even to be with Mom so that she wouldn't be alone with that man who scared me. I ran, my instincts told me to get far away, but how did I even end up talking about this?"

She gave Rafi a haunted, startled look.

"What was I talking about?"

"About things being simple."

"Simple, yes, lucid. So you could look into me and see all the way to the bottom. But that's no longer possible with me, my lens is dirty, or actually there are several lenses on top of each other . . . How much, tell me? How many lies can you stuff into one person's life before their brain starts leaking? One after the other they come to me, sometimes two a day, one leaves and two hours later the next one arrives, and I don't want you to think I'm doing it for the money, God forbid, if any of them makes that mistake and offers, he's off the team, there's no forgiveness for that, but for everyone else I'm the sweetest, honeyest thing, I'm innocent and tender and motherly, or slutty, depending on what the audience demands, Nina is up for anything, any initiative, the crazier the better, you cannot imagine, Rafi, deeper and deeper into the muck, and that's what drives my masters crazy, that anything goes, any fantasy and any whim—am I disgusting you? Should I stop?"

"I'm just filming."

"Keep filming, I told you, I have to have all these lies together, for once . . . My poor Rafi . . . What a life you could have had if your soul hadn't caught on the nail that I . . . Should I go on?"

The camera nods.

"And they can't believe their good luck, they can't believe that the skinny wisp of a girl from the department of so-and-so, the one they flirted with in the elevator, or on the subway, or in line for frozen yogurt—flirted unintentionally even, maybe just to be polite, to make her feel good—that this anemic owl is suddenly turned on and burning between their hands, and writhing wildly like they've slept with three, four, five different women, and the only thing she won't let them do is kiss her on the mouth, which is one way in which she actually does resemble her prostitute sisters. Oh Rafi, my sweet." Here she took a step forward and wrapped her arms around his neck and breathed desperately, then pulled herself together and stepped back and talked to the camera. "I'm rambling and rambling without saying the main thing, and the main thing is . . . What is the main thing, I can't remember now, what is the main thing, you tell me . . ."

"The main thing is that you're making all this up to depress me," Rafi said quietly, his fury barely held back.

"Oh, I wish"—she sighed—"I wish . . . If there was a way, some magic trick to put it back where fantasies belong . . . It's all true, Rafi, and you don't understand, you're too good and too pure to understand this sort of thing. Now listen and let me say the whole thing, because I will never get another chance to tell these things to anyone, and everything you're recording now you will hand over to me and I will throw it into the deepest pit I can find. The main thing I wanted to tell you, so you'll know, the main thing is the last moments before the next one up knocks on my door. That is the moment when my brain burns the hottest, you'll be surprised, but, yes, it's *before* he arrives, lecher number two, or three, do you see? The main thing is the ten, fifteen minutes before, when I imagine him getting off the subway, and I see him walking toward me, getting closer, and with every step he takes I reach out and halt him—slowly, darling—and he flies to me like an arrow but in slow motion, and he walks past the Korean girls' nail salon, and then there's the deli, and the Indian guy's grocery, and I'm almost dying with anticipation, oh Rafi, why didn't we stay at home together in my room on the kibbutz when we were kids, why didn't you lock me in there after we slept together until I could clear out all this poison, this drug?"

Rafi said nothing.

"And the guy is by the drugstore on the corner now, and he starts smiling to himself because my waves of warmth are wetting him, they rise up to him from the street, from the asphalt, and there are also . . . how can I describe this . . . circles of fire, like in a circus, I can't think of the word . . ."

"Hoops?" Rafi whispered disgustedly.

"Hoops," she said, savoring the word, "but he's the only one who can see them, all the other people walk past them without seeing them, they walk to their left or to their right, but he walks through my hoops of fire, he jumps through them easily like a majestic lion, with his mane puffed out, bursting out of his suit, and he knows, he knows, he feels that he is jumping through my rings of fire, he understands that he's lost his volition and what moves him now is only me, the strong magnet that is me, what am I doing telling you all this nonsense, Rafi, stop me when you get sick of it, how are you not sick of me, and now, look, imagine, be with me, don't leave me now, see with your own eyes, hear the ancient elevator creaking downstairs, see it slowly carry him up to me, ninth floor, tenth, eleventh, twelfth . . . And he wants it so badly, he is all one

big burning desire. It's me he desires, Rafi, me, do you understand? And I am consumed with desire for him to want me, I'm on fire because he is choosing me, choosing his little Nina, and I am inside his pure desire, and his dick is like the needle of a compass pointing at me, because it's me he's choosing out of all the millions of people in New York at this moment, and he is clear and unequivocal, and by the way, all my lechers are like that, there is no such thing as 'I don't know what's up with me today, this has never happened to me before,' no such thing. He'd be disqualified on the spot and a replacement would be found, because I—Rafi, my darling—must be wanted. Do you understand? Do you?"

Rafael sighed. His head was aching, as if someone had drilled into it. "You're drunk, Nina. Let's go back to Vera's, we'll make you some strong coffee—"

"Wanted and desired, and wanted again, until there's no room in my brain for anything other than the fact that I'm wanted. That's my condition for acceptance. The choice—I have to be chosen—" She shouted those last words and then sobbed.

Rafi swallowed. For the last few minutes he'd been outside of himself. Now he felt as if a hypnotist had tapped him on the temple and woken him up. And the pain.

"Well?" she said after a few moments of silence.

"Well, what?"

"Say something, spit at me, crush me under your shoe like a cigarette, call the kibbutz out for a stoning. I can't believe what I've done."

She crumpled and sat down on a manhole cover. Held her head between both hands. "I can't believe it." She groaned. "Of all people—you? Give me the camera."

"We'll talk about that in the morning. When you're sober."

And to his surprise, she agreed. She looked up at him with her torn eyes. "At least say something. Don't leave me bleeding like this."

He sat down next to her, took a deep breath, and held her to him.

"You don't think I'm contaminated?"

"I don't know what to feel."

"You think I'm contaminated."

"Once, when we were . . . When we'd just started, I made a vow." He sighed. "Well, I don't know why I'm telling you this. I took a vow that I would always soak up your poisons until you were completely clean, and then, this is what I thought, we could really start being."

"And now?"

"I don't know. I think I've soaked up as much as I can."

"As much as you can—or more than that?" Her voice cracked.

Rafi did not answer. He thought perhaps it really was time to get her out of his life.

"I understand," she said. She clung to his arm, leaning on him. He thought about her body, about the life of her body. She'd once told him you could write two completely separate life stories: one about her, and the other about her body.

His hand on her shoulder was lighter than usual.

"He's cooling off," Nina noted, "I disgust him."

He was awash in her desperation, in the fact that she'd gone so far, so far beyond anything he could comprehend. He felt her falling, plummeting into the abyss. All at once he turned her toward him and kissed her on the mouth.

And kissed and kissed. And she did, too. They kissed.

Then they broke away and stood looking at each other.

"So," she said without breathing, "did you soak up some poison?"

"It's like it's our first kiss," he murmured.

A group of girls walked past. "Get a room!" one of them yelled, and another added, "In assisted living!"

Nina and Rafi laughed.

"My first kiss in a very long time," Nina said.

"Your mouth is so sweet."

"We kissed . . . What did you do to me, Rafi?"

"I kissed the woman I've loved my whole life."

A soft sigh escaped her. "You're so screwed up," she said, suddenly furious, as if he'd casually ruined a complex plan she'd been working on for years. But she quickly pressed up against him with her whole body again. "Run," she said, "save yourself." They kissed again. "We're already nine kisses deep," she murmured. He laughed and she was happy. He kissed her again. "Is that a goodbye kiss?" she asked. He kissed her again. She rested her head on his arm. Her eyes were closed, her lips extended. "You know how sometimes you start eating something and only then realize how hungry you were?" Her body went slack and she dripped into his arms.

"We'd never been so close in body and soul," Rafi told me after I finished watching the footage and wanted to die.

The next morning, earlier than planned, without saying goodbye to my father or to Vera, she flew back to New York.

"So we arrive to Belgrade, my father-in-law and me, and it's night, and we must travel into Croatia, my country. First I want to visit my and Milosz's home in Zemun, which is right next to Belgrade, where we lived before war began. I want to be even ten minutes in my beautiful apartment and take some clothes and things we can sell for money to help us find Milosz.

"But in Belgrade there is curfew, and the German army is already there, and there is a pontoon bridge to cross the river to Zemun. I see an army vehicle with Hungarian flag, so I scream in Hungarian: Take me! And they take me and my father-in-law over the bridge. And then we are in Croatia, and it is dark, and we walk to my house, there are tall houses with four floors, and I see that my blinds are open, and clothes of German soldiers hang outside on the line. I go upstairs in darkness and get to the door, and on the door there is a red sign with that bird of theirs and it says: OCCUPIED BY GERMAN ARMY.

"I open a little the door and peek inside, and there is light, and soldiers, and prostitutes, and my beautiful crystal glasses are getting smashed, and I shut it quietly, go down back, and say to my father-in-law, 'We wait a little and then I go in.' And he says, 'You are crazy, *snaja,* I am not letting you go back in there, because I promised your husband I take care of you.' And I say, 'I must get my things to save Milosz, and I have a plan.' He says, 'But where will you look for Milosz? Maybe there is no more Milosz?' And I say, 'There is Milosz and I will find him.' So we make big plans, and we both do not think of how we are in the middle of Croatia and my father-in-law is in Serbian clothes, and I am dressed like a Serbian farmer. When we remember that, we are very unhappy.

"I think to myself: I cannot do anything right—is this proof that I don't love Milosz enough? Then I see next to my feet, maybe two meters away, on the sidewalk, lies a shape of human being, and says to me, 'Miko, how did you find me here?' And I say, 'Milosz, how did you know to come here of all the world?' Milosz says, 'I knew you will come to our apartment to take things so that you can get to me.' And I say, 'Milosz, you look very sick, are you really alive?' He says, 'I am alive but wounded badly. I crawled here for almost two weeks.'"

"Not true," whispers Nina.

"What's not true?" Vera retorts.

"Is that really what happened?"

"That is what happened."

"You two are such a story . . ." It's hard for me to decode what she means.

"Yes," Vera agrees with strange joy, "we are a story."

"Go on, Grandma," I urge her.

"Milosz tells us that his division fell apart, and Croatian fascists took Serbs like him hostage and shut them in gymnasium in Bjelovar, and Milosz jumped out of the window and fell on his stomach where he had the operation. The stomach opened up, and he started walking and falling on the street, and he is still in Serbian uniform, and then he sees clothing store belonging to Gruenhut—a Jew! He knocks on the door and says, 'Mr. Gruenhut, open up for me!' This Jew gets scared, but he opens. And Milosz says to him, 'My wife is Jewish, Vera Bauer.' 'Bauer? I knew Clara Bauer from the Bauer *kompanija*—she must be your wife's mother! Come in quickly!' So this man gave him food and burned Serbian army uniform and gave him Croatian clothes, and Milosz slept there for a few nights in the storehouse, until he said, 'I must go now to meet my wife.'

"This is what Milosz tells us, and I notice he talks to me like a woman, in female, not like a man, maybe because his father is with us, or maybe because he misses me so much, and meanwhile we three of us sit in the dark on the sidewalk, and I resist from hugging him or dancing around him, and he also resists touching me even with tip of his fingernail because of respect for his father. Then we see soldiers and prostitutes coming out, drunk, singing. I tell the two men: It is my world now. I will go in. If there is someone there, drunk or prostitute, I will kill them. I take my gun and I go into my home, and there is no one there, everything is destruction. They ruined my apartment, those prostitutes and soldiers. I start throwing to my father-in-law from the window my mother's jewelry, which I hid in marmalade jars, and I found also some money and silverware. Two suitcases I filled and threw down, sheets and the eiderdown I still have today, which Rafi, when he was little, and later Gili, they liked to sleep with it even in summer."

Rafi says that blanket smelled like overseas. I remember how I loved to feel it enveloping me. I film Nina's silence.

"So that was how I stole my things, and I went back down to Milosz and his father, and I said: 'Now we will very slowly take Milosz back home.'

"Now, what is the problem? Problem is that Milosz almost cannot walk. He leans on me, he is in pain. His wound from the operation is open and leaks out pus and dreck, and he holds with both hands his stomach so the guts don't spill out. But we are together, so everything is all right. His father walks a few steps in front, like he's not looking, not seeing how I stroke Milosz's hairs so they don't fall in his eyes. And I think in my heart: If only we can walk like this all our lives, more than that I do not ask. But Milosz has no more strength and so I carry him on my back, because his father has an injury in his back from World War First.

"We get to the bridge, it's three o'clock at night, we wait until there is some light, then they put the bridge down and let first the farmers with land in Serbia go across. I go up to a farmer who has cart and two cows. We have injured man here, I say. I have silver forks and teaspoons and all this is yours. He tells me: Put it all here. We get onto his cart and he takes us over the bridge, and after the bridge there is market, with farmers already there. I leave Milosz and his father and take my ring with diamont—"

"Diamond," Nina says distractedly, "it's pronounced *diamond*."

"But that's how I said."

"You said *diamont*. Never mind, go on."

"That's exactly—*diamont!*"

"Okay, don't get mad," says Nina and tilts her head back, hissing to herself: "Forty-five years in Israel, and she still talks like an immigrant."

"And there is also a *hostelry,*" Vera says. "Is that the right word, Nina? Or is that an immigrant word?"

Nina laughs. "You win, Mom, I'm just . . . Go on, just continue."

"I go inside and I shout: Which man has horse with carriage, I will give him this diamont ring! The innkeeper examines it and says: 'This is worth three carriages with horses.' 'I need only one carriage!' So we put Milosz on the carriage. I wrap him very well with the sheets and eiderdown from my apartment. I tell the innkeeper to go to Milosz's village and that I want to enter the village at night, so no one will know Milosz is back, because someone might inform and they will take him again, and I will have to find him again. So that's how we arrive, and his mother, my mother-in-law, quickly slaughtered a sheep, took off its fur skin, wrapped Milosz inside, and sewed it up with a big needle, and Milosz fell asleep inside for almost two days. When we took him out of the fur, he already had some color back in his face, and we put him in a small room without windows and only me and his mother took care of him.

"Poor Milosz, he suffered more because of me than because of him. 'How do you survive, Vera? All this life is not right for you at all!' And me—what do I care? I'm with you! Everything is right! You are alive? You are next to me? Then everything is fine!"

Rafi points to a road sign: forty miles—or kilometers—to go. The rain has lightened up a little. The lime sails down the road with the ease that comes after great effort. Rafi stretches out, filling the space of the car with his body and his yawn—like the MGM lion's roar. We drive in silence for a long time. I think Nina starts to nod off.

"And all the time I also worked there in the village," Vera recounts quietly, almost in a whisper, to the camera. "In the fields, in the vineyard. Milosz was sick and lay in bed, and his mother told me, 'You must do two rows, also for your husband!'—'But it's your son!'—'But it's a mouth that eats!' That is the logic of farmers, and that is what I accepted."

I focus on Nina's face. The tension and anger have melted away. She listens with her eyes closed. Smiles.

"Every morning I looked at the chicken's bottom to see if she has an egg, and I cooked food for the pig—potato peels and pumpkin, with bran, and in the mornings I baked for everyone bread from cornmeal, big loafs, I hardly could get them out of the oven. And I would cook food for the men in the field, cabbage or beans, that is their national food. Meat is almost never. Only for holidays. Sometimes chicken. They slaughter a pig maybe once a year."

She rubs her eyes. Nina, next to her, dozes off. With a sudden resolve, Vera sharply pulls Nina in to lean on her, head to head.

"I liked to be in the village," she says into Nina's hair. She takes Nina's hand and slowly strokes it. "I liked it there, Nina. Everything was good for me. I bathed in the cellar, in a big barrel. Feet they washed every evening, and as their daughter-in-law, I had to sit on my knees, take off their shoes, take socks off my father-in-law, and bathe his feet in water."

She almost whispers. I hope the Sony is picking it up. Maybe the words matter less now. Her lips are close to Nina's ear, as she tries not to fall asleep. Future-Nina seems to have disappeared. There is a sense that things are being restored. That they are finally rooted in time and family.

"And to me everyone in the village told things. Because somehow I knew how to get inside them. Everything was interesting to me. Every person was to me special. So Milosz's mother told me that her mother-in-law is evil and terrible, and the mother-in-law told me that Milosz's mother cheated on Milosz's father while he was in World War First . . . And to me this was all very interesting, I wanted to swallow everything . . ."

The camera is on Nina. She smiles to herself, her eyes almost shut, seeking a comfortable place to nest in Vera's body.

"—and I went in the cemetery to talk to women who sat crying on their husbands' graves, and I asked them: Tell me, please, kind neighbors, who was this precious man? Tell me about him, please. And I remembered everything. I still remember like it was yesterday.

"See, Ninaleh," she whispers, "I so wanted to soak in everything that belonged to Milosz, his whole world. I needed to understand everything so that I could understand him, because that is his root . . ."

Her mouth is on Nina's cheek. Nina opens her foggy eyes, perhaps trying to remember how she got here, and slowly surrenders to sleep. Something in the picture is heartrending: Rafi drives her, I film her, Vera tells her a story. The three of us awake, and she among us, falling asleep.

"They liked me there because I was not a 'madam.' I walked through dirt and stinking, and instead of a toilet they had hole in the ground, and there were no beds at all. When me and Milosz came at first, they borrowed from the next-door village two beds and softened them for us with straw, and fleas were hopping around, and in that time girls were not shaving legs yet, and I had hairs, and all between them—fleas."

"Grandma, that's gross!" I laugh.

"Gross is today," Vera says dryly, "then everything was different. There was poverty and there was war and there was Balkan. But I wanted it, I wanted to be part. For the first time in my life I felt I was part. I cooked food, and they all went to work, and at lunchtime I put a big stick over my shoulders with pots hanging on sides, and I walked through the fields to the vineyard, and I sang and I was happy and it was best in the world because Milosz was close to me, and he slowly came out of all his troubles and illnesses. The farmers in the fields said: 'Hey, Miloslaw, who is that woman walking there? Who is singing like a bird?'—'Oh, that's Novak's bride! She is bringing them food!'"

Nina is asleep. After a few minutes Vera falls asleep, too, her head on Nina's. I turn off the camera. My father and I drive the rest of the way in silence.

A colorless, unfocused sadness descends on me. (Written on a windowsill at night, looking out on a little marina. The Adriatic Sea. A town whose name I won't even try to pronounce again, otherwise I'll need jaw surgery.) The only thing in the minibar is white light. Flocks of dry leaves and plastic bags fly around on the promenade. It's an unattractive coastal town with a row of seaside hotels, and restaurants that are still open, empty but lit up with bright neon, emitting billows of noxious yet slightly tempting smoke from grilled meat, all with long freezer cases piled with mountains of ice cream in frightening colors. In three other rooms in the hotel, Vera, Rafael, and Nina are asleep. Tomorrow morning, if the sea permits and the storm doesn't kick up again, we will sail to the barren island that lurks somewhere out there in the fog. That is the island where significant parts of my childhood and youth took place, even though I've never spent a minute on it. And that is where this voyage will end, and I will be able to go back to being me and not a hologram of the mess created by my father and Nina with every move they make, every time they talk to each other, look each other in the eye, hug, sigh.

And all at once it hits me: they are still making me.

Middle of the night. When they're not crowding around me, I am with Meir. I can't stop thinking about me and him and what's going to happen. I swore I would erase him on this journey so as not to lose my mind, but I can't do it. I think it might help a little if I write about him. Or about us. No, about us is not good for me now. I'll write about the niche we carved out for ourselves. Not the sexiest start-up, let's put it that way, it's the latest in low tech, but it works for us and it keeps our heads above water when I'm in between film gigs: on the mountain across from our house, among the pine trees, we bury dead pets. People—mostly from the area, but not exclusively—bring us their dogs and cats and parrots and hamsters. Once we even buried a pony, and twice a donkey. We've buried a trained falcon (we found a beautiful urn for him, illustrated with a bird of prey), and we have a whole plot full of rabbits. Usually the funeral is attended by a parent and a child, but sometimes the whole family comes. I always join in. Meir needs time to warm up, and meanwhile I set out a little table with a thermos of coffee and a pot of tea and juice and cookies and fruit, and a bouquet of flowers. Meir takes the animal out of the family car's trunk. Usually it arrives wrapped in a sheet or a blanket, as we request. All of Meir's beauty comes out in those moments—quiet, tender fatherliness.

No, there's no doubt.

I'm the problem. It's me I don't trust.

The grave is prepared ahead of time. Meir places the animal in the ground and covers it, which is always a difficult moment for everyone. Then he puts a piece of cardboard on the grave with the name of the dog or the cat or the parrot. Sometimes the family asks to include a picture of the pet. Sometimes they want us to add their last name to the pet's name. And there is always a little ceremony (we arrange it with the families ahead of time), where a little boy reads a farewell letter to his hamster, or a teenage girl plays the guitar for her dog. If the family hasn't prepared anything, Meir spurs them on. He asks questions about the pet, and about the family. It almost always brings up memories, and there is laughter and also tears. It's nice to see how he melts away their distress.

After the ceremony, we encourage the family to walk around the graveyard. It lifts their spirits. They feel that their beloved pet won't be alone. When they leave, we sit by the grave for a while longer, drinking tea and talking about the family we just met.

Recently we've been having some trouble. Someone, probably one of the neighbors, snitched on us, and the Jewish National Fund is threatening to sue us and destroy our place because it's state-owned land or something, and the income tax authority is coming down on us, too. Never mind, we'll figure it out, chin up.

And then comes a knock on the door.

Nina stands in the doorway with her hands behind her back: "Don't throw me out."

I move aside for her. She walks in. It's 1:30 a.m.

She puts a bottle of whiskey on the table. There's a white polar bear on the label, and at least two fingers are already missing from the bottle. She asks for permission to sit on the only chair in the room. I sit down opposite her on the edge of the bed.

"Can't fall asleep," she says.

"I can see that."

"Lousy hotel."

"Really? I think it's fine."

"Doesn't give any . . . I don't know. Any sense of home?"

Laughter flies out of me like spit.

"What?" she inquires. "Did I say something funny?"

"No, it's just that if I were you I wouldn't go around using words I don't understand."

"Oh, you're so witty."

It's like we have to start walking the whole path toward each other from the beginning every time. She drinks and hands me the bottle. I never drink, and at home with Meir, alcohol is the devil I purged. One of them. But I wet my lips and cough my soul out. It's so strong it brings tears to my eyes.

"There's a pub in my village," she says, "actually there are two. One says it has the best whiskey in the world. The other one, which I like more, says it has the best whiskey in the village. In the evening, at the end of the day, I like being there. Not just me. As soon as evening falls, especially in the dark season—four months without sunlight—people are drawn there. A sort of need to be together in a warm porridge. Humanity."

I listen.

"Sometimes there are guys there from the Arctic satellite station, sometimes also the miners. The encounter between them, just to be there . . . And almost every evening we sing."

"*You* sing?"

"I hum."

She drinks. Rather generous swigs.

"Around the village," she continues, "there are enormous mountains, monsters, and they're covered with snow, and it's totally dark for four months—did I mention that? So dark you can hardly see a foot ahead. People walk around with flashlights. The weirdest thing is walking by the sea in that darkness. Hearing it without seeing it."

"Is it pretty?"

"Is it pretty . . . ? You can't think of it in those words. Overall, words are not the strong suit of that place."

"Explain."

She thinks for a moment. "No. That would spoil *there* for me."

Her directness is good for me. I think she and Meir would get along excellently, as long as she didn't try to fuck him.

"Still, give me a hint."

"It's like the end of the world and the creation of the world together."

"Are you happy there?"

"Happy? I can't say. I like how it's all just a little bit. Succinct. I've never been as calm inside, within me, as I am there."

A sigh escapes me. My man, my succinct man.

"And because everything's diminished," she says, "you become attentive to the tiniest things. It's all signs."

"Yes," I say, "I know the feeling."

We're both making an effort. Fumbling around for the place where we can occur.

"How long have you been there?"

"Two years. Since I ran away from America."

"Ran away?"

"A misunderstanding with the tax authorities," she says with a laugh. I laugh, too. We have a common enemy. Any minute now we'll be discussing VAT and business deductions. "But I was planning to leave anyway. I had to move. I'm a person who moves."

"I've noticed."

"And there up north, something calmed down."

"You know," I say after a suicidal chug, "I look at you and I think: It simply isn't possible that this woman flung me out of her life when I was three and a half."

"It's a fact."

"And you don't even . . . I mean, you aren't considering apologizing?"

"No. No. Definitely not."

"No?" I practically scream. She has some nerve.

"There's no apology for that, and even if I did apologize, there's no forgiveness. That horror is something I have to live."

Eyes in eyes. There is something moist in her look, and for an instant I believe her. Then I think about the life poseurs, from the book that taught me about "the ideal marriage" ("people who are extremely impoverished in the realm of emotion and play the part of affectives. They are known as 'life poseurs'"), and I believe her slightly less.

"Tell me more," I say.

"About what?"

"I don't know. About that place."

"The thing they have more than anything else in the mountains around there is bears. Polar bears. White ones. Beautiful ones."

"For real?"

"Absolutely. About two thousand of them. Every few weeks one of them wanders into the village to look for food in the trash cans, or to devour humans. We have a bear alert on our phones, but someone still gets eaten every few months. There've been four since I've lived there. It's part of the deal."

"What deal?"

"The fear."

I signal for her to explain.

"It's not like being afraid of someone who flips you off at the light, or of a man walking behind you down an alley. It happens in a totally different place in your body."

"But don't people have weapons or something? Guns?"

"If you leave the village, you have to take a rifle, but you need to know how to use it. You have to have done target practice."

"Do you carry a rifle?" The idea of her with a weapon makes me nervous.

She laughs. "At night, when I walk home from the pub, I don't."

"On your own?"

"I'm alone there."

"Oh."

She gives me a probing look. It's a little absurd, but she seems to be considering whether I'm worthy of her trust or not. "I walk down the main street and shout for a bear to come."

"You shout out loud?"

"People think I'm drunk, but that's when I'm sharper than ever."

"You walk around calling bears?"

"In Hebrew, too, just in case there's a multilingual bear around."

A polar bear pounces on her from behind while she walks alone at night. In utter silence it tears her to shreds. Massive nails rip her delicate body. It doesn't care who she is. It doesn't care that she's beginning to forget names. That she once abandoned her daughter. For it—she's just meat. In my hallucination she doesn't shout, doesn't call for help. On the contrary, she smiles a terrible smile—the smile of someone who just wants to be meat. And I think of the lechers, and the Korean from Jerusalem, because they also devoured her. Over their shoulders, when they're on top of her, I can see her terrible smile, the smile of a skull, and I think: How much foreignness can a person contain and still be herself?

"Where were you?" she asks. "Right now, just this moment, where were you? What did you see?" Her gaze digs into me feverishly, desperately.

"Not yet," I reply, "give me time to get used to this."

"We have a coal mine, possibly the last one in all of Scandinavia. They shut down all the others because of pollution, but they left us free to pollute."

"Have you ever been down the mine?"

"I worked there."

"You worked in a mine? You actually mined coal?"

She laughs. Takes a drink. "I cooked for them. For a few months. Lots of carbs." There is a strange magic in the way she talks, especially after the whiskey. A dreamlike distance, continual, as if she's talking about someone else.

"Do you even know how to cook?"

"I'm a wonderful cook, Gili. I wish you'd let me cook for you one day."

I feel a sudden beesting on my tongue. "Tell me, Nina, there's something I have to know."

"Anything you want."

"How many days did you breastfeed me?"

Her hand flutters over her blouse button. "Why does that matter?"

"No reason, just tell me: Three or four?"

"Not even one."

"Oh, really?"

"When I was pregnant, I got eczema on my nipples and I couldn't breastfeed."

So Rafi lied to me. But if he was going to do that, why was he such a cheapskate?

"I'm sorry, Gili."

"No worries. It's all good." But it's hard to describe how painful this is. "Can I ask something else?"

"Whatever you want, Gili." She enjoys saying my name.

"I still don't understand—what's your connection to that place?"

"The village? Nothing."

"Nothing-nothing?"

"Nothing."

"Just a place you happened to end up in?"

"No. It's a special place. The most moving place I've ever been in."

"But?"

"There's no but. It's moving, and it's indifferent to me. Doesn't give me the time of day. Doesn't make an effort. Doesn't care whether someone like me exists or not, or that any minute I'll be gone. It's not the indifference you get on the streets of New York or New Delhi. No one there cares about me either, but in the mountains, in the north, with the sea all around, it's a way of totally uniting—with nothing."

"And that's good for you?"

"It's hard to understand, right? It's the best for me."

"Explain."

She gives me a simple, warm smile. "You won't let me off the hook. Forcing me to think. It's been a long time since I really thought. Let me tell you what's good for me there. It's good for me that with every breath, a little more of me gets erased. There is less Nina to be. What's that look?"

"Nothing. It hurts to hear."

"Hurts? Really?"

I nod. How can it not hurt. A person isn't made of stone.

Nina purses her lips. "I want to tell you something, but let me finish saying it."

"I'm listening."

"You, by your nature, no matter how much you deny it, are a belonging person."

I can't tell if there's mockery in her voice, or if she's jealous of me, or what. "Me? Don't make me laugh." But I think she's right. And it excites me to think that she's even given me any thought, that she has opinions about me.

"You belong, Gili, and you have your own place, and you have people and you have reasons and you have landscapes and colors of earth and smells and Hebrew, and you have Vera and Rafi and Esther and Chana and Shleimaleh and the whole tribe. And me?" She laughs. "I'm a leaf in the wind. Or rather—I'm that bird that never touches the ground. I can't think of its name . . ."

"Albatross. But that's just a myth. It does touch the ground sometimes."

"Me, if I do touch it, it's only to gain momentum to fly up again."

"And I have love," I say, and I think this might be the last time I'll be able to say it in the present tense.

"Yes. Rafi told me." She nods gravely. "And soon you'll have a child."

I say nothing.

"Oh dear," she says, "I shouldn't have . . ."

"I'm not pregnant."

"Oh, you aren't?"

"No!"

"Strange. I'm not usually wrong about that."

"But where would you even come up with the idea that I'm—"

"I don't know. I have a sense . . . Pregnancy always turns on all my alarms."

"I can't believe you're even allowing yourself to—"

"Wait, give me a second. Let me explain. When I saw you yesterday at the airport, when I fell on you, and I'm sorry, again, but it just threw me off when I saw you like that—"

"Like what?"

"Continuing the fucked-up dynasty."

"But I'm telling you I'm not pregnant!" I scream in her face, and we both stare at each other, horrified by the scream that ripped a hole in the air between us, and it's true that for a moment I am almost tempted to believe that she senses something invisible, a mother's heart—as if!—but even if there is something, *and there isn't,* she's the last person who'd be able to sense it in me.

I walk to the window, slightly unsteady, open it, and take a deep breath. Cold sweat breaks out all over my body. That's it, she needs to get the hell out of my room and my womb.

She murmurs behind me, "But when you are, at least make sure it's a boy."

I'm so furious at her that in my despair I start laughing. After a moment she joins in. We laugh slightly hysterically. I don't fully understand it. It's a laughter that changes colors in the course of being laughed. They used to have candies like that, when I was a kid.

"But tell me," I say after we both calm down.

We look at each other. I have to find out what she sensed in me.

"Ask, Gili."

I take in some air. "Do you really think I'm capable of being someone's mother?"

"Gili," she says, "you'll be a good mother."

"I will?"

A whole life can be pressed into those two words and the question mark.

"Yes," she says with utter confidence that comes from somewhere I don't know. "A good, belonging mother."

Later, much later, she says, "Rafi told you about those men."

"Yes."

"It's something that I—"

"I really don't want to hear about it now."

"Let me say it. For two and a half years I was in that story."

I stiffen, grieving the lost moment of grace. "That's your business."

"Listen, please. For two and a half years I was like . . . You know, what do you call someone who walks in their sleep?"

"A nymphomaniac?"

That hurts her. I can see it. But she hands me the bottle with a strange sort of tenderness. I suckle down more and more.

"Every time I lose a word, I panic," she says.

"Of course."

"Tell me honestly, Gili—can you tell?"

"No."

"I keep having this feeling that I'm, how should I put it . . . Do you understand?"

"No."

"Like I'm constantly playing almost the right note."

I don't respond. It's amazing how well she can feel something that she doesn't know.

I go back to the window. A cold breeze blows in. Nina comes and stands next to me. We look at the night sea, with its white shivers.

"But about a year ago," she says, and by now I recognize the swipe of the cynical blade inside her words, "someone finally turned up who wants me and only me, and insists on me, even unto death, and I don't need anyone else anymore."

"Who? Another boyfriend?"

"The disease."

How sad that in the end it was the disease that restored her expressions, not my father. She puts a hesitant hand on my shoulder. What am I supposed to do with that now. I drop my shoulder and wriggle away. Nothing happens. She stands by the open window hugging herself.

A soft knock at the door. Followed soon by three loud knocks, and then someone impatiently turns the handle. There is only one person who would barge in like that, tolerating no barriers. I open the door and lean on the handle, slightly dizzied by the last few moments. "I had a feeling you were all here," she grumbles and walks through me into the room. It's the same way she bursts into our house every few weeks, unannounced, with bags full of food. She sits down on the edge of the bed. She is wearing her wool hat with the leather earflaps, and a coat over her pajamas. "Great," I say, "let's have a slumber party." Vera sniffs, detects the whiskey, and hurries over to it. She takes a swig. A not-insignificant one. Wipes her mouth off with her hand. "It's no slivovitz, but not bad." She offers me some. I refuse. Grandma scrutinizes me: "Are you all right, Gilush?"

"I'm fine."

"You were talking, you two?"

"We were talking," Nina says, and I realize with horror: I didn't videotape our conversation.

"What's the problem," Vera says, taking off her coat and hat, "videograph it now."

"Dad has the camera. Should I get it?"

"No, no," they both call out together, "leave it, let him sleep."

Vera glues the bottle to her mouth and drinks. She and Nina hold the bottle by its neck, not by its body, and drink with the same exact motion. She passes it to Nina. They're both going to be wiped out tomorrow. They'll do the whole island without remembering they were there. And I'm not filming this.

"Tell me something, Vera," Nina growls, and I identify a slight tattering of her mind from the whiskey, "explain to me, and you, too, Gili, you're a girl with your head on your shoulders and you understand about people, don't you?"

"Not at all."

"Explain to me why I'm still stuck there, on Goli? Why can't I simply accept it?"

"What's simple about it?" Vera gripes.

"There was simply a dictatorship. And just like in a hundred other dictatorships through history, they threw a woman named Vera Novak into the Gulag for three years, and on the way they also screwed up her daughter's life. Big deal, what's the story? What's the fuss? It happened, it's over, on we go. Chin up!"

She looks into Vera's eyes like someone who has decided to stare straight at the sun, come what may. I curse myself for not having the camera. Rafi will be furious at me for not calling him, and rightly so. But I can't tear myself away from the two of them, not now, not when lines are being drawn.

Also, I couldn't stand having anyone else here. Just the three of us.

"And why have I been stuck in this shit for almost sixty years?" Nina snivels. "Fifty-seven years of being stuck at six and a half, isn't that a little over the top? Isn't it crazy?" While Nina talks, Vera nods to herself and emits a sort of inner hum, as if she's rehearsing her answer. "Fifty-seven years, stuck in a reeducation camp, isn't that a bit much? Shouldn't I have been reeducated by now? Gotten over it? Forgiven? Put it behind me and moved on? No, really—" She puts her fists to her mouth, refusing to give in to the tears. "It's just the three of us here now, just us, no world, we're the world, and I want you to both tell me to my face, once and for all, what is it about me that's screwed up? Where did my software get messed up?" She looks at Vera with eyes wild with pleading, and with terror.

Vera takes a deep breath and straightens up. She's going to talk now. It's going to happen.

But then, all at once, as if her last remaining drop of stabilizing substance has run out, Nina collapses. She sobs with her mouth open, loudly, snot streaming. Vera wipes Nina's face and puts her head on her shoulder. Nina is exhausted. Vera looks at me over Nina's head, and I remember how she used to talk about her ("Nina is weak, Nina is spoiled"). How close we were to speaking the truth.

With drunken eagerness, Nina suddenly hugs Vera and kisses her on the cheeks and head, and kneels down before her and kisses her hands, and begs forgiveness for everything she did to her. All the heartache and the worry and the shame. She waves the empty bottle around. Demands that we fill it. Vera and I stand her up and walk her to the bed and lay her down. I remove her shoes. Her feet are small and delicate; no man would run when he saw her shoes next to his own. But she, too, like me, and like Vera, has a right pinkie that climbs over the next toe a little, as if clinging to it.

She bolts up in bed: "Majka, tell me how I was born!"

"Shh, shh, lie down, my girl. Why do you want to hear how you were born now?"

"Now! Now!" She grabs Vera's sleeve. Anyone would think she was asking for proof that she really was born.

I grab my notebook: if there's no footage, at least we should have words.

For example, these four words: Rafi will murder me.

"Ninotchka," Vera sits down on the bed next to her and holds her hands, "you were born on June twentieth, 1945. In Belgrade. On that night we happened to have friends visiting from my town Čakovec. They were Communists like us, and when war almost started with Stalin, all the ones who were pro-Stalin Communists were straightaway sent to the front so that they, with their body, will find the land mines. So then, at night, when the Danube froze, they all ran away."

"You see, Gili?" Nina laughs with her mouth wide open. "I ask about my birth, and I get the Danube. And frozen, at that."

"No, no," Vera protests, "you'll hear why in one minute. In 1945, friends came with brigade from Russia. And in the evening our good friend Pišta Fišer came to stay with us, and he was so tired, and I'm running all over the house with contractions, not letting him sleep. Poor Pišta Fišer came to sleep one night, and that's when I have a baby!"

"Such lousy luck." Nina laughs through her tears. I fall about laughing, too.

"You laugh," Vera says, "but your birth was terrible . . . Twelve hours! We Bauers have very big babies. Gili is the only one born small, premature, but I was almost five kilos when my mother had me, and all my life I only got another forty-two kilos. And in pregnancy I looked like a monster. Nina, you were sixty centimeters—giant! And you were such a beautiful baby, and you looked on me with open eyes like you already wanted to talk to me . . ."

Vera strokes Nina's hair in a circular motion, smoothing over her face. "Already when you were born you had curlish hair, and skin like Milosz's. Like a peach."

I go back to the open window. It's still dark, but the sea is calmer. On the breakwater, next to a little boat, a man and a woman of a certain age dance under a streetlamp on the pier. There is no music playing as they do their strange, erotic dance, synchronized, moving close to each other, then away, their arms spreading out and gathering in. I feel terribly homesick.

Behind me, from the bed, Nina murmurs, "Tell me more about us. About me and Milosz."

"He used to coach you, remember?"

"I don't remember anything."

"He was always doing with you, how do you say it—*proba*. Practice. Teaching you to find streets in town, to look at a map, to hold a compass, to be independent. To be like a partisan in your own town. From the youngest age he would tell you: Now go to Jovanka, a few streets away, and give her this paper. And the paper said: 'Jovanka, just write down that you saw her.' You would come back after ten minutes: 'Daddy, the bell over there is very high, I cannot ring.' And Milosz said: 'It's not my business how you reach! Do you have brains? Then think.' And you went back there, and as soon as a neighbor went into the building, you followed in like a cat without him noticing."

"I did that?" A bright smile spreads over Nina's face. "I don't remember anything. That whole period is gone, my whole childhood is gone . . ."

"Yes," Vera says.

"Because of what happened afterward."

"Yes."

"How you went to Goli Otok."

"How I was put on Goli Otok."

"And you left me alone, both of you, you and Dad, in one day."

"So clever you were. You picked up everything fast."

"You trained me."

"God forbid trained. We just prepared you. Your father, he had a saying: 'Every person, his turn in the game comes only once.' And that is how he lived. So many times he was in danger, and in war, and life was also war, and everything was the logic of war, so that he, under his conscience, he knew he must prepare his daughter, and he had everything planned, including that he would in one moment need to commit suicide because of something. On the edge of a knife: that's where our life was."

Nina shuts her eyes.

"All in all," Vera says softly, to herself, "with me life plays a lot of games."

Nina has fallen asleep. Vera strokes her face again gently. Irons out her wrinkles. "I'm very tired now," she says to herself and lies down next to Nina.

I suddenly realize they were out fishing, that couple on the pier. They must be a husband and wife, back from the sea and folding up the net.

"Turn off the light, Gili, and come, too, because soon we must get up."

In any other universe it would never have occurred to me to get into bed with Nina, but I lie down next to her. The three of us share one pillow, which crowds our heads together, but the blanket is big enough.

I look at the ceiling. Nina's body is warm. She snores softly, and after a moment so does Vera. Meir claims I snore, but he's absolutely unwilling to sleep in separate beds. He can't sleep without spooning me. His arm surrounds me and he cups me all night. Sometimes it's stifling and sometimes I like it.

I think about what Nina said. I put my hand on my stomach. I'm dead scared.

At some point I can no longer hear Vera snoring, or breathing—that's all I need now. I sit up and see that she's on her back. Mouth open. Eyes wide, staring. She doesn't see me, and I'm convinced that this is it, she's gone, we've lost Vera a moment before her return to the island. Then her eyes focus and look intelligible again. She props herself on her elbow and whispers to me soundlessly, over Nina's body: "I think she already knows." I whisper back: "She'll only really know when you tell her yourself." "No, no, it would kill her." "I'm telling you she knows, Grandma, even without knowing, she knows." Nina gives a little sigh, and her mouth twists as if she's about to talk, or cry, or perhaps she's searching for a word that slipped away in her dream.

Then she stills.

Still is the furrowed brow, still are the cheeks, still is the mouth. She smiles to herself, pulls the blanket up to her chin, and turns over on her side, facing me.

They walk her. The sun beats down on her shaved head. She falls asleep midwalk. A woman with a foul-smelling cigarette puts her arm around her from behind and shoves a big rough hand under her armpit. Every so often the woman fondles her breast, crushing, pinching, and when she tries to shake off the hand she gets a quick, sharp slap.

"They're taking you," she tells herself out loud, "watch out for her." But after a minute she falls back into a slumber. All she knows is that she must put one foot in front of the other. They drag her like a rag doll. "But where are they taking you," she wonders. Her voice is hoarse and shattered, she's not convinced it's coming from her. "And what are they going to do to you there." The warden's laughter rouses her. "You've really lost your marbles," the warden explains good-naturedly, "you weren't like this when you got here. I remember you, I was at your interrogation once, you were tough as nails." Judging by the sound of the footsteps and the breathing, it's just the two of them, her and the warden. They've been climbing for a long time. It's a tall mountain. "There are all kinds of mountains on the island," she says to herself and nods gravely, counting on her fingers, so rigid she can hardly bend them, "there's the mountain at the camp for men who work in the quarry. And there's the mountain where you push the rocks. And there's the mountain for the quarry men, and the one where you push the rocks . . ." The warden laughs and pats her back, practically knocking her over. Vera tries to smile, she feels a smile is in order here, but she doesn't understand what the joke is. She thinks she heard the sound of metal hitting rock. Maybe a rifle. Maybe they're going to kill her. The path must be narrow now, because the warden has to walk behind her. She directs Vera with punches on her shoulders and back, right, left, waking her up every time she falls asleep or stares into the darkness inside her eyes. She trips on a stone and falls. Her hands break the fall, she gets up, licks the blood. "Tasty," she grunts, "bedbugs have the right idea." Out of breath behind her, the warden groans, "You still have the strength to crack jokes?" "What's the joke," Vera wonders.

Then a sharp right turn and a shadow falls on her swollen eyelids. She must be in a narrow cranny between two boulders. A cool breeze runs over her face. She slows down. Her body naturally slows. Her skin thirstily inhales the shade and the coolness, the back of her neck tenses for the slap.

"What happened, whore, why did you stop?"

The terrain grows rocky and rough. Vera and the warden breathe heavily. Sweat pours. The warden stops. So does Vera. The warden curses because of something Vera doesn't understand. The warden leans on Vera with one hand and takes off a shoe. The smell of shit spreads. She must be wiping her shoe on a rock. She curses some more, spits. "Turn around, whore." The warden thoroughly cleans her shoe on Vera's shirt. Vera hears a cork popping. The warden has two canteens on her belt. Vera hears water trickling. The warden is washing her hands. Now she hears strong, large gulps. Vera's mouth is dry. Full of sores. Her tongue is thick and heavy. "Maybe she'll give you a drink," she says, "maybe she's kind. Maybe she's your good mother? No, she's bad. She's a bad mother, doesn't take good care of you." The warden rolls around laughing. "You're really something," she says and gives Vera a friendly whack on the back of her head, "the girls told me you were like this, but I didn't believe them. Honestly? That's why I leaped at it when they asked who was going to take you up. Your whole brain is open like there's no lid, hey? It all spills out." Vera stops and shrinks back. What the warden just said worries her. "I think I've been a little bit not here lately," she whispers hesitantly, and the warden screeches with laughter.

Another sharp turn, left this time, and an even-steeper incline begins. They climb up, using their hands and feet, groaning, coughing. Then all at once she's in an open space. Maybe they've reached the top. A refreshing wind, a wind not-from-here, caresses her face. There is also a strong smell of the sea, different from the way it smells when she's in the barracks with all the women and their stenches. One bucket for thirty girls. Far below she hears waves crashing against the shore. There must be rocks there. A pretty sound, so pretty it hurts.

"Stand here, whore. Face this way!" A hard slap. The warden coughs—the wet, thick cough of a smoker. She spits.

"What is this here," Vera mumbles, "think fast, Vera. What are they going to do with you. Maybe throw you in the sea. The warden hears everything. Watch out for her."

"Exactly, whore, I hear everything. Stand up straight and shut up for a minute, I get it. It's not funny anymore."

Sun. The heat fries Vera's brain. It'll all be over soon either way. Too many signs. In a few minutes she won't be. Goodbye memory of Milosz, goodbye memory of Mother and Father, goodbye soulmate Jovanka . . . Goodbye Nina . . . Who knows where you are now. What they did with you. If I think about you I'll die before they shoot me. The warden holds her shoulders from behind and moves her a little to the left, then right again, then slightly back. What is all this, what are these movements, like some dance she's making her do.

"Stand up straight, trash."

"What is she doing. What does she care how you stand. If only she'd tell you what's going to happen." Her stomach turns. She's sweating, but now it's a cold sweat. The warden raises Vera's arms up to the sides. Not satisfied. She holds the arms up higher. Not satisfied. She punches her arms down against her body. She curses. Vera must have made a mistake. Vera herself is one big mistake. "How come a little raisin like you survived out here?" the warden spits out. "Legs straight! Back straight!" Vera puts her legs together. She whispers, "What is she doing? Maybe they told her to take a picture of you before they throw you in the sea." And with that thought she begins to tremble. Everything in her shakes, even the eyelids, the lips, and what's left of her beautiful cheeks. Her body is afraid, dying of fear, but she's not. She doesn't mind being done. On the contrary. She's only ashamed that the warden is seeing how cowardly her body is. "Two steps forward, trash." Vera doesn't know what she's walking toward. With the toe that sticks out of the hole in her boot, she feels for the edge. The warden scoffs: "You should have thought of that before you decided to betray Comrade Tito, whore." "Quick," Vera yells, breathing heavily. "Who should I think of now? How much time do I have? Where's Milosz? Where are you, my love, my life? Where is my little Nina, who was thrown out onto the street? Just like that. Took her and threw her on the street."

Silence. Vera is unable to guess where the warden is standing. Which side she's going to hit her from. And if it'll be a bullet or a fist. In the blazing sun, a circle of coldness darkens around her. The terror of death. It's not the first time this ring of cold has closed in on her. In the war she was in the forests with the partisans. Twice the Chetniks caught her and sentenced her to death, and she managed to escape. She faked passports and smuggled arms and people, one thousand five hundred people she saved, she and Milosz together, and three times she saved herself from being raped. After the war she and Milosz worked in counterespionage for the National Liberation Army of Yugoslavia. She truly did not know fear.

But back then she still had eyes.

Something jumps up in her head and she grows sharper, extricates herself from the dullness through which she's been staring for the past few weeks, since she went blind overnight. Up until that night she withstood it all: the interrogations, the torture, the fake executions, the hunger, the thirst, the hard labor, the temptation to inform, to turn someone in, because that's what they wanted, names, names. Who told a joke about Tito? Who wrinkled their nose when someone told a joke about Stalin? Even the horrible thoughts about Nina and what might be happening to her on the streets did not break her. But then came the blindness and finished her off. A few dozen women went blind that night, the whole left row of huts. A plague. They brought a doctor from the mainland, who diagnosed nyctalopia: night blindness. Because in the daylight hours the women could see again, and they all got better after being given vitamin A. But Vera never recovered. She could not see at night or day. "It's your punishment," Commandant Maria told her, and she would lift Vera's eyelids with the tip of her whip every morning: "Think very carefully, *banda,* about what you're being punished for."

In the first few days, Maria and the wardens thought she was lying, faking blindness to get out of working at the rocks. They beat her, starved her, and put her in isolation for ten days, three feet square, no bed, no chair, no window. Concrete floor, four walls, and a bucket. She slept diagonally. What did she care. Even if she ever got off the island, she would never be able to see Nina again.

—

"Why be afraid?" Vera scolds her miserable body that keeps on trembling. She hopes the thoughts are staying inside her head. For the past few days what's in her head has been blending with what's outside it. "But where's the warden? Behind you? Took a few steps back to gain momentum? And me, how am I standing? Facing the sea or the mountain? Which way will I fall?" Silence. The warden must be having some fun with her. But maybe not, who can tell in this place. Maybe she's crossing herself? Or praying before she pushes her? Vera sighs. She asks herself if Milosz taught Nina how to fall from a great height without getting hurt. He always used to prepare her, train her for all sorts of imaginary predicaments, and in the end what happened? What happened is that life was more surprising than him. What was it her mother used to say? "God has a big imagination for troubles." She says goodbye to her mother. They hug. Her mother was taken almost ten years ago, in Auschwitz. Prisoners who'd been in Auschwitz and were brought to Goli Otok said it was harder here. There, it was clear who the enemy was and whom you had to watch out for. Here the method is to turn every woman into every other woman's enemy. So you can't trust anyone. Where is the warden? Vera's body diminishes itself, her back shrinks, the back that is about to take the blow or the shot. Or maybe she'll shoot her in the head? And which thought will be the last one? Milosz, Milosz. She'll fly up in the air for a few seconds and crash onto the rocks below. She won't shout. There are women who came to the island pregnant, and gave birth or miscarried, and they took their newborns or fetuses and threw them into the sea. That thought reminds her of Nina again. Since going blind she hasn't been able to see Nina in her mind's eye. Instead of Nina's face it's always a blurred spot. As if Nina is punishing her, blurring and erasing herself. But now Nina is clear and sharp and smiling, and maybe that's a sign that Vera made the right decision. That Nina also understands that Vera did the right thing. Here is the beautiful, innocent, trust-filled face of Nina. Here are the pure green eyes, which you can dive into and feel that man is essentially good. Oh, Vera sighs desperately. "You can do it now," she shouts at the warden, "you can do it, but quickly."

"Want a cigarette, whore?"

Vera groans. A cigarette? Where did she come up with that? From the exact same unexpected place where the punches and the slaps come from, just because someone feels like giving them to you. Or maybe it's part of the execution protocol? Vera manages to bring in Milosz. She sees him as if he's standing here next to her. The high, light forehead, constantly teeming with thoughts and ideas. The funny big ears. The incomparable eyes. Milosz speaks in his pleasant voice, with his fast speech, *tik tik tik tik*, like a man running on a path of stones in a river. "Hey Miko, I knew you'd find me in the end." "Even in death I will find you, Milosz," she says with a smile. A match is lit next to her, then the sharp smell of smoke. A cigarette is shoved into her mouth. Her lips shake so badly they can hardly hold it.

She inhales hungrily. The cigarette stinks, but it gives a good burn. She wonders again if the warden is arranging Vera's body in this meticulous way so that it falls into a particular place on the rocks. She hears the canteen being uncorked. Maybe they give convicts one final sip. A gurgle of water nearby, down below, near her feet. Water spills. A sharp smell bursts into her nostrils. The smell of wet soil. And not just soil—Vera sniffs longingly—but rich, fertile soil. Where is there soil like that on the island? Did they dig a grave for her?

"Every two or three hours someone will come and arrange you the right way," says the warden and knocks Vera's forehead to straighten her head up.

"Arrange for what? Commandant."

"And you'd better be in the exact same place where I put you, down to the millimeter. Or else you're done." The warden pulls the cigarette out of Vera's mouth and flicks it into the gulf. Vera imagines herself leaping after it. It would be wonderful to fly. To be a burning spark. But apparently they're leaving her here for a while longer.

Without the cigarette the sun feels even harsher. Milosz has vanished. Nina has vanished. Her eyelids are puffy, but the smell of the earth is sharp and good.

"Listen up, trash: the one who comes at midday will take you to the rocks to shit and eat. You get ten minutes."

"Yes, Commandant."

They're not going to kill her. Not now at least. They didn't bring her up here to kill her. Wonderful relief spreads through her body. It was just a scare. She scared herself. Imaginative people suffer more on this island than others. She's never had much of an imagination. Nor a sense of humor. Before she got to Goli, she wasn't even capable of thinking about something that didn't exist. Yet when she got here, she made up an imaginary game that kept her going: she has to roll the rock up the mountain because a pharmacist is waiting for her at the top, with medicine for Nina. Poor Nina is sick, she has a fever. Nothing serious, maybe the flu, or even chicken pox, healthy children's illnesses. But she needs something for the fever, so that she doesn't suffer, and the head pharmacist said she'd wait for Vera one more hour, no longer. So now she's racing against time, not against the rock, the rock is just in her way. And she pushes and pushes, and groans and splutters and pushes. Nina is waiting—

Until she finally holds her head up and breathes easy, because she's reached the pharmacy at the top of the mountain, made it at the last minute. The head pharmacist smiles at her and hands her a bag with pills. And now Vera has to roll the rock back down, and that's the hard part. She has to stand under the rock, which weighs more than she does, and lodge her feet into the ground to stop its momentum and make sure it doesn't crush her. She's already seen women here splattered under their rocks, but that's not going to happen to her. She calculates every step because at the end of the descent, in the field of rocks, Nina is waiting for her medicine. Waiting desperately, and Vera will give her the medicine and see the smile on the little girl's face. Nina can count on Mother. Then she has to go back and join the line of women pushing rocks up the hill, to the pharmacy that will shut in an hour, to get medicine for Nina's flu.

But she was unable to fantasize anything else. Pathetic, her imagination. From the pharmacy to Nina, from Nina to the pharmacy. How could you compare that to Milosz and Nina with their make-believe games, and their fantastical creatures with eyes on the ends of their fingers, and the black bird that only flies over someone who's told a lie, and all the stories Milosz used to invent. Vera would sit in the next room, darning socks or knitting, wondering where Milosz and Nina came up with these notions. Because with Vera he only spoke about things from life, from reality, about the principles of socialism and class warfare, while with Nina a man from another world came out of him. And how they laughed together, he and Nina.

Her body stretches out with relief at not having been killed. The cowardly body cracks its joints, takes a deep breath. She yawns, a chain of enormous yawns. She can't stop herself. The body demands that gaping of the mouth and the deep inhalation. She's alive.

"Look at her," the warden comments, "still has teeth left."

She tries not to think about the sun. The blazing yellow ball hangs exactly above her head and fries her, vaporizes her. There won't be a drop of fluid left in her body. Her blood grows thick and slow. The bedbugs lose their mind over this blood. When she worked in the swamps, after she'd just arrived, the leeches clung to her legs, slowly swelling with blood, and then they would pull away, fat and sated. Some women tried to eat them, Vera did, too, but they tasted awful. At least here there aren't any leeches. But the sun. Women who confessed in interrogations, women who gave names, who told stories, who made false accusations, were given permission to wear a hat, or to turn a shirt or rag into a hat. That was how you could tell who had confessed and started collaborating with the

UDBA. Vera and another ten or twelve women were still
bareheaded. She was careful not to talk to any of them.
They were no less dangerous than the others. And they
tried, they exchanged looks with her, blurted words of
encouragement, or obstruction, when they passed her on
the way up or down the mountain, each with her own
rock.

It's been two or three hours since the warden left her on
the cliff top. Or an hour. Who knows. Maybe they've
forgotten you. She's talking out loud again. Has to hear a
human voice. Why are they making you stand? What kind
of work is this, not moving, just being? Is it a punishment?
What are they doing with you here?

And then, when her legs are practically buckling—
footsteps. Light and fast, tapping up the rocky path. A
warden. Not the one from the morning. Sounds younger.

"Move yourself, *banda*, Comrade Tito is giving you a
break for food and toilet."

Grabs her arm with a strong hand, pulls her away,
marches her. They walk. She must put one foot in front
of the other. A canteen is shoved into her hand, and then
a rough, rusty tin plate. Vera smells bread and potato and
something else—tomato? Could it be a tomato? It must be
a holiday outside. What month is it? Her dry mouth fills
with saliva. Her mind is addled. It's been more than a year
since she tasted a tomato. She mustn't eat yet. The warden
is humming a love song to Josip Broz Tito. Vera bites hard
on the insides of her cheeks. A restraining technique.
Sometimes the wardens keep them sitting in the dining

room, starving, for almost half an hour while they stand
there singing their songs, frothing themselves up.

"Hey, whore, are you really blind?"

"Yes, Commandant."

"Liar. Stinking *banda.*"

"Yes, Commandant."

"Why are you lying? Comrade Tito doesn't like liars."

A quick shadow passes this way and that in front of
her open eyes. A familiar shadow: that's how the wardens
check if she really can't see.

"*Yaou!*" the warden barks in her face. That was also to be
expected. As was the punch to her cheek. Don't cry. Vera
doesn't live here. The smell of tomato is heady. Soon she'll
be given permission and it'll be wonderful.

"Did you come here like this, or you got that way here?"

"Got what way, Commandant?"

"Blind."

"I came here healthy."

"I pray you don't leave here alive. Amen," she chirps.
"You have five minutes, scum. Comrade Tito says bon
appétit."

The morning's warden said ten. But the important
thing is she's allowed to eat. Vera crams the tomato into
her mouth with both hands. This is no time to save the
best for last. She licks and sucks. A soft, overripe tomato,
rotten, but bursting with juice and flavor. Her gut is
so astonished it starts to bubble. "Is there any paper,
Commandant?"

"Of course, just say the word. I've got some with pink
flowers on it—is that good enough for your ass, Your
Highness?"

Vera feels around. Touches a rock. Puts the tin plate down on the ground, crawls away on all fours. She remembers to take the canteen. Memorizes the number of steps and the direction. Crouches, pulls down, knows the woman is watching her. This would have been inconceivable once.

She has a moment of indecision. What's more urgent, drinking or pissing. The smell of urine is sharp and concentrated and makes her a little dizzy. There are maybe three sips left in the canteen. The water runs out long before the thirst. Fortunately she has no trouble with constipation. Some of the women here lose their minds because their time is measured on a clock. She wipes with her hand, then the hand on a rock. There's almost no soil on the island. All that's left from the winds are barren rocks. Even a leaf of grass you can't find here. Vera crawls back to the plate. It is kicked toward her by the toe of a shoe. The potato is practically raw, but it's big. She chews fast. How long does she have left? Mimi the cook used to make *restani krumpir* for little Vera. Roast potatoes. Just the name makes her salivate. She shuts her eyes and eats a potato cooked in its skin and mashed and fried in golden butter and garnished with curls of crispy fried onion. But the potato in her mouth makes the sound of an apple. Well then, she's savoring an apple. Who said she lacks imagination? She chews the apple and sees her childhood home, the kitchen shelves lined with jams and compotes, pears and plums and cherries boiled in water and poured into large canning jars. Tomato juice cooked until it boils, then poured carefully into bottles. She chews compulsively. She's an alchemist. Turning the potato into roasted red peppers marinated in oil with lemon and garlic. Into cucumbers pickled in the sun with dill. Into sausages smoked in the backyard. She smiles with her whole mouth. She is eating game meat marinated in spices for a whole week, not a moment less, so that it loses the gamy, wild flavor . . . Her head spins from the aromas. There is no warden. There are no bedbugs. There are no dead eyes that see only black with white flashes. There is no room in Belgrade with two doors and three colonels in uniform who tell her: You have three minutes to decide. Two. One. There is no thought that leaves her brain singed with a horrific mistake as large as life itself.

"Time's up, whore. Get up."

"But I didn't drink yet, Commandant. There wasn't enough water in the canteen."

"Your problem."

And she's moved again. A little to the right, back to the left. Small step forward, two back. This warden isn't pleased either. "Move your ass, whore. Stand here!" A marionette, a marionette, but in which play?

"From now until they come to arrange you again, you don't move, understand? Don't even breathe!"

"Yes."

Mistake. A slap, and a spit. Saliva dribbles down her arm. Abundant.

"Yes, Commandant. Sorry."

"And what did I say?"

"Don't move and don't breathe, Commandant." The sun bores through her shaved skull. There are parts in the brain that bubble like boiling water, and there is one place where she is suddenly sharp and alert, a partisan, a forest creature that will not miss a chance: the sips the warden took from the canteen before she spat on her. Four or five, it was. You could hear the water filling her mouth before she spat.

"Someone will come at sunset to take you back down to the barracks."

"Yes, Commandant." The warden's spit is crawling into the crook of her elbow, but the warden is in no hurry.

"Tell me something, but answer from the heart: You and your friends, did you really think you were going to bring Stalin down on us to beat Comrade Tito?"

"Yes, Commandant." If only she'd leave already, get out of here. When Vera worked in the swamps, they used to drink the polluted water. They stood there for days on end in the water, pissing and shitting in it, and then drank. The thirst beat out the fear of typhus. The warden's spit slowly drips down Vera's arm. She feels it sliding down cold, then warming, then slowly drying. Evaporating.

But the warden is intrigued: "So how did they not kill you on the spot, hey? How did they take pity on you? Were you a high-up's cunt?"

"No, Commandant."

"Traitors like you should die."

"Yes, Commandant." Just make her go already, please, please, let there be a miracle.

"That's what I always say. Comrade Tito is too kind, leaving scum like you alive."

"Yes, Commandant."

"Polluting our homeland's air."

"That's true, Commandant."

"Remember: don't budge, don't breathe!"

"Yes, Commandant."

Footsteps. Quiet. She must have left. But even if not, it's a lost cause. The tongue probes over her arm. Reaches as far as it can, all the way to the crook of the elbow. Nothing. Dried up, evaporated. The skin dry and salty.

Soon after sundown, a warden comes to take her back to the barracks. Vera can barely stand. The women in the barracks are curious. They want to know where she was, what she did all day. They know she can't talk. There are informers among them, and there are wardens disguised as prisoners, and there are provocateurs working full-time for the UDBA who have the ear of "the decapitator" in Belgrade.

Women circle around her, bump into her as if by mistake. Whisper. They just want her to tell them if it's harder up there than with the rocks. If she gets breaks. If she's alone. If she can see—or hear—the men working in the quarry on the other side of the island. Or at least smell their sweat in the wind? She doesn't answer. Drinks four mugs of water, falls on her bed, and sleeps. Until they come to wake her before sunrise.

Again they take her, the only one from the whole barracks, and again they position her. Stand this way, no that way, scum, move here, straighten out, arms up, arms down, spread your legs, close them, don't move now, understand? Yes, Commandant. You don't move until someone comes to rearrange you. Again the canteen is uncorked, and Vera's lips open like a newborn's, and the water is poured on the ground by her feet, and the smell of wet soil, and droplets on her arms, and they all evaporate before she can lick them.

Over the next hours, the next days, every so often, she hears from a distance, from the sea, the sounds of an engine. A boat or a ship sailing from the island to the mainland or to one of the nearby resort islets. Perhaps the passengers suntanning on the deck notice the tiny figure standing with its arms spread wide atop the bald mountain. They assume it's a statue. Or a little human-shaped lighthouse. Perhaps Commandant Maria put her up here so that the people on the boats would see her and think she was a symbol of something. But of what? What does she signify? The figure of a small woman. From afar she must look like a child.

Suddenly a twisted thought stabs her: she is a memorial. A monument to Nina. They put her up here because of Nina. Because Nina was thrown onto the streets. This way everyone sailing on a luxury ship will see, and they will know the punishment meted out to someone like her, someone like Vera, a woman who loved too much.

Two hours later, at 4:15 a.m., I wake up feeling tight in my chest. Waves of anxiety flood over me. I lie waiting for the heart palpitations to subside. For a few minutes I am prey to all sorts of thoughts and pictures. Even my agreement with Meir—not to think bad thoughts about myself before 9:00 a.m.—doesn't work this time.

Nina is in a deep sleep. Vera is pressed up against her in a fetal position. I touch Vera's shoulder lightly, and she opens one eye, puts on her glasses, and sits up briskly, without asking, without complaining. I wrap her in Meir's sweater, which I brought to take fortifying sniffs of, and remember to grab a new notebook—I've already filled two—and at the last minute I also decide to take my stopwatch, which I carry whenever I'm on a set, hanging around my neck on a string; it can't do any harm.

Vera waits by the door, still not asking anything. All I need is one look to understand that she knows exactly what is about to happen. I don't let my excitement take over (which leaves me with only the nervousness). There is work to do, and we are going to do it. Nina rolls over and reaches out to my side of the bed. Looking for me. It's *me* she's looking for in her sleep. We stand watching, mesmerized, as her hand probes, trembles, relinquishes. She sighs in her sleep and we hold our breath: What will we say if she wakes up? How will we explain it?

We tiptoe out. I feel overcome with disgust. Enough, enough with the lies. We go down to the lobby, which is dark and bare apart from one spot of light on the front desk, and another above a planter containing a grand, regal coleus. I drag an armchair over for Vera, sit her down, and run to the elevator to call Rafi. A moment before the door slides shut, I take a picture of her on my cell phone: a little old woman in the depths of an empty lobby. I go up to the third floor. Looking in the elevator mirror, I see a horse. In my state of shock, I formulate a fast, objective verdict: large, brawny woman with dark bags under her eyes. Slightly gruff femininity. Thus determines the script girl who examines me for three floors without blinking, without pitying (but that's also because of the puffy vest and the cargo pants with all the functional pockets). In short, the face of a producer is what I've got now. I leave the mirror with a neigh and knock softly on Rafael's door, which he opens in a second. He's dressed for work. The Sony is on the bed.

It's as if he's been sitting up all night, waiting for me to come get him.

In the elevator, I manage to squeeze out a smile, and he immediately reads me: "Is everything okay, Gili?"

"Everything's fine."

"Nervous?"

"A little."

"Well, with good reason." He spots the new notebook, orange, spiral-bound. "You're not writing enough." I remind him that I was busy shooting the whole way here. "Still," he retorts, "the details, the little details."

"About the little details . . ."

"What about them?"

"Was Stalin really planning to invade Yugoslavia in '48?"

"I don't know. But that's what Tito believed. And there were signs. That's why he set up the Gulags, or whatever they call them here, for Stalin's supporters and spies."

"And in your opinion, were Grandma and Grandpa really Stalinists?"

"Vera and Milosz? She'll eat you alive if you so much as suggest the possibility."

"But you—what do you think?"

"My rule of thumb is to always believe her."

I laugh. "That must make life easier."

He mumbles something about people keeping questions bottled up for years until they no longer have the guts to ask them. It's clear he's not talking about Stalin and Tito.

In the lobby we quickly get organized. We position Vera so that she's well lit. Drag another armchair over for me. During my absence she had time to take off her sweater and comb her hair (it's thinning, have I written that? her pink scalp shows through beneath it, like a fledgling that has yet to sprout a feather), and of course to put on lipstick, mascara, and a little blush.

"Such a lady, Grandma."

"Lady, schmady. A girl should always look spick-and-span. I say this to you, as well." She eyes my pile of hair, all curls and springs. "Birds could build a nest up there," she adds.

"Grandma," I say, "you know what we want to do now, right?"

"Well, yes." She takes a deep breath. I straighten her collar, smell her sharp perfume (she had time for that, too), tidy her hair in the back, covering the sparseness. She finds a speck of dirt on my shirt. Her hand smooths over my arm and for a moment holds on to it. The atmosphere feels strange, like the moments before an execution, when the convict and the executioner smoke a cigarette together.

I start off by looking for a way to soften her up. "Now, Grandma, before we begin, I want you to tell me one nice thing about you and Milosz. Doesn't matter what, just a few words."

"About Milosz? I already told you everything."

"Then tell me again, something little, something funny. I need to hear that before we start." In fact this is a variation on an old trick I learned from Dad: a second before clapping the board, I go over and whisper a few words in the actor's ear. A key image from the scene, or a line from a poem that evokes it. Not all directors love that, but hey, this is *my* film.

And it's my grandmother.

Vera gets right into the game: wrinkles her face, hums a quick few words to herself, puts on a smile. The trick worked. "We used to dance a lot, me and Milosz," she says. I ask for details. "When Milosz got healthy from tuberculosis and all the plagues he had, and we went back from his village to Belgrade, and we had a beautiful apartment, and I wasn't yet pregnant, and so happy we were both together . . . We used to pull down the blinds and put on the record player and dance for hours! We had same movements, and same rhythm, like twins, and we spun in the same moment . . ."

Rafi gives a thumbs-up. From his perspective Vera is completely in the mood; we can start.

"And Milosz used to sweat so pretty, Gili. He had smooth skin, maybe I told you once, without one hair, skin like suede. And after he was out in the sun, he was like a Negro . . ."

Rafi, behind her back, points to his watch and slashes his finger across his neck, but you try stopping Vera when Milosz is in the air.

"And we would have fun with friends, and they would shout to see me dance, and do you know how I danced? On the table, I did *csárdás*! Here there were glasses, and I danced between them, and one glass did not drop to the floor! And I hold up my skirt . . ."

Well, my little trick has spun out of control.

"To this day, you know, I love to hear 'Magical Moments' on the radio. They put on songs that Milosz and I danced, tango and slow fox, and every time they give a song like that, I can't resist and I dance with him, and tears come from my eyes."

"Lovely, Grandma, that's great. Exactly what I wanted to hear."

"Really?" She grins. "So I helped you?"

"A lot! Now let's talk about that other thing, you know."

"Oh, yes." She sinks back into the chair.

"Grandma, I can't go to that island without us talking."

Rafael adjusts the angle at which the armchairs face each other.

"But what if she comes down?" Vera whispers. "Isn't it better that we do it in Rafi's room?"

"I hope she does come," I reply.

"No, no, no! It will kill her!"

"She has to know," I insist, even though for some reason I'm slightly less confident now.

"Has to?" She whips my knees with the sleeve of my sweater. "How can she has to if she doesn't know she has to?"

"She does know," I repeat what I whispered to her at night, "she knows even without knowing."

"Not possible. Either you know or not know."

"Grandma, listen to me: everything Nina does, everything she says, every time she breathes, everything that hurts her, everything that's screwed up for her, it all comes from that place." Vera pushes my words away with a cluck of her tongue, and I feel like grabbing her and rattling her to make something finally penetrate. "It's her life, Grandma! She has to know what her life is made of!"

She gives a long, dismissive sigh, and I know I'm right, but I sound like a Girl Scout troop leader.

"And you know what really bothers me more than anything, Grandma?"

"Well, let's hear."

"That I'm not completely sure who you're protecting in this secret—her or you?"

"*Me?* Gili!" My grandmother flares up, horrified. And for one long, effervescing gaze we are enemies, heart and soul, and it's intolerable.

"All this talk about how a person must always know the entire truth, and must, how you say it, *come to terms* . . . That's all very nice, Gili, and very clean and moral, good for you"—she claps her hands for me three times—"but I'm saying you cannot suddenly come to a sixty-three-years-old woman and say, Listen, honey, what you thought is not exactly how it was, and all your life you are actually living in a mistake."

"In a lie," I correct her.

"No! No! Lie is when someone wants to hurt you. And here is maybe, *maybe,* just someone who had no choice."

Rafi signals at me to tone it down. He's right. If we get embroiled in an argument, she'll clam up.

"And I tell you something more, Gili, and you should remember very well what I say: if she knows, she will not want to live—she will not want to live! I know my daughter."

"How about letting her decide for herself? She's not a child!"

"If she knows, she will go back to be like a child."

"So it's better to leave her in a lie until the end?"

Vera holds back. She blinks frequently. In her fading eyes I can read: It's not for much longer.

She crosses her arms over her chest. Rafi makes a winding-up motion with his hand.

"Okay, I understand. All right. Vera, please tell us what happened."

"Not like that"—she slams her palm on her thigh—"do not talk to me like that!"

"Like what? How was I talking?"

"Like you don't already know me."

We both breathe heavily, feeling bruised. It's hard for her; it's hard for me. It's hard for me knowing it's hard for her.

"Come on, Grandma," I say, my voice slightly cracking.

"Gili . . ." She cups me with her eyes, in the place where I always feel it most.

"I'm sorry, Grandma, I'm very nervous. Let's do this. Tell me what happened."

"Right, I will tell." She sits up straight and puts her hands on the armrests. "Rafi, is the cinematographer running?"

"In September '51, Milosz was in some horse race and he broke a shoulder bone, and he was half his body in a cast. He had sick leave, but went every day to visit his soldiers on the cavalry team. Then, one morning when he was home, phone call. His general calls him urgent. And he went, and did not tell me what happened there.

"But next morning, Milosz gives to Nina a ring. And I said: Are you crazy? How will we pay our bills? You see, Gili, that was only on twelfth of the month, and we were already in big restrictions! At four in the morning I used to go and stand in line for bottle of milk for the girl! For first leather pair of my shoes I stood in line day and night and day! Before that I had shoes of canvas that fold up like an accordion and the water all gets in . . ."

With outrageous distraction, she extends her legs and arches her left foot this way and that, eyeing it delightedly. And I remember how, as a little girl, I used to watch her, study her, having no other teacher for such things. I remember the way she smiled back then: the smile of a woman looking at her own lovely feet.

"And in that time, for example, so you can understand, Yugoslavia sent train cars full of frozen eggs to Czechoslovakia. Then ties were cut, and there was left one wagon in Belgrade at the train station, and they said citizens could come with bowls and take eggs, because they are leaking out of the wagon. And we went the three of us and took a whole egg, and all the way we laughed about the omelet we would make for all of us. So in such conditions Milosz goes out and buys a ring and gives to Nina?"

Rafi and I glance at the elevator every so often.

"The next day general calls him again. Milosz went first to buy wood and coal for winter. In his thought he was already preparing for me to be alone in winter, and then he said to me: The plaster cast scrapes my shoulder. Maybe you can put something in, at the top, something like bandage? And foolish me, I stuffed in bandages between the cast and his body." She shakes her head, as if still in disbelief. "At night he asked me forgiveness, because he has to write something urgent, and he sat in the kitchen and wrote about twenty pages. For Nina. Told her about the life he had, since his childhood in the village, and the school where he went in the city, and then the army and world war, and how we both rescued partisans from quislings, and he also wrote about me, very lovely things . . . How we met at the party, and how he waited for me at the station, he wrote everything so that Nina will know, and they took all that away from me, the UDBA, a few days later, when they searched the house. In my interrogation they read me his letter to Nina from beginning to end, trying to break me, but I wasn't moved even one muscle in my face—"

Rafael asks us to stop. Something in the lighting is bothering him. Too many shadows on our faces. He moves the armchairs again so that they're facing each other and closer together.

"Another thing he asked that evening—that Nina should go to sleep in our bed, next to him, and only then he moved her to her bed. Idiot me, I saw all this and did not understand he was saying goodbye to his life—how could I not understand?"

Her birdlike chest rises and falls quickly. I've never heard her retell these things like this. Not in such detail, not in this melody.

Here it is again, the powerful moment in a documentary film, when the interviewee, in the course of being filmed, changes her contract with the director and with herself and, without meaning to, begins to give herself genuinely.

"Next morning he says goodbye to me, gives kisses to me and to Nina, and goes to see the general, and he doesn't come home. It's two in the afternoon already, and I phone the minister of interior, but they say—No one here, everyone went home. With us, if Milosz was late home even one minute, he telephoned. I can already feel: something happened. I quickly take the bus to his friend, another colonel, and he looks at me: 'The army's security service took him, but we'll get him out, don't worry.' I do worry. Of course I worry. I run to see the minister's deputy. So you understand, because Milosz was commander of Tito's cavalry team, we knew all the crème de la crème, and this deputy I also knew from a holiday we were once together, and he even looked at me very nicely behind his wife's back. Never mind. So they tell me: 'Deputy is hunting. Come tomorrow.' I come tomorrow: 'He's at a doctor outside of town.' I understood then. Thank you very much.

"On Wednesday, seventeen October, I woke up Nina early and said to her: I'm going to look for Father. You get up now and eat breakfast that I made you, and I will comb your hair, and then you go straight to Jovanka and eat lunch and stay there with her girls until evening, and then I will come for you. Nina was sleepy and didn't understand why she had to get up so early, but she ate everything, didn't leave bite on the plate."

"Excuse me for a minute, Grandma, and Dad. Let's pause. I'm just thinking—have we totally given up on Nina's idea?"

Vera is annoyed at the interruption. "Which idea?"

"Of talking to future-Nina. To the Nina who will exist one day."

The three of us say nothing. If we're not addressing future-Nina, we must be filming something that's not going to end up in her film. Something that she won't be made aware of.

"I suggest we let Vera decide," Rafi says.

Vera thinks. Scrunches up her face. And then the authoritative wave of the hand: "Let's first go on, and in the end we decide."

"In the end? But we have to decide now if we're doing it or not."

"Where was I?" Vera skips over my question. "I see her like it's now, sitting at the table in blue pajama, drinking milk . . . Really, such a good girl she was."

Vera has made up her mind.

"She finished eating, got dressed, and I made her braids and wrote a note to Jovanka. When she left the house, I looked from behind the curtains, which I never did, but that day something went through my belly, to look at her, to see how she walks and how she skips down the sidewalk on hopscotch the children left, and how her body is lovely and small, and that she is like dancing when she walks."

Silence. Terrible weight. She sighs, bows her head. It is grief, this thing cutting through me now deep in my stomach. For the first time, grief for the child Nina. For the future she would not have. For the person she would never be. For me. I hand Vera a tissue, but she pushes my hand away.

"I am not embarrassed for my tears!"

"Film's running," Rafi murmurs.

"Suddenly I see standing outside this big man with leather coat, and I instantly thought he was from security services, and there was also a black car with engine on and black windows. And that man looks at Nina and nods his head at the black car, and still I had in my head—why is he looking that way at my girl? Why is he making sign about her to the driver? But also I thought: He's come to tell me that Milosz is getting out! After one minute he knocks hard on my door, and me, such an idiot, I say, 'Oh, thank God you came! Come in, would you like some tea?'

"He walks in, takes off his gloves, looks around the apartment, does like this with his gloves on his coat sleeve, and sits down, and suddenly he's nice—"

Vera demonstrates for the camera, mimicking the manners of a gentle, considerate man: 'Do you smoke, ma'am?'

"'Yes.'

"'Then first light a cigarette. Good. I'm sorry to inform you that he tried to commit suicide.'

"I shout: 'What? Is he alive or dead?'

"'I cannot tell you now. Come with me. You will receive all information at the military hospital, but before we leave there are some things I must know about ties you had with Russia.'

"And for maybe half hour he asks questions and I answer, I don't remember what, don't know anything. He asks about Russia, about Stalin, about spies that we supposingly were. It all gets mixed up in my head, I barely hold myself, until finally he says, 'Now we go. Take what you need for a long time.'

"I don't take anything. Only coat and bag. My whole body shakes. We go outside. The driver with black glasses sits in the car, and the man with coat suddenly shouts: 'Lie down, whore! So nobody sees you!'

"We get to the army hospital, it's all very fast, running, shouting, suddenly we stop and he says to me: 'You go in this door and I wait for you here, and it's best for you and your girl that you tell the right answer.'

"Answer to what? To who? He doesn't say.

"I go inside the room where a doctor colonel is standing, and two other colonels, who afterward I understood were army lawyers.

"They greet me nicely: Hello, ma'am, sorry for your loss. The one who is tall with bald head reads me a government document: 'Yesterday at sixteen-twenty hours, on sixteen of October, the guard left for one minute only, to the bathroom, and in that time Novak Milosz took out of his plaster cast some bandages and tied them together and hanged himself from the bed. His head was so badly twisted that he cut his neck and we could not help him. And we now request that you sign for us that you and him are Stalinists, and that you renounce your husband as enemy of the people, as Russian spy for Stalin.'"

"Wait, Grandma, slow down. I don't understand: They wanted you to confess that you were a Stalinist?"

"Of course they wanted!"

"And?"

"And what? I didn't confessed."

"Because you weren't."

"Exactly."

"So what happened?"

"Look, Gili, I was even willing to sign for them that I am Stalinist and that I'm also Satan himself, but not that Milosz is Stalinist and enemy of the people. Not that! Never!"

"I'm trying to understand: Because you were unwilling to say that Milosz was a traitor, just because of that, they sent you to Goli Otok?"

"Yes."

So I wasn't wrong and I wasn't hallucinating. When I lay in the ICU with no blood in my veins, she told me. Perhaps she thought I was unconscious. Perhaps she thought I was going to die and she wanted to finally get it off her chest.

In all the years since then, I've known it, I've felt it, but I didn't have the courage to ask her if it was true.

"Anyway they cared about me less," she says now, "they wanted Milosz. He was important, he was a big hero in World War Second, he was the commander of cavalry for Tito, and they wanted only for his wife to say before everyone that Novak Milosz is a traitor and supporter of Stalin against Tito."

"And if you'd said it?"

"Said what?"

"I don't know . . . That he, say, supported . . ."

"Gili!"

"I'm just asking, Grandma. Let's say you—"

"Absolutely not! There's no let's say! My husband was not a traitor! He was idealist! And the most honest and pure man!"

"Yes, of course, we know that—"

"No, you don't know! No one knows like me. Only me in all the world knew what a soul he was! And only I can say about him, no one else is there for him, Gili, and that is why I will not sign for them even if they throw me on Goli, even if they kill me, even if they take Nina—"

She stops. Her eyes are on fire. Her small head trembles with fury.

"But let's say, Grandma, let's just say you were willing to state that Milosz had betrayed them—would they really have let you go?"

"I don't know. Maybe yes. That's what they said."

"And you would have gone home to Nina?"

"Maybe. Yes. But then Milosz would be considered an enemy—"

"We know, but—"

"What is 'we,' Gili?" She peers at me over her glasses. "Is this also some interrogation?"

"No, it's just Rafi and I who want to know. Let's take a step back, Grandma."

Even calling her Grandma sounds grating.

"Ask." She takes out her compact mirror and tidies herself. "Ask, go on."

"I'm asking again, because I have to understand. You wouldn't say that Milosz was a traitor, and that is why they put you on the island?"

"What choice did I have?"

I give her an anguished look.

"Rafi." She talks to him, but her eyes are on me. "You promise me, yes?"

"Promise what?"

"That what I say here is absolutely not going in the movie Nina wanted."

Rafi doesn't answer. The loyalty of the orphaned little boy wavers. I skewer him with a look, but Vera is also good with skewers.

"Look"—he squirms—"I think we ought to have this material for once in an organized, comprehensive form."

"So you don't promise me?"

"I suggest we not make that decision now."

Her hands tighten on the armrests.

Rafi asks, "Do you want to go on?"

"I don't know anymore what I want and what I don't."

Interesting response, I note. "Come on, then." I lean over and slowly stroke her arm up and down, our family's Reiki treatment. "Tell me exactly what they said to you."

"Is that so important now? They said things."

"Yes, it's important. It's the most important thing."

"Then ask."

"What happened in that room?"

"What happened there? Let's see . . . That tall officer, with bald head, he said to me—and this I remember every word: 'We are honest with you, ma'am, the situation is that because your husband himself did not say one word in interrogation, did not confess anything, then he has no charge, and you can demand his pension for you and your daughter, but that is only if you sign for us.'

"I said: 'You want me to say instead of him that he is a traitor?' They said: 'Yes.' I said: 'And what else?' He said: 'Nothing. Just that tomorrow it will say in *Borba* and in other two or three newspapers that Novak Vera renounced enemy of the people, traitor Novak Milosz.'

"And they see me quiet, and the lawyer colonel says, 'Novak Vera, here in this room are two doors. One on the left is to freedom and to go home to your girl, and one on the right is to Goli Otok prison for many years with hard labor. You have now three minutes to decide.'

"And my brain, it's dead. My whole body is not alive. Prick me with a pin, Gili, I feel nothing. Milosz is dead, my great love is dead, what more is there for me to want."

She digs through her bag for a cigarette. Fishes out a crumpled pack of Europa. I haven't seen her smoke in years. I think about little Nina, who by that morning hour had probably reached Jovanka's house.

"Then the doctor colonel says: 'You maybe have not understood. You maybe want to drink some water and think more clear.'

" 'I don't want anything, only to die.' " She can't light the cigarette and I help her.

" 'Listen, Novak, again I tell you we are showing our cards to you: for reasons of security we do not want anyone to know that he died with us. He will be buried in the grave of unnamed. After you sign for us, you take your daughter and go with her to live in different city. You just give us here on paper a little scribble, and then you are forbidden to talk about it all your life. Even with your daughter you must not say anything. Now you have two more minutes to think.' "

"Go on, sign already," I hear myself suddenly murmur in a ghostly voice. Rafael is horrified, but Vera is so lost in her story that she doesn't seem to have heard me.

"I told them: 'I don't need two minutes or half minute. I will not renounce my husband. My husband I loved more than my life. My husband never was enemy of the people. You do what you want.' " She ashes into the lid of the cigarette pack.

"Then the second colonel, not the tall one, said: 'If so, then you go tomorrow on the ship to Goli Otok. You know what is Goli Otok.'

" 'I know.'

"And he said: 'Nina, your girl, will be on the street.'

"I said: 'That is your decision.'

"He told me: 'No, that is only your decision.'

"I said, 'I ask you very much, kind people: Nina has nothing to do with this, Nina can go to my sister Mira, or to my sister Rozi, or to my friend Jovanka. She must not be on the street.'

"And the colonel said again: 'Listen to me, woman. You will go to Goli Otok with hard labor, and Nina, your lovely little girl, will be on the street, I give you my word. And the street is the street.'"

Vera puts her hand to her chest.

"Grandma, would you like to take a break?"

"No. I want to tell."

During my inglorious career I have been, among other things, a researcher on several documentary films. Over and over again I've seen interviewees standing at this crossroads: either reveal the dark secret, or perpetuate the lie. It's amazing how many—mostly people on the verge of death—choose disclosure, simply because of a conviction that the truth must be preserved in some place in the world.

"Gili, what do you want to ask?" says Vera.

I gather up all the strength I don't have. "Tell me, Grandma, what did that mean, 'she'll be on the street'?"

"I don't know."

"Think."

"I don't know."

I try a different approach: "You said you asked them not to involve Nina?"

"Correct."

"Do you think, say, that you should have asked for a little more?"

"I asked as much as I could. That was the most I could."

"Yes. But maybe if you'd just been a little—"

"I don't know how to beg." She purses her lips. Looks away from me.

"Grandma, I'm sorry, but I have to ask. Did you ever hear about girls the UDBA threw on the street?"

"No."

"Not a single one?"

"I don't know. Maybe they said something about one or two. Maybe it's all rumors. That was a time of rumors."

"And what happened to them?"

"I don't know."

"What did the rumors say?"

"I didn't hear."

"Grandma—"

"Can we go on now?" she practically shouts. Her lips tremble and she does not wait for approval. I suddenly realize how badly she needs to tell this story—for it to be heard at last, to fully exist in the world.

Precisely because of how open and frank everything is now, I feel that a giant mistake is amassing: Why are we filming this conversation behind Nina's back? Why even now, a moment before we go to the island to finally cleanse ourselves of what's been polluting our family for three goddamn generations—what are we doing instead? What are we doing to her again?

"And they said to me: 'Novak Vera, think careful one more time. You have one minute to think.' And I again said: 'I don't need even one second.'

"And the doctor colonel said: 'You choose dead man over living girl? What sort of mother are you? What sort of woman are you? What sort of person are you?'

"I told him: 'I am not a mother anymore, I am not a woman, I am not a person. I am nothing. Mother and woman and person Novak Vera is dead. You killed her reason to live. I won't sign for you. Do what you want.'"

"Sign it!" I bark uncontrollably. This time Vera hears me. She leans back and gives me a long, dark glare. She nods her head with bitterness and disappointment, as if having discovered that beneath all my servile layers there is treachery in my blood. As if she's always known that at the pivotal moment I would betray her.

I remember what she told me when I was a young girl: "Don't let them twist my story against me."

That moment—

How there can suddenly emerge, out of that familiar, beloved visage, the face of a stranger. An enemy. Because we're at war, Grandma Vera and I. That is clear. Her eyes warn me not to cross the line. Beyond it lies desolation, *homo homini lupus,* with no preferential treatment for grandchildren. But this time I don't give in: I look her straight in the eye and watch her face pull back into sharp angles, and for the first time since she began telling the story, perhaps even since I've known her, I detect fear.

An unruly particle of her mind that was chained and muzzled for almost sixty years seems to have slipped out of her control, and it's screaming inside her head—What did you do? Good God, Vera, what did you do.

"The doctor colonel goes to the right side door and opens it, and there stands the one with the black coat, and someone hits my head from behind, I don't know who, and I walk to the one with the coat, and he grabs me, hard, like this—" She grips her arm and shows the camera. "And I want him to take me to Nina, to tell her what happened, so she will know to stay with Jovanka for a few days, and then Jovanka will take her to my sister Mira, or to my sister Rozi . . ."

She chokes up. She resumes talking but chokes again. Swallows down the tears.

"But the man with the coat says to the driver: 'Take the whore straight to jail.'"

She sinks back in the armchair, her shoulders drooping. "My sweet Ninotchka," she whispers to the camera, to future-Nina who has popped up again, "how can I sign it? How can I tell everyone that your father was a traitor?"

"Because he's dead," I answer, "and Nina is alive."

"Milosz was not a traitor, Gili."

"How could you, Grandma?"

"I loved him."

"More than you loved your daughter?"

"More than I loved my life."

I can't take it anymore. I get up and pace around the empty lobby in circles. When I walk past my father he whispers, "Ask her if she would do the same thing today." I go back and sit down opposite her.

She leans toward me, hiding her mouth with her hand, and whispers, "And you? Didn't you commit suicide once because of a man?"

"But I didn't kill another person."

She flinches as if I'd slapped her. She lights another cigarette and offers one to my father. Not to me. She orders him to stop filming, and he obeys. Her hands are shaking. What am I doing to her? If she acknowledges what she did, she will crumble into a heap of sawdust right here. Rafael shares the cigarette with me. We both quit smoking years ago, after his heart attack, but now we pounce on the opportunity to singe our tongues and the roofs of our mouths.

"I am not a liar," Vera murmurs to herself in the smoke, "not a liar. I even once in my life never lied! So maybe one single time I did not tell Nina all the truth, but that was for her good, so that she wouldn't—oh, look who's here!" she exclaims and coughs out smoke that engulfs the three of us. She waves. "Hello, Nina, honey, we're over here! Good morning, how did you sleep?"

Nina steps out of the elevator. Disheveled, a little dazed, yawning. "How long have you been here?" The suspicion wakes up long before she does, scrunching up her eyes.

"We were just shooting something to prepare for Goli," Rafi explains with a helpless chuckle. His expression makes him look ugly. Vera and I follow suit with our own helpless chuckles. We stink of dishonesty. "Grandma was telling all sorts of anecdotes before we go to the island."

"Oh." Nina's nostrils widen. She picks up information from the air and filters it through, but she's still too sleepy to decipher it. She takes the cigarette from Vera's hand. "But when did you come down? I didn't hear a thing. Is there any coffee? My head is exploding from the whiskey."

Rafi and I dash over to the empty reception desk and ring the call bell. A sleepy clerk says he'll try and find something, but there's no real chance because the kitchen isn't open yet. Rafi and I lean on the counter, looking back at Vera chatting with Nina. "What whiskey?" he asks, but I ignore the question. Nina says something; Vera throws her head back and laughs.

"I didn't get to ask if she'd do the same—"

"I noticed."

"It's too bad you didn't remind me before."

"Yes."

"And you knew that's how it happened, didn't you?"

"How what happened?"

"That they gave her a choice."

"Yes." He enlists all his powers not to avoid my eyes.

"So in fact you knew that Nina wasn't just abandoned."

"What . . . I don't understand."

"That she was abandoned *and* betrayed."

That word stabs him deep down inside.

"Do you understand? She didn't just abandon her daughter—she betrayed her. Her own daughter, my mother. She betrayed her."

"Yes. That's what it is," he murmurs to himself, "abandoned and betrayed."

The two women are in a cloud of smoke that curls up to the lamp above them. Vera smokes with short, frequent drags. Nina—slowly, pleasurably. She runs a questioning look over us. Rafi and I signal to her that there's a problem with the coffee. She signals that maybe we should go out and find a café. We signal: Okay. She signals: Just let me finish my cigarette. She inhales lustily. Rafi and Vera and I swallow her up with our eyes.

That strange, evasive quality of hers.

She is here and she is not here. Seen, but also remembered.

After three or four days, or a week, who knows, who can remember, a new warden takes her up. She leads Vera by a rope, and walking behind her is almost tolerable, with no collisions and no falls, as if the two of them have learned to coordinate their steps. Judging by her voice, this warden is very young, and judging by the funny, drawling accent—she's from Montenegro. It's hard to believe how garrulous she is. She's been through her reeducation. Been through all the stages. She started off like Vera, as one of the *bojkots,* the women considered nonhuman and shunned in every way, advanced to the *bandas,* the scum of the earth gang members, and got all the way to the *brigadas,* the ones who confessed to crimes they did or did not commit, agreed to act as informers, and were taken back under the wing of Comrade Tito.

The warden is cheerful: she's getting out of here soon. She will train as a seamstress and get married. She already has a groom waiting in her village. He's a little chubby, but a good man with a desirable vocation: he's a cooper. They'll have five kids. Vera listens to the pretty sounds she makes as she talks, but she's constantly on guard: this warden can't really be talking to her like this. Vera should stay quiet and not even listen. Stop any thoughts from popping into her head and escaping out of her mouth.

When they get to the top, the young girl laughs happily at the view of the wide-open sea, and Vera's breath stops at the sound of her voice.

It's like she's a child, Vera thinks.

"Let's see, whore," says the warden sweetly, "do you already know where to stand in the morning?"

Vera shakes her head and points to her eyes.

The girl laughs. "I forgot. I'm such a nitwit. Stand here. Now don't move!"

"Commandant," Vera whispers, "why am I here?"

"What do you mean 'why'?" She lands a single blow on Vera's chest, but not a very hard one. Just going through the motions.

"What are they doing with me? What am I doing here?"

Silence. Now she's really gone too far.

"Didn't they tell you?"

"No."

"No one told you?"

"No."

She laughs in surprise. One can imagine her strong white teeth and her red gums. "Then why should *I* tell you?"

Vera bets the whole pot: "Because you're a human being."

She hears a breath cut off in an instant. Like a baby's short whimper. There is something about this girl that, on Goli Otok, is almost inconceivable. "Look, it's not . . . I'm not allowed . . ." And then a quick whisper into Vera's ear: "Commandant Maria's plant is up here, you know that, right?"

"No."

"They didn't even tell you that?"

"No."

"Commandant Maria brought it from home."

"Home?" Vera has never considered that Commandant Maria might have a home. This is all very confusing. And what does she mean, a plant? What is a plant doing here?

"She's from a village near Rijeka."

"But what for?"

"What do you mean 'what for'? So it'll grow."

"What?"

"The plant. Her sapling."

"I don't understand," Vera whispers in despair.

"Nothing grows in this place, right?" The girl says what Vera already knows. No sapling could set roots in these barren rocks.

She hears the canteen being uncorked. Water pours out plentifully. A few drops spray onto her arms. She licks them thirstily, knowing this warden won't hit hard.

"Is it big?"

"What?"

"The plant."

"You have a lot of questions. Enough, shut up, whore."
Vera pictures her young face scrunched up in the anger of
regret at having been tempted into kindness.

"Please, Commandant, just tell me that, I have to know."

"It's tiny," the warden grumbles. "I'll gouge your eyes
out with a teaspoon if you tell anyone we talked." Then
she laughs. "Well, you don't have eyes anyway. Now don't
move, do your job here and shut up, understand?"

"But what is my job?"

The girl leaves. Vera doesn't even wait for her footsteps
to get far away before she hunches down. The smell is
dizzying. Wet, rich soil, soil from another world. She does
not have the courage to immerse her hands in the soil and
stir it around. She quickly stands up, frightened and happy.
She stretches her arms out. Who ever thought there could
be such hunger for earth? She hears herself laugh. It's been
a long time since she heard that sound.

There is a little plant here. The thought delights her,
excites her. As if a baby had been placed in her arms.

At night a woman pushes up against her on the bench.
Vera wakes up, startled. They must be coming to take her.
Interrogation, or worse. The woman silences her with a
touch to her lips and whispers: "I know what you're doing
up on the mountain."

"Who are you?"

"Never mind. Don't shout."

"How do you know?"

"Wardens talk. There's a plant up there, isn't there? A
sapling? Something of Maria's?"

Vera keeps silent. She has no doubt that this woman is an informant. Someone trying to get her in trouble and earn a few points.

"Get out of here," Vera whispers, "or I'll shout."

The woman's voice flows hurriedly into her ear: "When I got to the island and ran between the two rows, you were the only one who didn't spit at me."

Vera connects the voice with the face and body. A tall, noble-looking woman, thin as a skeleton, with crazy, frightening blue eyes. She ran through the lines holding some sort of round instrument close to her chest, probably a mandolin. They all saw that she was trying to protect the instrument, and this inflamed them even more. They hit her so she dropped the mandolin, and kicked it viciously until it shattered. Vera got ten lashes because she was only pretending to beat the woman.

"She put together a place up there," the woman whispers into her ear, "Maria. Her own private whore-house with a sea view. She brings girls at night."

Forty lashes, this conversation could cost. No one makes it out alive, or sane, after forty lashes.

"And she said she wants to see a little green up there."

Vera doesn't understand. "At night?"

"Why not? Or maybe it smells good? Did you smell it?" A deep breath, warm vapors on her ear. The woman sighs. Vera's body slackens slightly. A forgotten emotion is mingled in that sigh. The woman whispers: "Goldman. Professor of musicology, Goldman Erika. Nice to meet you."

Vera is dying to say she's also pleased to meet her. To taste the words of politeness. She says nothing.

"From the minute I heard there's a plant on the island," the woman says softly, "I felt better immediately. Like there's hope of getting out."

Vera tries to understand what she's hearing. The woman's words don't always cohere into intelligible sentences. After the last weeks on the mountain it's hard to conduct a logical conversation. Logic, in general, is a demanding and exhausting affair. You have to sustain a chain of facts that come in a particular sequence. Vera turns her face, searching for the woman's ear. "But what am I doing there?"

Again the dance of the faces, she has to turn her face to the wall, so that the other woman can whisper in her ear: "Didn't they tell you?"

"No."

Someone in the corner of the barracks, near the bucket, cries in her sleep. She promises this is the last time she'll be late for school. The two women freeze. Vera feels the woman's beating heart on her back.

"Just tell me," the woman whispers, "did you touch it?"

Vera is astonished. It hadn't occurred to her to touch it. Nor to smell it. So powerful is the fear of the wardens.

"Touch it once for me. Promise." The fervor of her whisper tells Vera it might have been this request that made the woman take such a risk. Vera is despondent at the thought of how cowardly she herself is. She hadn't even dared to smell it. A familiar taste of error sours inside her. Of the wrong choice. Of a terrible incompatibility with reality, reality as it is known by everyone else. Goldman Erika suddenly kisses Vera on the earlobe, on the cheek, a soft kiss and then another, painfully pleasant, and in an

instant, moving as smoothly as a little animal, she slips off
Vera's bed and vanishes.

The next day at dawn, after the warden has watered it
and positioned Vera and left, Vera tries to focus her gaze on
it, but all she sees is darkness with the occasional crack of
white. She must not move. She tries to smell it from where
she was positioned, but the scent of wet earth is strong
and fills the air. She distractedly touches her earlobe, her
cheek, the spots where she was kissed, and suddenly Milosz
flickers inside her—just for an instant, but that's enough for
her. He has finally come. He took his sweet time getting
here.

All at once she drops to the ground, squats on her heels,
and feels around until she touches a little mound of stones.
She runs both hands over it as though she were blessing a
child's head. With her fingers she studies the mound. It's
arranged in a circle. The plant must be in its center. She
still doesn't dare touch it. It's enough for her to know that
it's here. She carefully enters the circle with her fingers and
touches the damp earth, but is instantly driven to a frenzy
and sinks her fingers all the way down to their roots. A
feeling of marvelous abundance floods her. This soil—such
ample goodness. Whoever touches it will be protected
from evil. She holds her muddy fingers up to her face
and inhales deeply. She puts a damp clod on her tongue
and dissolves it, and without thinking she swallows and
splutters and laughs. Her fingers are drawn back into the
circle, and now they hover over something soft and delicate
and slender.

A small, short plant. Tiny leaves. After months of
pushing rocks, her fingers are rough and crude, and she can

barely feel the leaves. That is why she touches them with the inside of her wrist. Unbelievable softness.

She strokes them, without pressing, she doesn't want to cause any harm, God forbid, but she touches enough so that something of the plant, a faint, unfamiliar aroma, will cling to her fingers.

She smells, inhales. The richness is almost uncontainable.

Hearing a sound, she leaps up to her feet. False alarm: down in the gulf, in the sea, a wooden beam clattered on the rocks.

A little sapling. Tiny leaves. Leaflets, full of life. Perhaps there's also a stalk, though she's not sure now, and she needs urgently to know: Is there a stalk? More than one? And how are the leaflets arranged? Crowded? Spacious? Or in pairs, facing each other? How did she fail to notice these things? She's too afraid to lean down and touch it again. But the touch lives in her: like thin velvet, because the leaves are downy. Everything is so delicate. Vera sighs longingly. It's so slight and fragile, and it's clear to her that the little sapling doesn't stand a chance in a place like this, in this sun, without a drop of shade.

Then there is a short period of time, like the instant between a strong blow and the pain, or between the moment bad news is uttered and when it seeps into comprehension, and in that particle of time Vera feels nothing and does not think, but she knows. An ugly, crude laugh bursts out of her, a vomit of laughter, and her body recoils from the plant, and she just wants to run away, not to be anywhere. How stupid she's been—a blind cow. Because she suddenly understands what she's doing here on the mountaintop, what they're doing with her and how they're using her, using her body, from sunrise to sunset.

Yesterday at four in the afternoon there was finally a lull in the storm, and we sailed to the island. The forecast said it would only kick up again at night. By then, we thought, we'd be on a plane back to Israel. We paid a fortune to a man who owned a little fishing boat, the only person who would agree to ferry us to the island in such bad weather. He demanded payment in advance, and cursed and spit into the water after Rafi handed him the cash. He hated himself and his greed, but mostly he hated us. He would wait for an hour after we disembarked, he said, tapping his watch, not a minute longer, and then he'd sail back to the mainland with or without us. We did the math: one hour on the island, forty minutes to sail back, two and a half hours to drive to Belgrade—we could do it. It would be down to the wire, but we'd make our flight.

I'm trying to recount the events in an organized fashion, as they occurred, to maintain continuity.

For most of the passage we stood close to the bow. We swayed with the boat, the wind and seawater whipped at us, and the air stank of dead fish. The fisherman grunted about the approaching *bora*—the strong northern wind. The police were already closing off roads: the wind would be powerful enough to pick up cars.

And then I saw the shadow of the island through the fog, and my knees went weak.

I went into the cabin. I wanted to be alone for a moment, before stepping onto the island.

The rain made a surprising comeback. Heavy, dense rain.

This is what I wrote: The island is visible now. How does it feel? Some fear. A kind of awe.

I step back outside.

Nina says something to me. I can't understand. She shouts in my ear: Goli looks so much like her island in the Arctic. They both resemble the head of a giant crocodile lurking in the water.

The boat enters a little anchorage. Decaying wooden bridge. Wood beams floating around. Swollen carcass of a rabbit stuck in a clump of seaweed. Harsh, sweeping wind. Hard to talk and hard to hear. The rain prickles every inch of exposed skin like needles. The fisherman ties the boat to a small stone post on the shore and secures it against the concrete harbor wall. He doesn't help us off the boat. Rafael climbs onto the stone pier and holds out his hand. First Vera steps off, then Nina, then me.

I'm on the island. I'm on Goli.

Empty and barren. We're alone on the island. Only a madman would come here in this storm. The fisherman unties the rope and quickly sails away. I hope he's just looking for a safer spot to anchor for the next hour.

I still find it hard to grasp that we're on Goli Otok. The cold wind and the rain make it impossible to feel celebratory. Of course none of us thought to bring an umbrella, but it wouldn't have helped in this wind anyway. Vera darts among the puddles, agape. I'm afraid she'll fall, and then what? Rafi follows her with the Sony. I leave them. Again—I want to be alone to absorb my first encounter with the place.

I'm surprised to see a number of stone structures. Two-story barracks. This was not what I imagined. There's a train track, too, probably for transport between the island's two camps. I read somewhere that the Croatian tourism board wants to turn the island into a tourist attraction. But what most surprises me is the flora—trees and bushes. When Vera was here nothing could grow, and I imagine the changes happened after they shut down the "reeducation camp" and turned the island into a prison for criminal offenders.

Vera keeps pointing to things, slaps both hands to her cheeks: this was like this, and this was like that. Her eyes glimmer: "Here was the first time we got off the ship *Punat,* and longtime prisoners stood in two lines and made a *Spalier* for us, a sort of fence, like an honor guard, and we had to run between the lines, and old-timers screamed at us like animals and spat and hit with hands and with planks that had nails and with whips, and girls lost eyes, lost teeth, almost died. That was our welcome, and a month later we ourself stood in two lines and new girls ran down the middle. And here was Commandant Maria's hut, there is still its floor. Later they built all houses from stone. Where's Gili? Come see—" She pulls me by the hand, moving lighter than I do in this place, practically floating in her puffy down coat. "Here stood Maria when new girls arrived on the ship, and she screamed: *'Ispadaj!* Out!' Girls were so terrified they wet their pants. And here was headquarters, and here drainage ditch for the kitchen and latrine that we dug with our hands, here you can even see its line going down to the sea." Vera talks quickly, breathlessly. "And here was barbed-wire fence we put around, like as if someone would even want to come in here, or as if someone had strength to run away. The Adriatic Alcatraz, that's what they call it still now." Rafi hurries after her, filming and offering a supportive arm.

Nina is still in shock. I think she's taking the blow of the island harder than all of us. She gazes about as if she cannot understand where she is. I go over and link my arm with hers. It's hard for me to imagine that she might waste our single hour of grace here staring into space.

Vera claps her hands: "And this was toolshed. Here they gave us in the morning hammers to break stones. And here they kept the *tragać,* stretchers, and also on them we put rocks to carry up, and here was the yard for roll call, where they would punish you in front of everyone and you had to confess and be beaten in front of everyone. This is where we lived, in huts. Here is our row, here is my hut. Here stood my bed. Wooden bench with a bit of straw and bedbugs. Look, there are marks from beds on the floor."

Everything is ugly, the way violence is ugly. Doors ripped out, objects burned beyond recognition. Rust and ashes. A concrete surface sprouting crooked iron rods, barbed-wire spears twisting in shattered windows. Vera hurries along the walls, pointing and murmuring the names of prisoners who slept in each bed. Her feet step lightly, as if they're thirty years old again. She skips over cold mounds of embers, over planks with nails sticking out, over shreds of tires and rusty cans.

The rain stops. A pale sun comes out for a moment and disappears behind the clouds. The light is gray and murky. What will we even be able to see in the remaining half hour, and why did we put ourselves under this constraint? We're such a screwed-up family. Such an ungenerous family. What would have happened if we'd stayed on the mainland for one more day and tried to sail here tomorrow, when all the forecasts promised almost springlike weather? In other words, why does everything that has anything to do with Nina end up crooked?

All at once the initial wave of excitement tanks, as if it's been worn out. We keep walking around, but more slowly, and each to ourselves. We peer into collapsed buildings, walk through perforated walls. Vera points to the sky: it's turning black again. The clouds suddenly hurtle toward the island from all directions, like a mob hurrying to a fight. We're going to have a rough passage back.

I walk on a path paved with stones, feeling strangely limp. As if I'd had a strong desire that was sated too quickly. I reach a spot from which you can see the mountaintop: Vera's mountain. The cliff where she stood for fifty-seven days in the blazing sun is now hidden in a mist. I look for the place where the path starts climbing up, but it's covered by a giant puddle. There obviously won't be time to climb to the top. I won't be able to stand there for even five minutes above the gulf. I won't put my feet on the spot where she stood, and I will not retell the things she told me about those days.

From the window of one of the huts I see a strange scene: out on a large field stand a few dozen boulders, almost human-sized. They are all slightly rounded and seem to be hewn. They stand darkly, they stand *together*—not just side by side—and there is something troubling about them, as though they have a consciousness.

My father sees them, too, and he runs over. I don't remember ever seeing him run. He shoots the massive rocks from every angle. Then he puts two hands on one of them, tries something, and moves on to another one. He tries again, then moves to a third. He puts his hands straight up against the rock, takes a deep breath, and pushes. I run to help him. He makes room for me next to him.

The minute my hands touch the rock, something in me comes full circle and I burst into tears. I can hardly stop it. What am I crying about? About everything there is to grieve. In the rain and the wind Rafi senses immediately and he hugs me. He slowly strokes my head until I calm down.

Then we try to push the rock together. It will not budge. Vera walks out of the barracks and comes to help. I'm certain, absolutely positive, that the minute Vera touches the rock, it will start rolling upward. She stands next to me and puts her hands on it. The three of us groan and pant, but the rock is indifferent. I shout into her ear: "How did you push it?" She shouts back: "Nina is waiting for medicine!" I close my eyes and push with all my strength: Nina's waiting for medicine, Nina's waiting for medicine.

"Where is Nina?" Vera suddenly asks. Nina is standing some distance away, on a pile of gray rocks near the waterline. She motions for us to look away. She's trying to find a spot to pee. A minute goes by, two minutes. We turn around slowly and she's gone. Nothing but rocks and sea. The spot devoid of Nina fills us with terror. Rafi starts walking, then running, toward the shore. For a moment he disappears, too, then reappears, clambering up the rocks beyond a crease in the ground, and waves at us reassuringly: She's here. We walk over. She's lying behind a rock with her pants and underwear down, grinning. A little startled, completely soaked.

"I'm stuck," she explains, "I twisted my ankle on the stones."

Rafi wraps Nina in his coat and examines the rocks she's trapped between. "Are you in pain?" "No. Maybe a little." Her foot looks intact but twisted in a choreography I cannot comprehend. She tugs on Rafi's beard: "Hey, what exactly are you looking at?" "You have the legs of a young girl." "Glad you're enjoying it." "I'm going to get something." Rafi runs. A fast man erupts from him. I can barely catch up. Vera falters after us. I think she's getting tired. Nina is alone on the shore again, and we, as usual, feel it immediately. The us-square is always leaking from Nina's side.

Rafi shouts and gesticulates to explain what we're looking for: a stick or an iron rod to pry the rock off her foot. I check my watch: fifteen minutes to go. We won't make it. We seriously won't. A thought: Maybe Vera and Rafael should run to the dock and sail back to the mainland? Nina and I will spend the night here. I'll take care of her. In the morning they'll come back for us. I find a rusty iron rod, part of a collapsed barbed-wire fence. Rafi manages to extract it from the fence without getting injured. It's been ages since I've seen my father such a man.

The idea grows on me. I like the thought of spending the night here, alone with Nina, in the purifying storm with all the family ghosts. We hear the boat honking from the dock. The fisherman is also looking up at the sky and seeing what's coming. Rafi bolts over to Nina with the rod. She lies there, withering. I've noticed: all at once, sometimes within seconds, the life runs out of her. Vera always said Nina was spoiled. But it's not that. What does being spoiled have to do with it? How dare she.

Rafi looks for somewhere to anchor the rod. He says something to Nina and she awakens to him, laughing. She's lying there with her ass exposed in the pouring rain, and the situation amuses her. It's amazing how her dignity is untouched even in that state. It might have actually been interesting to grow up with her for a few years.

The fisherman honks irritably. We ignore him. At this point there are sparks of illicit cheerfulness flying through all four of our heads. Rafi sticks the rod in the ground next to Nina's ankle. His hands are covered with rust, and he washes them off in the rain. "One minute," Nina shouts at him, "one minute I wouldn't last in this place. How did she make it for two years and ten months?" Thunder rolls in over us. Nina is shivering. The top rock won't budge. The rusty rod isn't making a dent. Rafi tries to lodge it under the rock that's trapping her foot, to release it a little so her foot will have some wriggle room. It's hard for him to concentrate. "Can you smell my pee?" "Any minute now the rain will wash everything away." The boat's honks are becoming hysterical. Suddenly there's the sound of an explosion, and a red flare sails through the sky and slowly nose-dives. "Leave me here," Nina says, just as I was about to suggest they leave me here with her. "Yeah, right," says Rafi, struggling, "that's exactly why we brought you all this way." "Rafi, I'm serious. Do me a favor, stop that for a minute!" She pounds on his chest with both hands and he stops. He hovers over her, swaying on the rod that separates them. Their bodies do not touch. They look into each other's eyes. "Listen to me, think logically." "Leave you here alone? That seems logical to you?" "It's my logic. Give me one night here alone. A final act of kindness, Rafi."

The fisherman gives one more long, violent honk. Vera is standing next to me, looking sullen. Her hand feels around for mine and clasps it. The wind is going wild, and Vera's lips are blue. I wipe her glasses with my finger, then pull-push her against the wind into the closest barracks. All the windows are broken and the walls are threadbare, but at least there's a partial roof. I sit her down in one corner between two walls, as if she's more protected that way. God, I think, how could we bring a ninety-year-old woman to this place? How is she going to survive the night? Outside, on the beach, Nina grabs my father's shirt with both hands. The wind carries her shouts: "Tell me, what do I have to wait for in this life?" My father shakes his bison head. In moments like these he emits dense, furry growls. No, no, no.

"Pick up a stone, Rafi, I'm wiping you clean of everything. If you really love me, get a good stone and clobber me on the head." He leans all his weight on the rod. She shouts and scratches his face with both hands.

He gets up and runs back to the field of rocks. She twists her body backward to watch him. I leave the barracks and run to him. A punch of wind almost knocks me over. And another punch, from inside: she came here to die. Nina. In this place where she's lived her whole life. She came here to unite with her death, which has been waiting for her, right here, since she was six and a half years old.

Rafi waves his hands at me and yells for me to run to the anchor-age. I mime a boat that's already sailed. He yells, "Now!" I don't understand why, but he is possessed of a strength that can move things. I glance into the barracks on my way to the shore. Vera sits on the ground exactly as I left her. Her eyes are glazed. She looks halfway between human and bird. Rafi roars at me to hurry. I run. I remember how he used to be a force of nature on film sets. The actors were like puppets in his hands, and they didn't like it; they rebelled. That was another reason the whole thing fell through. I feel around under all my layers and find his nitroglycerin spray and aspirin in my shirt pocket. I run up a small hill. From the top I can see the boat sailing away, a black spot on the gray horizon. I take a picture with my cell phone, even though nothing will show up. It was dumb of me not to take the camera from Rafi. From up here I can also see Rafi running back to Nina with another rod, which looks more massive. He covers her with his coat again. So your ass won't freeze, my sweet, he's probably whispering. And she hits him furiously. Maybe she was really hoping we'd left her, the way she was used to. He talks to her. Strokes her hair. I keep filming them on my cell. Nothing will come out from this far away, but I can't not shoot—this is the film of my lifetime.

I climb down and sprint to the dock. Rafi was right. On the wooden bridge, at the top of the steps, is a large, shrink-wrapped, bright orange package with the Red Cross logo and another sym-bol, probably the Croatian coast guard's. Considering how large it is, it's incredibly light. I wave a thanks with both arms at the fisherman, but of course he's long gone and cannot see. I run back to Vera's barracks, where I rip the nylon off and open the pack-age. Inside, a treasure: a large blanket, which I spread out and wrap around Vera thoroughly. (I remember a thought running through my mind: I will know how to diaper a baby. I will know how to take care of him. I will stay with him, come what may. I have many flaws, but I'm not a person who abandons, and I'm not a person who betrays.) "Go see what's up with them," Vera says, and I run. On the shore Nina is smoothing my father's face with both hands, tidying his scruffy beard. He says something; she laughs. He tries again to pull her foot out, but it's useless, and I start to worry. What if she really can't get out? I'm not far away, but they are so lost in themselves that they don't see me. From my vantage point it looks as if the island is closing its jaws on her. Any minute it'll start to devour her. I want to go and take the camera from Rafi's backpack and shoot them. These are powerful moments, though I cannot penetrate their intimacy. My father is fighting a dragon: he sticks the rod gently under her foot and carefully presses down. Yesterday, in the hotel, I briefly held that delicate foot. Nina catches his eyes again. Poor, dear Rafi, says her face, I wish I could release you from it. From me. Right now the only one stuck is you, he answers. With both hands she pulls his face to hers. They kiss. They are indifferent to the rain and the winds and the gray sea. I have no words to describe the beauty of the moment.

Then suddenly there is movement. The rock on top of Nina's foot shifts. Rafi presses carefully. It's amazing what gentleness comes out of that clumsy body. In the thick rain, the two of them are now focused on each other. They use precise movements, forward and back, and her foot gradually breaks free until he is holding it in his hand, and he falls sideways onto his back, lies on the rocks, and laughs up at the sky and the rain. Nina laughs with him. There are streaks of blood along her shin and on her ankle, but she's not worried. She pulls up her pants, puts on the shoe that came off, and together, embracing and drenched, with Rafi's big coat as an umbrella, they enter the barracks and stumble over to Vera, who is covered up to her neck in a soft, red blanket.

Apart from the Red Cross survival kit, the fisherman also left us a few apples, a flashlight, some candles, matches, and hand warmers. He even left the flare gun. I am moved by the display of generosity by that unfriendly man, especially here on Goli.

"Come," says Vera to Nina and Rafi and me, and she holds up the edges of the blanket. "Come in, children, there's room for everyone."

Eight-thirty p.m. We sit on the concrete floor, slightly stunned by what we've done, leaning on the least decayed wall. From left to right: Nina, Rafi, Vera, me. We are all huddled under the blanket. We've eaten two of the three apples, passing them from hand to hand and mouth to mouth, gnawing them down to the seeds. The rain comes and goes, unpredictable, like everything else on Goli. There is no cell-phone reception of course, so we can't call the hotel and tell them we're stuck on the island. No one is going to come and rescue us in this storm. We don't want to be rescued anyway.

"Our flight's taking off now," Rafi notes. Vera wants to know if they'll refund our airfare, at least partially. "After all!" she demands, and her voice is already climbing up and arguing with an impervious bureaucrat from Croatia Airlines. "Is it our blame that we got stuck on the island? There was weather! You could barely put your nose out!" Nina gets riled up just as quickly: "And whose fault is it that we decided to set sail a minute before a storm?" Vera: "Is that our problem? That's force majeure!"

Those two—

A scene from the flight to Zagreb: Vera, Rafael, and Nina asleep in the row of seats behind me. Rafael is in the middle, mouth open, snoring loudly. Vera and Nina huddle against him, their heads on his shoulders. They both have their eyes open in their sleep. Not fully open, but about a quarter of a lid. You can just see the whites of their eyes. Honestly, it's a disturbing sight. I shoot stills and video.

Later, in the hotel, I watched the film and discovered something: in both of them, every few seconds, the eyeball slowly descends from its hiding place under the lid, appears halfway against the white background, then ascends and disappears again. I couldn't hold it in: I ran to Rafael's room with the camera. "Those two"—he says with a laugh—"they won't let themselves shut their eyes even in their sleep."

Before I left the room, he stopped me: "So, Gili, that's what I look like?" I pointed out that as compensation he has inner beauty, detectable only by a fortunate few. He threw a pillow at me and grumbled, "Time hates man . . ."

An hour, another hour. The sun moves across her body like
a slow flamethrower. Head, shoulders, neck. Everything
is burning. The sweat drips. Her lips are cracked and
bleeding. A cloud of flies buzzes above her. The bedbugs
are nicely fattened up on her blood. She doesn't scratch. No
longer brushes them off. Lets them drink it all. This body is
not hers. Neither it nor its pains. She is no longer human or
animal or anything. Since yesterday, since she understood
what she was doing here, her limbs and joints have been
rigid. Her legs wooden. She walks as if she's on stilts.

A day, another day, a week, two weeks. Even before
sunrise they stand her atop the mountain. There are
wardens who like her arms out to the sides. There are
others who demand that they reach upward. Sometimes
they spread her legs and order her to bend over with her
head down. At noon she sniffs at the tin plate but does not

eat. Her intestines have practically ceased functioning. In the afternoon they move her to the other side of the circle of stones, with her back to the sea and the slowly setting sun, which blazes until the moment it dips in the water. Then Vera stands extinguished for another hour or two, an unwanted object, until someone down at the camp remembers that she has to be brought back.

Here and there an outburst: pounding, unruly heartbeats. Almost always they presage Nina: walking to school, satchel on her back, skipping among the red fall foliage. Memories arise, things she said, gems that Milosz wrote in a special notebook, which was also confiscated by the UDBA. ("Why do I laugh when my friend tickles me, but not when I tickle myself?" "Is it true that even the worst person in the world once did something good? And is it true that even the best person once did something bad?") But even those tiny memories are becoming scarcer, soaked up in the wasteland of her existence.

For the past few days it's been Milosz who has appeared more often. She tosses and turns on the prickly straw in bed, and when he appears she starts to complain. Why did you do it, Milosz? How can I be strong like this for two and a half years, and yet you broke down after one day of beating? Why didn't you take some power from the love I gave you? She wants to stop complaining, but the words burst out: Maybe you didn't love me and Nina enough, if you were willing to go so easily? So quickly, Milosz? As if you were just waiting for the chance to get out? Milosz listens. He has only half a face, and it's impossible to know if that is because of the darkness in the barracks, or if that's what he looks like now. Then he starts talking and it's not exactly what Vera was expecting. "How could you do such a thing to our Nina?" he whispers. "How could you give them her instead of me?" Vera waves her arms in front of her face, to erase and eradicate the bad impression left by his words. "What sort of thing is that to say, Milosz? There was no choice, you know that. You would have done the same for me!" Milosz says nothing, and she begins to fear that he has forgotten what their love is. A frost starts to crawl up from her feet to her head. Only if Milosz has forgotten, only if he is watching them from the outside, like a stranger, like those ordinary, cowardly people who have not known love like theirs—only then could he be angry at what she did. But if he loves her the way she loves him, if he is deep inside their love, their extraordinary love story, then he cannot be angry. After all, he would have done exactly as she did, one body and one soul, the same thoughts and the same logic . . . And she shouts out from her heart: "I loved you more than anything in the world! I loved you more than my own life!"

A few women in the barracks wake up. They curse. She huddles. She is not afraid of anything in the world, but it terrifies her to consider that he thinks differently than her, that he doesn't understand her, and, if so, that perhaps their whole love was a mistake or, worse, an illusion. Perhaps it was not the absolute, pure truth, the most refined matter that exists, which only she and he had discovered—no, not discovered: they had created it, produced it every time his thought touched hers. Every time his body entered hers. She lies there frozen, helpless. "Ultimately," he'd once told her in a moment of despair, "love only loves itself." Such

terrible words. The little muscle in his cheek trembles,
perhaps with the effort to tell her that he loves her, too.
Or perhaps he is holding back from saying something else,
something that would cause her to cease living all at once,
like a candle snuffed out between two fingers. Milosz
does not say anything, only looks at her with one terrible,
terrified eye. As if he is seeing a monster. Vera fights
to wake herself out of the dream, if it even is a dream.
Milosz's half face looks squashed and long, and it pulls
back, the darkness sucks and swallows him, and then she
wakes up bathed in a cold sweat.

Dazed by the heat, without thinking, she kneels down
and touches the sapling. She counts out loud. More than
twenty leaves already. It's growing. Sucking up her life
force and growing. She scratches a leaf with her fingernail.
The smell sprays out, sharper than usual. Perhaps it's
the smell of the plant's fear, sensing that something is
happening? That its faithful guard is becoming a danger?
She holds a pair of tiny leaves between her fingers. She
gently pulls them: Should she tug more? A little more?
Perhaps grasp the stalk at its bottom and uproot the whole
thing and fling it into the sea? "Does that hurt, sweetie?"
she taunts, her mouth yellow with hatred. "You are my
catastrophe, my murderer. Why do I have to give my life
for you, my body for you?" She waits. It does not answer.
Suddenly, in her blindness, she spreads her fingers out and
slams her hand down as hard as she can on the soil next to
it, almost crushing it. She feels it trembling. Tomorrow or
the day after she will not be able to control herself. Its end
is nigh.

As is hers.

She's seen Maria giving orders to murder women for lesser crimes.

A day, and another day. Today Vera is more tired and grumpy than usual. No one came to let her relieve herself at midday. She has at least two hours to go before sunset. She shifts from one foot to the other, cursing the camp, and Tito, cursing out loud. Let Maria hear. Let her informants hear. The plant is getting on her nerves, too, with its comfortable, bourgeois coolness in this sweltering hell. Sitting there in her shade and flourishing, goddamn it, as if it really does not know at all and does not understand that she is burning alive here for days on end only to give it life. The fury seethes inside her. These characters, these parasites, she knows them all too well. She's been fighting against them ever since she can remember. She starts taking small, blind steps around its well. This is the first time she's dared. But now—let this spoiled brat feel what it's like, let it feel some bare sun. Let it understand what lies ahead if she decides to start a little class warfare against it.

Silence. What does she want from it? Every time she flees it, taking two steps this way or the other, she can feel its leaves moving, trembling. Even without seeing with her eyes she knows: it's looking for her. Deep in her gut she senses it seeking her, needing her, and then she hurries back to it. For some reason she cannot tolerate its anxiety for even one moment. But what is this thing? What is it doing to her, and how did it happen that a stupid little plant has become the focal point of her life? How has her entire existence been flowing into it for weeks, the way blood flows to a wound? Vera kneels down. She cups her hands around it. She strokes it, strokes it also for the woman with the crazed eyes. For her shattered mandolin. She forgets herself, forgets the warden who will be here soon and will catch her sitting down stroking the plant. She runs her fingers over the leaves, the delicate fuzz. It has never been as soft as it is today. Maybe it really does recognize her? She laughs. You've lost your mind, girl. She quickly checks to see how many new leaves have budded since yesterday, and if the stalk is any thicker. For some time she hasn't been pushing rocks up the mountain, and her fingers are a little more flexible and sensitive. She must tell Milosz about how she talks to the plant, how she gives it political speeches. So he'll see that she does have a sense of humor. He always said she didn't. She will make Milosz laugh, and he will forgive her. No, no, there's nothing to forgive: he will simply understand.

A day and another day. Or perhaps it's the same day? Or a week later? Today, for instance, the hours have started moving backward. She feels them peeling back. Someone forgot to come and rearrange her around the plant. She rearranges herself. The sun today is white-hot. The sea is a metal sheet that reflects the blazing sun back to her. You will not lose your mind. It's just a plant, and you are still slightly human. And remember that there is someone waiting for you on the outside. There is Nina, whom you have to take care of. Nina, though you must not even for one second wonder what she is going through, where she is, whom she's with, what sort of girl she will be when you get out and take her back from wherever she is.

Because there were stories. There were girls the UDBA kidnapped, yes, girls. Most no older than ten. Someone must have requested those ages. Sometimes they sent them back and sometimes not. They said the ones who came back were not the same anymore. They told a story about one girl who was sent back after three months with a note pinned to her shirt: "Tell her she dreamed it."

She hears the warden's footsteps. It turns out Vera is not standing in the right place. She must have walked around the plant a little. She gets the two slaps. She begs the warden to let her go and defecate. Threatens to do it right then and there, next to Maria's plant. The warden gives in. She takes Vera to the usual spot and says she'll wait by the plant meanwhile, to get some fresh air, and that Vera should call her when she's done. Vera tenses up, sensing that the warden used too many words. If only she could at least see shadows. She has a strange intuition: the warden is doing something up there. Maybe she's touching it? Or talking to it? Vera is dying to relieve herself, but she is anxious. Why would that woman come here and take her place? Besides, it's not good to confuse the plant too much, it's grown accustomed to Vera. She gets up quickly and feels her way back. The warden lets out a startled cry when Vera appears from between the rocks with the face of a bereaved mother bear. She beats Vera and knocks her to the ground and screams: "Jewish trash, *čifutka!*" She drags her over the rock face.

Then the warden lets go. She takes a few steps back. Breathes quickly. In an unsteady voice she hurls at Vera, "You should know, whore, that when you lose your mind completely, they'll replace you. *I'll* replace you!" Why did she say that? Had she heard something at the headquarters? Were they thinking of replacing her? Vera stifles a shout:

No one can replace her. No one knows it like she does, no one knows exactly what it needs at every particular moment.

Later, a week or two later, the same warden comes to arrange her again. Vera recognizes the footsteps and shrinks back, protecting her head with her hands. Today the warden does not yell or beat or curse. She only repositions Vera's feet. She lightly touches her back to straighten it. Touches her forehead and lifts her head up. And then, when Vera is standing in exactly the right spot, even before watering the sapling, she offers Vera the canteen.

"Drink."

Vera recoils. Bracing for the trap.

"Please," says the warden.

Vera lets out a strange sound, her body's response to the word. She puts her hand out to feel for the canteen and touches the woman's hand. What will happen now. What do they do to someone who touches a warden. Nothing happens. Nothing bad. The woman holds Vera's wrist and moves it to the canteen, wraps her hand around Vera's other hand, and closes Vera's hands over the canteen. Vera waits. Maybe now she'll be pushed over the cliff. The warden says, "Drink." Vera drinks. She drinks maybe half the canteen without taking a breath.

The other woman talks: "Don't you sometimes get the feeling he's constantly watching you?"

"Comrade Tito?"

"No." She laughs quietly, deeply. "This sapling. Doesn't it seem like he understands?"

"Understands what, Commandant?"

"This madness. How they're turning us into animals."

Vera stands silently, head bowed, the way you anticipate an especially vicious blow. Like a man with a noose around his neck waiting for the trapdoors beneath him to open up. Nothing happens. How exhausting to live in a place where everything is unpredictable.

"I have one like it at home, in Belgrade," says the woman. Her voice is so different from the screams on her last visit. "In a pot on the balcony. It doesn't like a lot of water. And by the way, you can make excellent tea from the leaves."

Vera does not speak. They must really have decided to drive her mad. Sent a talented actress to spur her on. Just the sound of her voice, so tender today, is enough to make a person die of homesickness.

"I envy you," says the warden quietly next to Vera's ear.

"Me?" Vera whispers. "What is there to envy, Commandant?"

"Because you have something to live for."

Vera hardly breathes. These words are so forbidden that there is no doubt this woman is from the UDBA. She doesn't dare ask the warden what she meant by saying she has something to live for. Did she mean the plant? Or maybe she knows something about Nina? Has she seen Nina?

The warden whispers, "I knew you and your husband."

"Where?" Vera whispers.

"Well, I didn't really know you. But I used to watch you in Kalemegdan Park, where you walked with your little girl on weekends."

"Please, please, I'm begging you, stop—"

The warden holds Vera's wrists. Her face is very close. She talks quickly. "Your man was so thin, a rake, but with a kind face."

"Yes." Vera fights against the choking sensation scratching at her throat.

"And his eyes . . . Weren't you afraid to look into those eyes?"

"No, I wasn't afraid. I wanted those eyes to see me all the time."

"You were a sweet couple, almost like kids, even though you already had a child."

Vera waits. The word "child" explodes inside her. "Her name is Nina, and I don't know where she is."

"And you were always talking, you and him. You argued and laughed. I remember once you were literally dancing around your man, and I didn't know anything like that from my husband, and I thought, What do they have to talk about so much?"

"About everything," says Vera, "there was nothing in the world we didn't talk about."

"And the little girl kept pulling your hands and your handbag and your husband's pants, trying to get you to notice her. She talked to the squirrels, to the crows, such a serious girl . . ."

"Yes, yes."

"And sometimes you would swing her up in the air together, 'Fly up high, airplane . . . ' "

The warden talks as if she cannot stop. Vera stands with her head down, arms drooping to the ground. Muffled sobs rock her body. If this is an UDBA trick, they have managed to break her.

"My husband," says the warden, "they killed him over nothing, over nonsense, and we did not have a child. We didn't have time for anything. I loved him, I think, but it was like I hadn't got to know him yet. I hope for you that your daughter is alive and that you find her." She touches Vera's shoulder lightly, then leaves.

A full, airy, luminous ball of world hovers in the air before Vera, and she takes a step forward and opens a little door in it and walks back inside. She nods her head at Jagoda, her good friend and desk mate from school in Čakovec. She smiles at Mimi the cook with the apron around her waist. She strolls past the police band playing in the park on the weekend, and eats hot chestnuts from a newspaper cone handed to her by the vendor on the street corner. Here is Father sitting at the cash register in the shop, winking at her as she walks by, and here is Mother in her armchair, reading, looking up and smiling at Vera. Here is the main street floating past, the houses of red-and-white brick, the maple trees. Here soon, around the corner, is Vera aged seventeen. Any minute now she'll be dancing at the high-school-graduation ball and she will meet Milosz, and life and love will open up for her.

There will yet be life, Vera suddenly knows. She walks out, head held high, from the floating bubble of the world and returns to the island, to the mountain, to the sapling. She kneels down and searches with her fingers. Surrounds it with her hands. "Don't worry," she says calmly, "I'm here, don't worry. I'm protecting you." The sun blazes more harshly than usual today. Perhaps it feels that Vera is stronger. She stands with her back to the sun. She locates

the familiar flame in the center of the sun wheel, the one
that burns the hottest. She sets it in the middle of her
back and holds her arms up to the sides, as if to separate
two people fighting. Thanks to her, thanks to the shadow
cast by her tiny, shriveled body, the plant and the sun are
almost equally matched. Thanks to Vera it has lived here
all this time. The burning intensifies. The sun swells,
filling with anger at Vera. Vera breathes deeply. Buttresses
herself against the blaze. Sweat rolls down her face and
body. Does it know, the sapling—perhaps thanks to a
mysterious survival instinct possessed by vegetation—
that she is the one rescuing it day after day? Does it, after
all the days and weeks she's been standing here, at least
recognize her scent? Does it correlate, through some sort
of neural network, her presence with something good? A
pleasant sensation spreads through her. Of all the hundreds
of women in the camp, she might be the only one doing
something beneficent.

That thought, those forgotten words. She stands up
straight and her arms open wider, like in a dance.

Then she turns around and, with the splendor of a brave
child, of a seven-year-old snotnose, faces the full sun and
soaks the blinding light into her eyes. She could drown an
entire sun in the black of her pupils. Then she gives the sun
a little bow—a victor's bow.

It is unclear to her how, but the three of them seem to
have attained a peculiar equilibrium: there is sun, there
is plant, and there is Vera, who feels like one of the astral
bodies.

—

In the silence that has fallen on the barracks, Nina shouts nightmar-
ishly: "But how did you stand it?"

"What?"

"This, this Goli. How did you not—"

"When you have to—you do."

"No . . . You're strong . . . ," Nina mumbles. "You're much stronger than me. You're made of different material."

"But you stood it, too," Vera says tenderly, "don't forget. And for
you it lasted exactly the same time that I was here."

"I didn't 'stand it.' I was crushed by it."

"No, Nina, don't say—"

"Of course I'll say. It's hard for you to hear, but I will say it.
Because you got out of here and quickly found work in Belgrade,
and then we went to Israel, and you built yourself a new life and a
new family, ready-made, and you had Tuvia and Rafi and the whole
kibbutz, you saw what that party on Saturday was like—"

"You also have your own life, and probably your friends—"

"Me? Look at me. I have a quarter of a Red Cross blanket."

She laughs through the sobs, and we laugh with her, cautiously,
with her always cautiously, so she won't think we're laughing at
her. Our guarded laugh seems to amuse her, because she sniffles
and laughs even harder, maybe in desperation, and we laugh with
her: Rafi in a deep bass that jolts his belly, Vera in cackles, and me
and Nina in choked-up creaks. We sound like a quartet tuning up
before a concert.

"Rafi," Nina says when we calm down, "you will take care of me."
It is neither a question nor an imperative: it is a statement of fact.

"Always," he grunts through his thick beard, "we settled that.
But for that to happen you'll need to be in Israel. I can't take care of
you long-distance, and I hate flying."

"I'll be in Israel. I have nowhere to go."

"Also, Ninotchka," Vera says, "don't be angry with what I want to tell you, but I can also a little, really, remember for you . . ."

I freeze. I can't believe she said that.

"What? What did you say?" Nina asks quietly. "You can what?"

"Don't be angry . . . I was just thinking, we two will remember everything, a little you'll remember and a little I will. We can go in together, share the pot. What do you think? Is it okay for me to say?"

Silence. I'm guessing Nina's response will send Vera running to the UDBA for shelter.

"Mom," Nina says softly, and she laughs and swallows down the tears and takes Vera's hand. "Mom, Majka, Mom . . ."

It turns out I'm always wrong about everything. About everyone.

Vera wipes her eyes and asks what project Nina is working on in the North Pole.

"It's not quite in the pole," Nina says, "but close. It's a project for preserving seeds of edible plants that are going extinct all over the world. But I don't work there anymore. My contract ended a year ago."

"Oh," says Vera.

Silence again. We study the new information. Afraid to say the wrong thing.

"I don't understand," Vera says, "then what have you been doing since then?"

"There's a coal mine in the village. I told Gili. I cooked for them a little. I worked in their laundry for a while. Then they shut down parts of the mine, and it turned out they didn't need me there anymore either."

"So what do you . . . What are you in now?" Vera stammers, unable to comprehend even a single day without work.

"There's always someone in the village who needs an extra pair

of hands. Laying tiles, drying sealskins, mopping the church floor."
She laughs. "If there's one thing I learned on the kibbutz, it's how
to mop floors . . . Odd jobs, nothing intellectually challenging. Five
or six days a month, enough not to die of starvation."

"But we talk every week," Vera says wanly, "and you didn't even
say."

"What is there to say about nothing?"

"You said you were working at a satellite station . . ."

"So I said."

"You were just lying?"

"Not just," she searches for the words. "I . . . The truth is, I didn't
want to upset you, Majka. You've had enough from me."

"So just like that? Nothing?" Vera looks very old.

"Nothing," Nina says.

Nothing and suddenly, I think. Suddenly and nothing. From
both those breasts I suckled.

Rafi asks some more about her village. I can see he's fascinated
by it, and the truth is, so am I. Nina relaxes under the blanket. She
tells us about the deep snow, about cages with dozens of sled dogs
that bark all day and night, about time, time itself, which in the
dark months takes on a different meaning there, "because what difference does it make if it's ten a.m. or ten p.m., it's all the same darkness, so you start developing your own internal sense of time." She
tells us about the people who ended up there, like her, each for his
own reason, each with his own secrets. "It's a place where no one
asks you questions, but on the other hand they're constantly bom-
barding you with gossip." "Just like kibbutz!" Vera laughs, and we
laugh with her, making the proper noises of a family. A ludicrous
one, but a family. I notice that Nina hasn't got any words wrong or
forgotten a single thing since we've been under the blanket. She tells

us there's a home on the island for kids removed from abusive families. She worked there for a few months as a cook. "I cooked them
all your dishes, Mom." "Did they like it?" Vera asks wondrously.
"They licked their plates clean. Do you know how great it is to eat
yufka in chicken soup when it's thirty degrees below freezing?"

"After three or four months of darkness, on March eighth, every
year, the sun comes back," she tells us. "The whole village wakes
up in honor of the day. They dress the children in yellow, paint their
faces yellow, decorate them with all kinds of sun-shaped pendants
and tiaras." Her voice is warming up, and we feed the flames with
questions. It does us good to ask her things. It does us good to hear
the melody of a question that knows it will be answered. In the pale
moonlight I see, or imagine I can see, the delicate pulsing of a light
blue vein on her neck. Forty-five years ago my father saw it and fell
in love with her.

"And then everyone flows to the church, from the children to the
elderly, they walk in a procession through the tall snow, and they
stand on the church steps waiting for the clock to strike eleven. A
bit of pale light starts to show on the edges, but not direct sunlight.
And we sing a song of thanks to the sun, which someone from the
village wrote. Then there is total silence for a few minutes, no one
says anything, even the kids feel that something special is happening. Then the priest looks at the clock and gives a signal, and we all
shout together: 'Here comes the sun! Here comes the sun!' And on
the third time, the sun appears, and its first ray touches us."

In the almost dark barracks, her face is lit up. I see her standing
among the kids with her eyes closed and hands held out, allowing the sun to touch her. I whisper to her from a Lea Goldberg

poem: "I shall be as a tree in the dark of the woods / On which the light chose to shine." She doesn't know it, but she repeats the words silently, like a prayer.

I watch her all the time. The way her body moves, her facial expressions. Tiny motions of withdrawal and gathering in, then suddenly a sort of propelling outward, forward, then embarrassment and hesitation, and another withdrawal. My mother tongue.

There is a constant nervous tremor in the air around her, as if wobbly pencil lines are continuously sketching her contours. Several times I've caught myself mimicking her expressions. I have no control over it. I must be learning her—thirty-six years too late—the way a normal three-year-old girl learns her mother.

"I heard you asked for me."

"Is that the commandant? Commandant Maria?"

The tip of Maria's whip travels over Vera's face and props up her tightened, infected eyelids. "They said you had something urgent to tell me."

Only now does Vera grasp what she's done: her concern for the sapling must have driven her insane. Made her act against the instinct possessed by every woman on the island—stay as far away as possible from Maria.

"I'm listening."

"It's the plant, Commandant."

"Which plant?"

"The plant that's here, Commandant." She deliberately points a few centimeters away from the spot where the sapling is planted.

"Let me understand. You called Commandant Maria up to the top of a mountain for a plant?"

"He's going to die, Commandant. He hasn't been right for a few days." Footsteps circle her slowly. She feels Maria's breath on her face, on the back of her neck. "The wardens water him too much, Commandant. His roots are rotting. Let me water him when he needs water. I know him."

"You know him . . ." Maria is amused. The edge of her whip tickles the plant, and Vera is horrified. "And I thought you finally wanted to sign some papers for us, give us some names . . ."

Vera says nothing. The stupidity of her act fills her with terror. She was so engrossed in the sapling that she forgot how the world outside operates.

"Tell me the truth, *banda,* wouldn't you like to lift the weight of betrayal off your heart?"

She shudders. "What betrayal, Commandant?"

"Wouldn't you like to cleanse your conscience a little?"

"My conscience is clear, Commandant."

Maria gives a slow laugh that horrifies Vera. "Someone who betrayed Tito will betray anyone."

Vera swallows. "Yes, Commandant."

"And tell me this, *banda,*" Maria says calmly, "how many days have you been up here?"

"With him?"

"With *him,* yes," Maria says, walking slowly around the circle of stones, the tip of her whip picking up blackened leaves and dropping them.

"A few weeks, Commandant. I wasn't counting."

"And how long have you been blind?"

"Maybe about two months, Commandant."

"And they probably told you this is a plant that Commandant Maria brought here."

"Yes, Commandant."

"A plant that Commandant Maria brought from home." She talks in a strange, slow tune, as if telling Vera a story.

The skin on Vera's back starts crawling. "Commandant, please let me take care of him. I know what's good for him, I have an instinct."

"In-stinct!" Maria rolls the word over her tongue, giggling. "Let's examine your instinct. Look at the sun."

"What did you say, Commandant?"

"Wait, let me understand, are you deaf now, too?"

"No, I just didn't hear what you said, Commandant."

"I said look at the sun and open your eyes wide."

Vera bows her head.

"Is that hard for you?" asks Commandant Maria, with sorrowful commiseration.

Vera nods.

A rough hand caresses the back of her neck. "How long have you been able to see?" asks Commandant Maria softly, and her fingers tighten on Vera's gaunt neck.

"It just started this morning, Commandant."

Maria laughs. "Come on, *banda,* you know we're after the truth here."

"Maybe since yesterday evening, no longer, Commandant."

"And you decided to keep the little secret to yourself, *banda?*"

The pain in the back of her neck is dreadful. It's hard to breathe. "No, no, Commandant. I was thinking—just until he recovers a little."

"What a kind soul you are."

"But, Commandant, he can still live, I really do know how to care for him."

"That's nice. Very moving." Maria wipes a clownish tear from her eye. "Now pull it up."

In some way she knew this would happen. From the moment she saw Maria emerging from between the two rocks, she knew that either she or the plant would not get out of this encounter alive. She gets down on her knees and begs. For the first time in her life, she begs. Not for her life, but for its life. She begs to the point of tears this time. She gets one lazy lash on the back of her neck, and another on her temple, above the ear. There is no point resisting. The plant is easily uprooted, as if it had no roots at all. The little leaves lie in the palm of her hand. They are almost black. How could the plant be so paltry?

With two fingers Maria takes it from her hands and tosses it over her shoulder into the abyss. Vera sees. It's been at least a week since she's been able to see. The light came back, the colors, the images. She won't dare believe it and won't dare celebrate. The sight of the little bundle flying over the sea and the gulf sends horror through her. Now it's her turn.

"Tomorrow morning you go back to work in the rocks."

"Yes, Commandant?"

"You should thank God and Comrade Tito that you're not down in the sea right now."

"Thank you, Commandant."

—

Vera followed Maria to the camp headquarters. For a few
hours she stood outside her office. No one came up to her
and no one spoke to her. Then a warden came out and told
her to leave. She was not punished; she was not lashed. The
next morning she rejoined the women rolling rocks up
and down the mountain. Their talk, the noise, the crying
and shouting, even the occasional laughter, were almost
as hard for her as pushing the rocks. One morning the
Punat docked at the island and off-loaded dozens of women
for reeducation. A senior warden's voice came over the
loudspeaker, naming the women who had finished their
prison terms and would be sailing to freedom. Vera's name
was read out. Vera stood there in disbelief. They called
her name again. Someone hit her on the back and shouted
at her to run to the office. No one explained why they'd
decided to release her. She had not confessed to a crime,
had not expressed remorse. She had not given them a single
name. She had betrayed no one, and yet they'd decided to
release her.

She was given her clothes and belongings—some of
them—that had been taken when she came to the island
two years and ten months ago. She was also handed thirty-
four undelivered letters from Nina, and two from her sister
Mira. From these she learned that an UDBA officer who'd
been fond of Milosz had made sure Nina was sent to Mira
on the day Vera was imprisoned.

By the time of Vera's release, Commandant Maria was
no longer at the camp. A few weeks after their hilltop
encounter, she'd been transferred to a new job in a different
camp. There were rumors that even the UDBA found her

murderous penchant too much. "After all," Vera was told
by a kibbutz member from the Yugoslavian group, thirty
years after the events, "the Goli Otok camps were intended
for reeducation, not for killing." But even after three
decades, Vera still believed that something in her had been
murdered on that island.

Night. Almost 2:00 a.m. A righteous thunder-and-lightning storm.
We talked, oh how we talked, so many questions were asked and
answered, so much we said. We've never talked like that, in every
permutation and combination, until sleep reaped us all, or so I
thought, because I suddenly hear Vera whispering, probably so as
not to wake Rafael and me: "You didn't tell me what it was like at
your aunt Mira's yet."

"Maybe you didn't want to hear?"

I can feel Vera's feet stretching the blanket down. Rafi rolls over
and somehow slips out from under the blanket and turns on the
camera.

"Why are you filming?"

"So we'll have it."

"Let him film, Mom."

"If it doesn't bother you . . ."

Nina signals to Rafi that it's all right.

Rafi murmurs that it's so dark he can only record sound anyway. I'm angry at myself for not insisting on bringing a sun gun
that would have given us some precious light. Nothing is how it
should be.

"Wait," I catch a ride on Rafi's coattails, "in that case, I'll write."

"In the dark?" Nina wonders.

"Whatever comes out comes out."

"Write, film," Vera grumbles, "I can't be bothered to argue with you."

"Forget about them, Majka, that's not what matters now."

Vera arrived in Belgrade in the early morning and went straight to her sister's house. She knocked on the door. It was seven-thirty. Her sister Mira opened the door, shrieked, and hugged her. Vera said she could see Nina over her sister's shoulder, sitting on a stool, drinking a glass of milk, and staring into space. Nina was nine and a half. According to Vera, Nina shot her a cool and utterly mature glance, and said into the room, "Vera's come back. What a sight you are." Vera wanted to explain that working with the rocks had made her muscles bulge and distorted her physique, but something in Nina's eyes petrified her and kept her quiet.

Nina remembered their meeting completely differently. She remembered that when she saw her mother at the door, she jumped up and shouted, "Mama! *Majka!*" and ran to her, and they stood hugging and crying with joy. Vera insisted that Nina did not get up and certainly did not hug her. And that she, Vera, also did not go over and hug Nina, for some reason. Nina finished drinking her milk and went to school. In the afternoon she came home, did her homework, and went out to play in the yard. Here, too, Nina's story diverged: she didn't go to school that day, she spent the whole day with Vera. They went to a movie together—she couldn't remember which one—and then to a café, where they "talked for hours" and occasionally sang songs from Nina's childhood. That whole first day they almost never mentioned Milosz, Nina recounted with surprise, and this was confirmed by Vera. There was one other thing they agreed on: Vera's sister Mira did not believe a word of what Vera told them about Goli Otok. She told Vera that if she didn't shut up, she and her husband would have to ask her to leave.

Rafi recorded, I wrote.

The story split off again in their account of the night: Nina said they slept in one bed, head to feet, and couldn't stop talking and laughing and crying, until Vera's brother-in-law, Dragan, came in his underwear and yelled at them to be quiet, and then they giggled hysterically. Vera had a different version: the hours went by and they lay awake in bed, in terrible silence. Vera couldn't tolerate it. She asked, "Are you a good pupil?" Nina didn't answer. Vera asked, "What is four times four?" Nina pretended to be asleep. Vera asked again. Nina answered, "Sixteen." "Good. What's five times seven?" Nina answered. And they went through the whole multiplication table. Nina did remember "something with math," but she was sure Vera had tested her at the café.

As for the rest of the time, their currents of memory united. They were in the narrow bed, the aunt and uncle had fallen asleep, and Vera asked, "Is there something you want to ask me, Nina?" Nina said there wasn't. Vera remembered that Nina's voice sounded cold and foreign. She felt as if a frost had enveloped the girl her daughter used to be.

Vera asked again, "Is there anything you want to ask me?"

"Why did you and my dad both leave me on the same day?"

"Because the police put us in prison," Vera replied.

Nina asked in a trembling voice, "Who did you and Daddy love more than me? Who did you leave me on my own for?"

"The police put us in prison," Vera repeated.

"And you couldn't get out?"

"No," said Vera, and in some sense that was true, but it was also the beginning of the lie that would grow and branch out until it strangled all of us.

—

After a long silence, Vera asks, "Were you unhappy there, Nina? With Aunt Mira and her husband?"

"Yes, you could say that."

"What was it like, my girl?"

And I—we—hear her story for the first time. The aunt and uncle had no children of their own, and she was not the girl they wanted. They hit her over every little thing, locked her in the cellar for hours, didn't let her eat at the table with them, instead put her on a stool in the corner. She would run away from home and "chatter," as she put it, with Serbian soldiers from the nearby military base.

Vera is incensed: "Mira and your uncle Dragan, even though they are in graves, they still don't forgive me that I made a child with a Serbian."

It also turns out—the wonders never cease—that in the years she was living with her uncle and aunt, she really did join a gang of lawless boys, all Serbians. She was small and thin and fast, and apparently indifferent to peril. She would crawl into houses through tiny windows and open the door for the boys. And she never got caught. If other things happened to her with them—she did not tell us. We did not ask.

The rain is no longer a meteorological phenomenon: it has distinct volition. It has a purpose. Waterfalls cascade through all the holes in the roof. We huddle together between the tributaries. Once in a while the thunder rolls over us like a train with lots of cars and makes the barracks shudder.

"But there's something I still don't completely . . . ," says Nina.

"What? Ask me."

"You told me so much about Goli and the other camps, and about the women's island you were on, Sveti Grgur—"

"I wish I kept quiet, but I couldn't. I was exploding inside."

"But do you know what I was thinking?"

"When?"

"Just sometimes."

"What were you thinking?"

"That there's one thing you never told me."

"A thing I didn't tell? I told you everything, my girl. I told you too much."

"For example, you never told me how you even got here. What happened before you—"

"I told you. I came on *Punat,* they opened a big door down below, and we all spilled out like dead fish into the sea."

"But what happened before that, Majka? Before Goli. Before the *Punat?*"

"What do you mean? We had our ordinary life, a good life, until one day . . ."

"But when they took you to the UDBA, did they interrogate you? Did they accuse you of something? Was there a trial?"

"There were interrogations. Trial—no."

"Did they let you say anything?"

"What do you mean 'say'?"

"Explain, defend yourself? Did you have a lawyer?"

"Lawyer? Are you crazy, my girl? Fifty thousand people they throwed like dogs with no trial in Tito's camps. Only here, in Goli camps, maybe five thousand persons died. Killed or suicide. So you ask about lawyer?"

"Tell me from the beginning. Everything."

Vera sighs and elongates her short stature. They are still under the blanket, sitting close together, almost cheek to cheek, still not looking at each other. Rafi is recording. "What is there to tell? It was the morning after your father, you know, hanged himself. They came to take me to interrogation, a man with leather coat. Still when we were at home he started questions, said they know everything about us. That your father and I were pro-Stalin and enemies of Yugoslavian people. And what are your ties with NKVD? And who of your friends in Russia came to you? And did you listen to Moscow? Did you listen to Budapest? Even asked why we gave you Russian name, all sorts of nonsense. Then he took me in a black car to army hospital, and there, well, it happened like always."

"What happened? I want to know."

"That's how things happened back then. They did not care about truth. They just wanted me to sign for them that I admit your father was enemy of the people, and I would not do it, and that's that—off to Goli."

"But who were they? Do you remember them? Their faces?"

Hey, I whisper silently to Nina, that's not the right question! Who cares who they were?

Vera also seems surprised. "Who were they? What do you . . . They were three colonels. One I remember, with a bald spot kind of, and he had actually sympathetic face. Spoke nicely to me."

"And you . . . Hang on, what was I going to . . . Did you ever try to find out where he is now?"

"God forbid, Nina! I don't even want to see their shadow! Even if they were the last person on the world, I won't talk to them!"

"You see, I'm the opposite of you. I would look for them and find them, even buried under the ground, and I would come and . . . and . . ."

"Well, and what? Shoot them with gun? What?"

"No, but I would throw it in their face."

"Throw what?"

In the window, a three- or four-jointed bolt of lightning frenetically cuts the sky.

"What, Nina?"

"Me."

Silence. Vera breathes quickly.

"What . . . What do you mean, you?"

"And Gili," Nina says, "and everything that happened to her because of me."

She said it. Rafi recorded it.

"Enemies of the people?" Vera hits her own thigh angrily. "I should sign that we were spies for Stalin? That we wanted to kill Tito? Liars!" On the wall above Rafi's head there is a scratched slogan: CON TITO. Vera juts her chin at it, snorting: "'With Tito we'll build socialism,' my ass!"

"So you didn't sign for them . . . ," Nina mumbles, looking suddenly exhausted.

"How can I sign something that isn't the truth?"

Sign already, I whisper again silently, and we can all go home, and draw the blinds and mourn Milosz, and ourselves, and together we can slowly repair what is repairable.

Nina gets out from under the blanket. Vera gathers more and more of it over herself. Nina kneels next to her, holding her hand. "But Dad was already dead . . ." Her voice is thin and feeble again. "And if, say, you would have tried, say . . . to offer them . . . maybe they would have . . . No, that's a silly thought." She snorts softly. Right in front of our eyes she is retreating, turning into a faded draft of herself. "But sometimes, Mom, I wonder—"

"Wonder what, Nina? Don't keep inside your belly!"

"What are you so angry about, Mom." Her voice is hollow.

"Not angry, Nina. Just my head is exploding from this talk. Like I'm being interrogated again."

Nina sits on the cold floor, distractedly stroking the blanket on Vera's tiny body. "No one's interrogating you . . . What is there to interrogate? Who even has the right to interrogate you . . . No one has been through what you went through."

"No, Nina, you don't understand—in the contrary! Interrogate, ask anything. It's good. I need to talk."

"But understand that I'm not interrogating you. Just trying to do something . . . To understand, to repair backward a little."

"You cannot repair backward. That you already know."

Nina looks at me and I at her.

"What happened, happened," Vera mumbles, "and that is what you live with."

"But let's say, Mom, I'm just asking, even so, if they had, for instance . . ."

"What are you asking? Say directly, Nina."

"No, I was just thinking: if they had—"

"What? What could they offer me?" Vera shouts bitterly and pounds her fists on her lap. "What could I give them for not to betray your father? To not let them dirty him and to prove to them that I say the truth? What did I have to give them?"

Silence. Vera and Nina glare at each other. At the edge of my nerves I can feel them getting swept toward a blind, dark spot, which only they can see in each other's eyes.

"Ah . . ." Nina emits a strange voice, light as a feather, as if somewhere inside her, with unimaginable tenderness, something has clicked into place.

"My head," Vera murmurs, pressing her temples with both hands.

Nina shuts her eyes and her head falls back. Her thin eyelids flutter with alarming speed. As if in an instant she has fallen into a deep and total and dream-filled slumber, and in her sleep someone is slowly running a hand over her forehead.

Then she opens her eyes. "No, I have to get out of here."

"It's pouring," says Rafi, "I'm going with you."

"No, no, no one is going with me! I need to be alone. To breathe. Have to breathe. Just tell me one thing," she says, getting up, darting around the room aimlessly, and I can't help thinking of the headless chicken I'd wished her to become. How could I have been so cruel.

"Tell me, Mom," she practically shouts, "couldn't you have at least asked them to let me come with you?"

"What?"

"Couldn't you have asked them to let me come with you?"

"Where?"

"Here. To Goli."

"For me to ask UDBA to take you, too? Are you mad? Never there was a child on this island, never! And I not for any fortune in the world would take you to this hell!"

"But that way we wouldn't have been apart," Nina says as she walks to the doorway.

"What?"

"That way we would have never been apart."

"How?"

"Because we'd have been together, here."

"But why on earth would they agree . . . It's not possible, Nina, no, it's not . . . They never took children to Goli."

"I know. I read all the books about Goli."

"Even in imagination I don't want to think that you would . . . No . . . That is the most horrible for me. More horrible than me myself being here." She gives Nina a terrified look: "Again I must ask you, and answer me with clear heart, Nina, and not with spite: Was it so bad for you at my sister and her husband, that you would want to come to this hell?"

"You really don't understand, do you?"

"I know how they treated you, but—"

"It has nothing to do with them."

"It doesn't?"

"All the time, every minute you weren't with me, I wanted to be with you."

"Even if they would kill me, Nina, I wouldn't ask them—"

"I would have gone to the pit of hell with you," Nina whispers from the doorway of the barracks, "just to be with you all day and all night." She runs her hand up and down the door hanging on one hinge. "That's all I thought about. To be with you, to be with you."

Vera looks down. All this is beyond her strength.

"Please don't follow me," Nina says and walks out.

The air seems to be pulled out with her.

So stifling.

The rain and wind are going wild, as if new prey has been tossed at them.

"She doesn't want to know," Vera says to herself, "she doesn't want to know."

"I'm going out," says Rafi.

"Dad, no. Please. Let her be alone."

"She'll end up doing something to herself," Vera murmurs.

Rafi and I sit on the wet concrete floor, in opposite corners. I lose my mind with worry for her.

Suddenly Vera speaks: "They buried him under a number in cemetery near Belgrade, and after I came back from Goli, I wrote letters to Tito to let me bury my husband. Maybe twenty letters I wrote, and finally Tito asked Moša Pijade—his Jewish deputy—Who is this woman who is not afraid of Tito? Give her already her husband, but she must do it alone."

Every time a bolt of thunder or a pelt of rain shakes the barracks, a spasm of pain runs through Rafi's face. He's stopped filming. I signal for him to continue. There are sounds here that I can use as voice-over, and there is Vera's story.

"I went with my parents-in-law, Milosz's parents. They came from their village with horse and carriage and with a coffin they made. My mother-in-law wove beautiful kilim rug, lots of colors. We came to the cemetery of the unknown. I looked until I found him, number 3754, and I took off the top stone with a shovel, and I knew him immediately from the teeth and jaw, how people always thought he was smiling. Our wedding ring was gone." Her speech is staccato, one word does not touch the next. "There were bones there and lots of leaves and mud. I cleaned all that off him and put him inside a sheet, and brought him to the carriage and put him in the coffin on the kilim, and we traveled to the village. One word we did not speak all the way. After we were traveling for maybe an hour, my mother-in-law says, 'What are you made of, Vera—iron or stone?' And I thought in my heart: Of love for Milosz. I said nothing, and we spoke no more until we got there and until we put him in ground of his village. I had to do it. I could not leave him under a number. And I knew no one else would do it. So this way Milosz has a grave with a name, which Nina can visit, and Gili, too, if she wants, and also Gili's boy or girl, which maybe there will be one day. I had to do it so that everyone in the world will know there was such a Milosz, there was one person who was thin and sick and not very strong in his body, but a hero and idealist in his soul, and the most pure and deep person, and my friend and my beloved—"

—

When we couldn't take any more, and were about to go out and look for her, Nina came back. She faltered into the barracks, wet and frozen. She could barely stand up. We hurried over, wrapped her in the blanket, rubbed her back and chest and neck, her stomach and legs, with six hands. Each of us contributed something—dry socks, a shirt, a scarf. She stood between us with her eyes closed, shivering, almost falling over. I warmed her hands by blowing on them, her long and slender fingers. I massaged her neck and shoulders. Rafi kneaded her with massive force. I could see it was hurting her, but she didn't say a word. He soundlessly muffled a sob.

She slowly thawed out under our touch, then opened her eyes.

"Cry," she said to Rafi softly, "cry. There are things to cry over."

As I write now, it is eight years after that night. I try to imagine what happened to her while she was alone outside the barracks. I see her walking quickly, then running, up and down the paths of the abandoned camp, going into huts, running to the beach and touching the black water, running back to the field of boulders. She knows her way around this place, perhaps more than any of the cities and houses she's lived in and left or fled. Here is home; that is clear. It's a hellish home, but it is where her longings and pleadings and pain were directed all those years. Here is where her soul was deposited. Here, I think, is where Nina was when she was gone.

She tires out. Walks through the rain, indifferent to it. Trips over stones and gets up. Mumbles Vera's words over and over again: "What could I give them so as not to betray your father?" "Me," Nina splutters, "I am what she gave them so as not to betray Dad." Every time the thought strikes, it launches her again like an electrical current. Unbearable pain bursts out in every limb, all the way to the tips of her body. She runs again, incapable of standing. Of course Vera gave them herself, too. Almost three years of hard labor and torture. "But it was me she sacrificed," Nina murmurs, tasting the words, as I do along with her. We are suddenly together out there, the pair of us swept along in the storm like two leaves, the abandoned girls whose bitter blood never clots. "She could have chosen!" Nina yells into the wind. "They gave her a choice, and she chose, her love chose, and I knew, I felt it all these years, under my skin I knew. I wasn't crazy, I knew."

I imagine her stopping at once, looking around in wonder, like a newborn who has come into the wrong world.

For a moment the island comes to life. As if giant floodlights were switched on with a roar and everything was bathed in light. Women in prison uniforms run, shouting. Screaming with pain in interrogations. Sometimes laughing. Sometimes even joking around with the wardens. Roll calls, and megaphones, and lashes, and choruses of women singing songs of praise for Tito.

When Vera comes back to the barracks after being interrogated, Nina tends to her wounds. When the wardens force Vera to stand all night next to the *kibla,* the bucket where the prisoners relieve themselves, Nina stands next to her. When Vera chops wood brought to the island for heating and construction, Nina runs for some goat fat to spread on the ax. What's left of the fat, they stealthily rub on their cracked lips.

"If I were thirty years younger," Nina said after we finished kneading and rubbing and thawing her, "I'd get pregnant by this rain."

We laughed warily. We did not completely understand. Of all the things in the world, that's what she chose to tell us? She looked at me, smiling. "I'm hungry. Starving."

I gave her the last apple and a few rice crackers. Vera dug through her bag and fished out sandwiches for us all, God knows when she'd made them and how she'd known to keep them for this minute. We wolfed them down. We laughed at ourselves and at our hunger. Nina laughed with us. Her eyes glimmered. What happened to her outside? I couldn't understand. She was a different person, I sensed. Something in her had changed, released. Everything in her was suddenly exposed, naked, strong. On her face I saw neither anger nor vengeance. I searched. Neither resentment nor hurt pride. What I found was huge relief. Clarity.

"Mmm," she said with her mouth full of mozzarella and tomatoes, "what a wonderful sandwich."

"Enjoy it," said Vera, "you can have mine, too."

The wind died down. The rain stopped. It had been quiet outside for several minutes. The storm seemed to be abating. Nina sat in an almost dry corner of the barracks, covered thoroughly with the blanket, sated and warm. She smiled at Rafi. "What a night . . ."

He went over and knelt next to her. They talked quietly. She laughed. He hugged her to him. Honestly, it was a little annoying, after this whole night, for them to share secrets. Her hand drew something on his knee. His large paw gently stroked her head.

"Come, Gilush," said Vera and packed up the napkins and put them in her handbag, "we go for a little walk. There are still places we haven't visited."

"But why don't we all go together? I thought we'd go up to the cliff together—"

"Gili, honey, do you need every little thing explained?"

And only then did I understand, idiot that I was.

We left them in the barracks and walked to the shore. We stood facing the sea. It was dark, but the moonlight shone through the clouds. We crossed the field of boulders. In the dark their terrifying presence was even more colossal. We stood at a three-way crossroads: to the men's camp, to the quarry, to the mountain. I asked Vera if she would go up to the cliff with me. She laughed. "Ninety-years-old woman will go up hill!"

But it was hard for her. Both because of the terrain, and because something in her had weakened. I lit the way with the Red Cross flashlight. We circumvented the large puddle and found the path. It was narrower and steeper than I'd imagined. Where it was possible, we walked arm in arm, and sometimes fully embraced. In the narrower parts she walked in front of me, and I kept stroking her back and neck. I made my touch on her as soft as I could. Every few steps we stopped and waited for her breath to steady. Twice I suggested we go back down, but she refused.

She remembered everything that had happened to her on this path fifty-four years ago. She said she could have done it with her eyes closed, and not just because she was blind back then. At a certain point she regained her strength and simply dragged me after her, this ninety-year-old woman. Her tiny body was carried ahead. Her body and everything it had been through.

And then we were at the summit, and we breathed a sigh of relief, just as she had described. Cool darkness surrounded us. We could hear the sea down below. Vera whispered that she'd never been here at nighttime.

She became very quiet, clenched her fist to her mouth. She held on to me hard and showed me the place where she'd stood for almost two months. With her finger she drew the little circle that had surrounded the sapling. I positioned my feet outside the circle, in one of the places where she'd stood casting her shadow. It was not easy to fit into her little shoes.

The sea pummeled the rocks. Vera sat down on a large hewn stone, looking very old again. I said we would not talk now, and that I wanted to stand there until the sun rose, and even after.

I stood for maybe an hour. Very slowly, as if in prayer, I ran the story about my grandmother and the sapling through my mind. Every time I opened my eyes, I saw her looking at me with a steady gaze, conveying a current of something to me.

Then we heard Nina and my father calling us from below. We drew them up to the mountaintop. They came, out of breath but also slightly glowing, and sat down on a rock next to Vera. Nina leaned on Rafi. The backpack with the tapes we'd filmed was slung over her shoulder, and I saw that this made her happy and proud.

Even when they arrived, I did not abandon my post on the cliff edge. I felt that Vera was pleased by this. Once she got up and corrected my position: "Here is where I usually stood in the afternoon," she explained. Nina asked, "What is that? What are you doing?" Vera said, "I had a little plant here that I took care of, we'll talk about it when we get down." Nina, with a forced smile, said, "I see there are stories I haven't heard yet." And again the heart pangs I felt every time Nina stumbled on an invisible barbed wire.

The sky grew lighter and Rafi started filming again. Nina got up and walked around, approached the edge of the cliff and looked down at the sea, pulled back, and looked again. She said into the gulf: "I don't think I've ever been this happy." Then she looked at me. "Gili-Gili, it's good that you came to be with me here, Gili."

"Yes, I'm glad I came."

And she said, "This place is slightly my home, after all."

Vera shook her head and suggested we walk down. "We'll talk about everything there," she said, "I want to be down below already."

But Nina seemed not to have heard her. "I want to film you all," she said. She took the Sony from a surprised Rafi and laughed. "Let me feel like it's my movie, too." She asked which button to press, and he showed her. I saw the disquiet in his eyes. She asked what the flashing red light meant, and he said the battery was almost dead. She had two or three minutes left, at most.

My body tensed. I wanted to go over to her, but I couldn't. I didn't have the strength to move. She looked at us through the little screen on the Sony, walked in a circle around us, and filmed.

She walked lightly, floating. I remembered what Vera had said about the morning when they took her in, and she watched Nina dance down the street, skipping over the leftover hopscotch chalked on the sidewalk.

Nina ran the camera over Vera and Rafi and me. With each of us she moved from head to feet, slowly, as though she were conducting a sort of system scan on us. And perhaps that is exactly what she was doing.

"You see, Nina," Nina suddenly spoke to future-Nina, "now we're all here together, your mother, and your daughter, Gili, and Rafi. And you were with us on the whole voyage, too."

There were thin strips of light in the sky, like a hand with its fingers spread out. Nina filmed them.

Vera repeated, firmly and irritably, that we should go down. "The sun here, as soon as it comes out, it burns. Five minutes later it'll be fire." In the growing light, her face was becoming gray and lifeless.

"One more minute, Majka," said Nina as she filmed. "Rafi, my precious, my love." She smiled at him through the lens and he returned a confused smile. "All the love you had for me . . . You know, don't you?"

"Know what?"

"That it's the greatest gift anyone ever gave me."

He bowed his head and swallowed heavily.

She looked happy, radiant. Her bright, dreamy happiness confused me.

"And you know, don't you?" she asked him again.

"Know what?"

She stopped and stood close to the edge. "That better than this moment, it will never be."

Rafi said, "Of course it will, Nina."

And I heard her say quietly, to herself, "I suddenly want time. Loads and loads of time." Her face changed abruptly. I saw the struggle and the dreadful indecision, and I silently shouted one single shout, and she looked at me as if she'd heard.

With one swift motion she took the backpack off, shut her eyes, held her arm all the way out, and dropped the backpack into the abyss.

I heard the camera shatter on the rocks. There was silence, then a whoosh of waves retreating. Nina collapsed all at once, fell on one knee at the edge, stunned by what she'd done—or by what she hadn't. I reached her at the same moment my father did, and together we pulled her back, into us.

By the time we reached the bottom, frightened and holding on to each other, I knew I would not allow everything we'd made on this journey to be lost in the depths. Later, for years, every time I was drowning in grief over my lost film, I would tell myself: If there are no pictures, there will be words.

But years went by before I was able to sit down and write.

And meanwhile things came and filled up my life.

We named the little one Nina. She's five and a half.

She is my speck of earth.

Ours.

Acknowledgments

Eva Panić Nahir, who inspired the character of Vera, was a well-known and admired figure in Yugoslavia. She is the subject of a monograph and a biography, as well as a Serbian television series conceived by author Danilo Kiš, in which she recounted the horrors of Goli Otok. That was the first time the public was exposed to the history of Tito's gulags, which had been silenced and denied up until then. Eva became a symbol of almost superhuman courage, epitomizing the capacity to sustain one's humanity under the harshest conditions.

Eva first told me her life story more than twenty years ago, and repeated it many times since. She and I developed a profound friendship. It was impossible not to like her, and not to be in awe of her power and humanity. It was also difficult, at times, not to balk at her principled and hermetic rigidity. She wanted me to write her story, and that of her daughter, Tiana Wages. One of the most precious gifts of this book was my acquaintance with Tiana's wisdom, optimism, and bravery. Both women were generous enough to grant me the freedom to tell the story but also to imagine and invent it in ways it never existed. For this—for the liberty of imagination and invention—I thank them from the bottom of my heart.

My gratitude also goes to the author and translator Dina Katan Ben-Zion, who guided me when it came to the Serbian and Croatian languages and their echoes in Vera's Hebrew.

To the filmmakers Dan Wolman and Ari Folman. To Elinor Nechemia, continuity girl and script supervisor. Profound thanks to my friend the director and film scholar Aner Preminger for his help and devotion. Thanks to close friends and family members who read the manuscript and offered suggestions and improvements. They all gave generously from their time and experience. Any errors in the book, on any topic, are mine alone.

I thank my guides on my journey to the Arctic region, and those who joined me on my travels to Goli Otok, above all my sharp, opinionated friend the historian Hrvoje Klasić.

The family of Rade Panić, Eva's first husband, hosted me warmly in his birth village. The small but cohesive club of Eva's fans in Belgrade—Tanja and Aleksandar Kraus, Vanja Radovanović and Planinka Kovačević—welcomed me and revived past times for me.

Thank you to Eva's beautiful family: Emily Wages, Yehudit Nahir, and the illuminating Smadar "Smadi" Nahir. Profound gratitude to the directors Dr. Macabit Abramson and Prof. Avner Faingulernt, for their moving film, *Eva*.

For their generous assistance, I thank Seid Serdarević, my Croatian publisher, and Gojko Bozovic, my Serbian publisher.

Thanks to Ženi Lebl for her wonderful book, *The White Violet* (*Ha'sigalit Ha'levana*, Am Oved, 1993), and to Aleksandra Ličanin, who wrote *Two Loves and One War of Eva Panić Nahir* and led me through Eva's childhood streets in Čakovec.

And of course thanks to Dr. Van de Velde, author of *Ideal Marriage,* and Prentice Mulford, author of "The Law of Marriage," both of which appeared in a joint volume translated into Hebrew by M. Ben-Yosef, whose words are quoted here (and yes, it is a real book).

The facial expressions of everyone I spoke to on this journey seemed to change when they spoke of Eva. Her vigorous, turbulent spirit and her uncompromising personality, at once tender and absolute, live on palpably, four years after her death, in anyone who was fortunate enough to know her.

David Grossman
February 2019

A Note About the Author

DAVID GROSSMAN was born in Jerusalem, where he still lives. He is the best-selling author of many works of fiction, nonfiction, and children's literature, which have been translated into thirty-six languages. His work has also appeared in *The New Yorker*. He is the recipient of numerous awards, including the French Chevalier de L'Ordre des Arts et des Lettres, the Buxtehuder Bulle in Germany, Rome's Premio per la Pace e L'Azione Umanitaria, the Premio Ischia International Award for Journalism, Israel's Emet Prize, and the 2010 Frankfurt Peace Prize.

A Note About the Translator

JESSICA COHEN translates contemporary Israeli prose, poetry, and other creative works. She shared the 2017 Man Booker International Prize with David Grossman, for her translation of *A Horse Walks into a Bar*, and has translated other major Israeli writers, including Amos Oz, Etgar Keret, Ronit Matalon, and Nir Baram.